A Hunting She Did Go

IRENE SEDEORA

To Tejinder

A hunting we will go, a hunting we will go,
Heigh ho, the dairy-o, a hunting we will go
A hunting we will go, a hunting we will go,
We'll catch a deer and give a cheer *
And then we'll let him go!

Thomas Arne
1710-1778

*4th line alteration, Irene Sedeora

A Hunting She Did Go

October, 1997, Midville, Illinois

Davina Reed 52, had that bloodied dream again. When she awoke and rubbed the sleep from her eyes the fear and disturbing images remained, portending some unknown threat.

In the middle of May she had separated from her husband, Tom, so she couldn't talk to him about the recurring dream and its meaning the way they used to discuss such things. She got dressed in a sweat suit and headed out into the backyard. Beneath the tall pines she maneuvered her slim, fit body through measured movements of Tai Chi, her latest diversion.

Somewhere on a branch high above, a dove trilled *coo-coo-coo*. She made slow motion moves to its sad song.

Suddenly a doe appeared in the bushy ravine. It stood like a statue staring at her and then turned and sprinted away followed by its fawn. It happened so quickly Davina wondered if her eyes had deceived her and the sighting had merely been a mirage.

From inside her pocket the ring of the cell phone interrupted her musings. She pulled out the phone and walked back across the yard.

"Hello."

"Uh, Davina Reed?" The voice cracked loud and nervous in her ear.

"Speaking."

"I'm Keith, a friend of Jed's."

"Yes, I remember you."

She had met Keith months before, briefly when she had picked the two of them up from an Alcoholics Anonymous meeting after Jed's driving license had been suspended and Jed's wife was visiting her parents back east. She recalled dropping Keith off in downtown Peoria.

"I can't get Jed to answer the door. Do you have a key to his house?"

"Maybe he went out of town without telling you his plans," she said. This was her day off work at *Queen Anne's Lace*, the gift shop she co-owned with her friend, Meg and she didn't want it spoiled.

Silence, then, "Uh, no, I peeked in a window of his garage and his Corvette's still in there and his truck, too. We were gonna go fishin' this morning. Jed told me you had a key. I don't wanna break down the door or anything like that."

Davina climbed the steps to the deck, slid open the door and stepped inside.

Her younger brother, Jed was in his 40's and increasingly caused her concern. Since his pending divorce Jed seemed in a hopeless downward spiral.

She found it ironic that she and Jed were almost simultaneously splitting from their respective spouses.

"If you're really worried, call 911."

"But Jed would be pissed if I did that and it turned out he was just in bed with a hangover. Anyway, Paxtonia don't have 911. Why don't you start on over? And I'll see if I can find an unlocked window on the ground floor. I noticed the upstairs bathroom window was open, but I'm afraid of heights."

Something about his nervous chatter seemed odd.

"Meet me there in a half hour but keep on trying to wake him. I'll get there as fast as I can. Maybe Jed changed his mind about going fishing. Or someone could have picked him up when you were asleep and you didn't-"

"Just get here." Abruptly, he hung up.

She plopped on a baseball cap over her newly tinted hair. It was supposed to be auburn. It looked red. Maybe it's time to find a new hair dresser, she thought as she picked up her shoulder bag and car keys.

She backed her Ford Escort from the garage and

stopped to push the button on the remote on the visor. She saw a hand lift back one side of the drapes in the front window of the house next door.

She gasped. Her eccentric neighbor stood staring in her direction, his rail thin body buck naked.

Then he dropped his hold on the drape and disappeared from view. She imagined the old goat laughing his head off at the shocked look on her face.

"Get a life weirdo," she muttered.

Soon she took the ramp to I74 and sped toward Peoria. She crossed Murray Baker Bridge and exited on the Adams Street off ramp.

Davina's palms were wet against the steering wheel as she worried about Jed and drove along Highway 29 that aligned with the Illinois River. In the distance a sail boat oscillated in the morning sunshine. Intent on calling Jed, she picked up the cell phone but the battery was dead.

She had forgotten to charge it, and the charging cable she kept in the glove box had been missing for at least a week.

Her mind kept replaying the phone conversation with the man who had phoned her. Something seemed not right.

Had the recurring, disturbing dreams of blood she suffered lately, been omens? Although it was warm inside the auto, she shivered.

As she neared Paxtonia she passed a big sign that advertised a bar and grill with the name, Froggy's, and then a grain elevator.

Minutes later Davina drove past Main Street lined with its several businesses; a supermarket, Shell gas station, antique shop and a Dairy Queen. Paxtonia offered few employment opportunities. Most working townspeople commuted to jobs in Peoria, as did Jed. On the edge of the northern part of town Davina turned on Third Street where the corner gas station had closed but the pay phone booth remained open. A man was standing inside talking into the receiver. She drove two blocks and took a right turn.

Thirty yards before Jed's house she drove past a green house with a realtor's For Sale sign stuck in the weed filled lawn.

Jed's rental house, a decrepit Victorian type built in 1910, surrounded by several massive oak trees was located near the end of the street. On the lawn a pair of painted concrete deer left by the previous tenant stood with soldier like attention appearing amazingly lifelike.

A mobile home, vacant and boarded up was an eyesore on the weedy lot adjacent to the land with the once stately house. Davina recalled that Jed had told her that he liked the privacy the old house and its location provided. To her it was simply depressing.

She took the gravel road that led to the detached garage and parked in front of the closed door. A bicycle leaned against the side of the garage. The bike was old with flaking blue paint and a light attached to the handle bars. She wondered if Jed ever rode it.

Keith had said he would meet her and he was nowhere in sight.

As she walked up the sidewalk to the porch, she noticed all of the windows she could see didn't have screens.

When she walked across the porch the floor made a rasping sound. She stuck the key in the lock, turned the knob and the door creaked open. She stepped inside and the bright sunlight cast her shadow eerily upon the woven roses of the frayed carpet.

It was in that faded beauty of a house Jed moved after his marriage to his wife, Shirlee broke up in April. There were no homey touches, not one picture, poster or painting on the walls. In the living room next to a worn leather sofa, Jed had placed a couple of folding lawn chairs and several still unpacked cardboard boxes.

If a stranger looked upon the scene he could wonder whether someone was moving in, or moving out. She remembered the room with the spare furnishings and boxes from her visit in June and it looked the same.

In a corner of the room a long time body building interest held by Jed was evident by the weight lifting bench and bar bells, along with a carelessly tossed hand towel on the floor. Davina could imagine Jed on the bench resolutely pumping iron.

"Jed!" Davina called out. "Are you here?"

She walked into the kitchen and on the counter saw empty beer cans and an open pizza box. Two flies feasted on the three leftover slices of stale pepperoni pizza. The sink held a pile of unwashed dishes and the carafe of the coffee maker was an inch high with dark brew.

Davina turned and hurried back to the living room. Inhaling deeply and with dread she climbed the stairs, again calling his name, a chilling response, the silence.

At the top of the staircase and to the right she found the master bedroom door ajar and slowly pushed it open, seeing then the bedroom scene: a laptop computer on a corner desk, the monitor screen black, sheets and comforter tousled on the empty bed, the side table lamp lit, a *Scientific American* magazine sprawled open on the floor. Davina crossed the room and reached out to the doorknob on the door to the adjoining bathroom. It was jammed and when she pushed she managed only a crack opening. Gathering all her strength she slammed her body against the door and shoved herself inside.

Shock overwhelmed Davina.

On the floor Jed lay on his back. His lifeless hands clutched an arrow protruding from his chest. Blood mapped his white T-shirt and had trickled down to the tiled floor.

Chirp, chirp came from the wide open window, where a sparrow perched on the windowsill gazed upon the bloody scene.

She bent down and touched the shaft of the arrow

11

briefly, as if to pull it out, then took her fingers away in horror at the realization her brother was dead.

She heard a noise, straightened up and spun around. She bumped into someone dressed in camouflage clothing, a cap and a scarf wrapped around the head with only the eyes barely visible.

Forcefully, the disguised figure pressed in, covering her mouth with a cloth that took her breath away with a sharp overpowering smell that engulfed her. She wiggled, kicked and tried to escape.

The stranger pulled her out of the bathroom and back into the bedroom.

A woozy feeling consumed Davina. She fell to the floor, hitting her head hard against an unrelenting metal object.

She slumped into darkness.

● ● ●

"Hello there, are you okay?"

Davina opened her eyes and struggled to sit up. Her head ached terribly.

"What happened?"

She looked up at a man who appeared to be in his early sixties with curly grey hair gazing down at her, his face a reflection of concern.

"You tell me, we found you here on the floor. Come take a look at her noggin," he called over his shoulder to a paramedic carrying a first aid kit and wearing surgical gloves. The paramedic came and squatted down next to her. Then he asked some simple questions including what day, month and year it was and directed her to look at his moving finger. "And please tell me, who is the president of the United States?"

"Bill Clinton. Thanks, but I'm okay," Davina said, but she wasn't so sure. She felt stunned.

The paramedic examined the big bump on Davina's head then said in a calm and soothing tone, "I think you'll live, but be sure to see your family doctor and get an x-ray or scan for a possible concussion. When you fell your head must have hit that miniature iron cannon on the floor. I'll put a cold pack on it." He prepared an instant cold pack by hitting and then shaking it and told her to hold the pack against the bump on her head.

She recognized the replica cannon her head had struck and near it her shoulder bag. The cannon came from the gift shop, *Queen Anne's Lace* that she co-owned. The heavy iron barrel rested on a wood base with wheels. She had gifted the cannon to Jed when he had admired it back in May when he stopped in the gift shop just after he and Shirlee separated.

A realization crept in through the pain. She was at Jed's house and a horrifying image flashed before her eyes and she saw again his hands clutching the shaft of the arrow protruding from his chest. "Jed, oh Jed!"

"Your memory's coming back, now is it? I'm Leo Donovan, the police chief of Paxtonia and don't you worry Miss, we'll get to the bottom of this. Please relax and let me help you up."

In her fuzzy mind she thought how refreshing, if not a little silly, to be referred again to as a Miss as his burly arms heaved her up from the floor.

"Who would want to hurt my brother?"

"Officer Hedges, after the photographs are taken, dust for fingerprints and don't mess up anything."

"Officer Hedges' face reddened.

Donovan's firm lock on Davina's arm guided her out of the room and then down the staircase where she sat on Jed's leather sofa and dabbed a tissue at her teary eyes. Donovan pulled up a lawn chair and sat down carefully as if he feared it would collapse beneath his hefty body. From his pocket he pulled out a packet of breath mints and popped a couple into his mouth.

"Have a mint?"

"No thanks, maybe later after I throw up. I can't believe that Jed's"–she couldn't make herself say the word, dead.

Donovan put away the mints, pulled out a cigar and tore away the cellophane.

"I know it's a nasty habit, but do you mind if I smoke?"

"Yes, sorry but I'm allergic to tobacco smoke. Besides it's really terrible for your health."

"I'm trying to break my addiction but without much success." He jammed the stogy into his mouth, the unlit cylinder an accent to the words he uttered. "Now show me some identification and tell me what happened and how you ended up on the bedroom floor. "

Davina showed him her driver's license and tried to sort the thoughts tossing around inside her head. As she began to tell the events of the morning that brought her to the discovery of her brother's body, the police chief jotted down notes in a small notebook. Davina told him she didn't recall breakfast, or driving to Paxtonia, but she did remember the phone call.

"This morning I got a phone call from a guy named Keith but I don't know his last name. He was a friend or acquaintance of Jed's. They may have met at an AA meeting. He began hanging around with Jed more after Jed moved to Paxtonia. Keith said to bring a house key, that he'd meet me here, but when I arrived, he wasn't here. I unlocked the front door and came inside. I called Jed's name, checked the kitchen and came upstairs."

It was like a movie unreeling inside her head as images came back and she began to remember.

"I pushed hard against the bathroom door and finally got it open. Then I saw Jed on the floor, the arrow in his chest and all that blood and a bird sitting on the windowsill and then someone grabbed me. I tried to get away and this person put a cloth over my

14

mouth and must have knocked me down. And that's all I remember."

He scribbled in a small notebook. "What did this person who came up behind you look like?"

"I couldn't tell; it happened so quickly. He had a camouflage cloth draped over his face. I could only see eyes and I can't even describe them."

"Is it possible your brother would harm himself?"

"Definitely not."

"It's improbable, but not impossible. I once heard of a guy who used his foot to pull the string of a bow to shoot himself. We'll get to the bottom of this, don't you worry. By the way, did you two get along?"

She felt angry but she nodded and then readjusted the cold pack against her head. "He was my brother and in spite of his faults and failings I loved him."

"Can you think of anyone who would benefit from his death?"

"I don't want you to think I'm accusing her, but I suppose his wife, Shirlee. They were separated but still legally married, and in the midst of a divorce. She would get any life insurance money. His son, Scott may have been a beneficiary, too. I don't think Jed changed his will and removed Shirlee. He was hoping they'd get back together, or so Jed told me. Jed's brilliant, he graduated top of his class at the University of Illinois. He got his Masters degree from U of I, and then his doctorate at Harvard University."

"Harvard, that's so? Tell me more about your brother, Jed Davidson. Is that his legal name?"

Somehow, even though her head was throbbing through the coldness of the ice pack, Davina didn't think the police chief seemed duly impressed with the importance of the man on the floor of the upstairs bathroom, his hands in a death grasp around the shaft of the arrow, and she felt compelled to convince him of Jed's intellectual capabilities and of his scientific accomplishments, that he was more than a drunk with a messed up life.

"James Eliot Davidson is his legal name. Jed's his nickname, made up out of his initials. Jed was doing fine professionally in his job. But when Shirlee and he split up last April he sort of went crazy and started drinking again. Booze was always his weakness. He rented this old house. The use of a boat came with the rental and he told me sometimes he'd go fishing with Keith." She glanced up at the ceiling, tears pooling her eyelids. "I can't believe this has happened-Jed shot by a bow and arrow-Who would want to harm him?"

Donovan's hazel hued eyes gazed at Davina sympathetically. "I'm very sorry for your loss," Donovan said, "but we'll do a thorough investigation and find out who's responsible." He flipped shut the notebook and clicked the retractable ballpoint pen. His manner and words calmed Davina and she thought what a kind man he must be. Although he stood tall and burly in appearance, he radiated an old fashioned gentility, a man of substance, rough around the edges, but the type she imagined who would open car doors for women, and carry their packages without them even asking.

"Too bad you don't know this Keith's last name but don't worry we'll track him down. Somebody's sure to have seen the two of them together. We'll find out who he is and what he knows and why he didn't stick around for you when he said he would."

"Do you know who phoned the police?" Davina asked.

"It was an anonymous caller who said they thought someone was burglarizing this house." Donovan glanced down at her hands and Davina surmised his eyes recorded the absence of a wedding ring. The wedding band was where she had tossed it the day Tom had left—at home at the bottom of the fish aquarium, algae now beginning to grow around the golden circle.

"Are you a married woman?"

"I'm separated from my husband, Tom. He's having a mid-life crisis. He's sorting things out in a cabin on the Illinois River. But it's a temporary situation-- I think."

The chief removed the unlit cigar from his mouth. "Temporary situation, hm."

Lieutenant, Jerry Caldwell came into the room and handed a sheet of paper to the police chief.

"We found this in the computer tray. I dusted it but couldn't find any prints."

Donovan's eyes skimmed the paper, and then he passed it to Davina. "Take a look at this; it appears to be a suicide note."

Davina read the printout. It was a rambling half page about a screwed up life and how he couldn't live without his wife who had left him. She noticed there were a couple of misspelled words. There wasn't a written signature, only JED, in capital letters.

"This is a fake," Davina said firmly and handed back the paper. "I don't think Jed typed this. Davina felt anger and anguish mingled with doubt about her conclusion. Could Jed have typed it?

A small town like Paxtonia had limited resources for a murder investigation and she wondered if Chief Donovan and his department could thoroughly investigate Jed's death.

Davina came down the front steps of Jed's house with Chief Leo Donovan just as the man she knew as Keith arrived on the crime scene. He got out of a beat up Ford pickup and walked to the crime scene tape. No cop stopped him as he lifted it, ducked beneath, and then strode toward them.

"What's happening? Is Jed okay?"

He wore his oily, blond hair pulled back in a ponytail fastened with a leather cord. A thin mustache crawled above his lips like a hairy worm and acne scars peppered his angular face. The fold of one sleeve of his T-shirt carried a pack of cigarettes. His faded jeans were held secure by a belt with a silver buckle bearing the profile of an Indian chief that shimmered in the morning sunlight.

To Davina he didn't seem the type of person Jed would have anything in common with, except for their addiction to booze.

"Why didn't you meet me here like you said you would?" Davina felt Donovan's eyes studying her as she confronted the ponytailed man.

"You called me this morning. You said to meet you here and bring a key so we could check on Jed. You said you were worried about him but you weren't here. Where were you?"

"I dunno what you're talkin' about. I got here now so we could go fishin'. I seen the squad cars—are you Jed's sis?" Keith unfolded from the sleeve of his T-shirt the pack of cigarettes, pulled out one, stuck it in his mouth and proceeded to light it with a match.

Davina felt stunned. "So you didn't lure me over here, follow me inside, chloroform me and knock me down?"

"Nope."

He sucked on the cigarette, inhaled deeply then vented a puff of smoke.

"Well, Jed's *dead*. Somebody either shot him with a bow and arrow or stabbed him with the arrow. I'm beginning think it was you."

"I don't know what you're talkin' about."

"Why didn't you stay away from him? You were a bad influence." Davina's voice splintered into a sob.

"Calm down, Ms. Reed," Donovan said. Then he pivoted toward Keith.

"Don't I know you?"

"I can't say I've had the pleasure."

"Let me see your driver's license."

From a rear hip pocket Keith pried loose a billfold attached by a chain to his belt. He removed the license and handed it to the police chief.

"Stay put for a minute," Donovan said to Davina.

In the sky shifting clouds dimmed the sun and the wind caused golden brown leaves to cartwheel across the withering grass.

"Step over there by those fake deer," Donovan said as he nudged Keith's elbow. "I want some answers."

Davina gazed at the garage and noticed the shabby bike that she had seen upon her arrival leaning against the side of the garage was now gone.

Beyond the yellow tape stood a woman in a faded housedress and a young boy who fussed with a pot bellied pig on a leash. She assumed they were from the neighboring green house that was for sale.

The front door of Jed's house opened and a gurney bearing a black body bag, oversized to cover the body and the protruding arrow was wheeled across the porch by attendants, and then carried down the steps. Keith tried to rush forward but Donovan stopped him.

"Stay back," he ordered.

"But I loved Jed. He was like the brother I never had. Can't I see him and tell him goodbye?"

"This isn't the time," Donovan said. He glanced at Davina. "I'd like both of you to come to the Paxtonia police station right now and give your statements."

In a small interview room at the Paxtonia Police Department Davina wrote down on a yellow pad what she had told Chief Leo Donovan and handed it to Police Officer Patricia Hansen, a woman in her mid-thirties who wore her hair short and her perfume heavy. The perfume contained the scent of patchouli whose musty dirt damp odor reminded Davina of her hippie days. Hansen avoided the use of lipstick but not thick eyeliner, mascara and smoky hued shadow and gave off an air of authority.

"Wait here while I type this up," she said. "It won't

take much time. Then after you read it and sign your statement you are free to leave."

Davina watched Hansen close the door. Bored and anxious to leave, she looked around the small room and to pass time, counted the slats in the mini blinds covering the window. Then she shut her eyes and tried to meditate, in her mind picturing a man and woman in a boat, he rowing, she trailing her hand in the water.

"Peace and love, love and peace," Davina murmured over and over but she found her effort useless for all she could think about was Jed, her only sibling gone forever.

Fifteen minutes later the door opened and Police Officer Hansen and another woman came into the room.

"This is Nadine, our dispatcher. She agreed to be a witness to your signature."

Hansen gave the computer printout of her statement to Davina, who quickly scanned the document, scrawled her name and stood up.

Davina went into the hallway perplexed and heartbroken over the events of the morning. Why had Keith lied and pretended not to know her? She looked up and saw Police Chief Leo Donovan coming toward her. A cigar clinched between his teeth smoldered an ashy knob.

"Ms. Reed, wait up, I need to secure your brother's rented house. May I have the key to the front door? When we finish our investigation, I'll personally return the key to you. Can you give me the contact info for Jed's next of kin for notification?"

"Yes." She pulled from her shoulder bag a key chain with one key, and a small address book. She handed Donovan the key and then flipped pages until she located Shirlee's entry. "Here's his wife's current address and phone number."

He jotted down the information on a slip of paper.

"You said Jed and his wife had a son?"

"Yes, a teenager. His name is Scott. I'd like to

drive out and tell them before the news of Jed's death reaches the local news media. It would be just awful for them to hear of his death on the radio or TV.

"It's our responsibility, not yours to notify the next of kin. It's an unpleasant task but we won't do it over the phone. Don't you worry Ms. Reed; a police officer will go out to the wife's home in an hour or so." He looked at her intently and Davina thought his eyes lingered longer than warranted and she wondered if he felt she had something to do with Jed's death.

"The crime scene tape will stay put for a couple of days until we finish up our investigation. We have a small police department here in Paxtonia, but I assure you we are well qualified to get the job done." His glance covered the vicinity of her face and then paused on her hair for a moment.

His attentiveness reminded Davina of how the previous day she had walked out of Flo's Hair Care with a red hair color that when she noticed it made her consider changing hair dressers.

She had thought she left the shop with her usual auburn with red highlights but Flo had seemed distracted and hurried, and behind in her schedule and the chair in which Davina sat was turned so her back was to the mirror. Davina was distracted too, thinking of her troubles with Tom. But away from the shop's dim lights and driving home, a glance in the rearview mirror with the sunlight drenching the car interior, she noticed the red hair that to her seemed much too artificial.

"Ms. Reed," Donovan mumbled, "I really like your hair. It looks nice." As if embarrassed he hurried off.

She followed him. "Thanks, but please wait. I have a question." He stopped and removed the cigar from his mouth.

"Yeah, what do you want to know?"

"Will there be an autopsy on my brother's body?"

"Yes, when there's an undetermined or suspicious

death, an autopsy is always ordered. We don't need any permission from the next of kin either."

"Please, I'd like to know the autopsy results when you find out. I know it's not a suicide. Is Keith still here?"

"He says his last name is Thorne and he's still being questioned, but I think his interview is just about finished. He should be coming out soon. Even though we are a small town police department, believe me, we are trained like the big city departments. We're professionals and fully capable to do a good job. We'll handle this."

"Okay, but Keith *did* phone me. He lied and I want to know why." Her words trailed after him for Donovan was already walking down the hall. She noticed for the first time he had a slight limp in his gait as if he might be troubled with arthritis. He opened a door and went into another office.

Davina bit her lip in dismay. No matter what Donovan said, she would try to discover for herself who had killed Jed and why.

Heading toward the exit she saw her reflected image in the plate glass front door, Flo's blunder, a rosy glow above her puffy eyelids. She pushed open the door to a brisk October day, a day she would never forget.

On the sidewalk outside the police department, thoughts roaming through her head, she bought a newspaper from a machine and tucked it beneath her arm. Davina drove from the parking lot and moments later parked again, this time on a side street beneath the shade of an oak tree where she could still watch Keith's truck. "Come on, come on," she whispered as she hid her face behind the newspaper. "I don't have much time."

As the wind blew leaves across the street she sat in her car huddled behind the newspaper. She tried to read and also keep a lookout for Thorne.

While she waited she read that Nelson Mandela

and South African president F. W. de Klerk had been awarded the Nobel Peace Prize. That news pleased Davina, but she was unable to concentrate further and so she studied the truck. Beneath a tarpaulin the bed of Thorne's truck bulged with junk, including protruding fishing poles. She watched as Keith came out. With his back blocking the wind he lit a cigarette then got into his pickup and drove away.

Keeping a one block distance between the two vehicles, Davina followed his truck to a local diner, Grandma's Koffee Kup. She watched him park in front and go inside. Davina turned at the next corner, parked and exited the car.

She hurried to the diner and went inside where she found Thorne seated in a window booth. Scooting in opposite him Davina stashed her shoulder bag alongside on the seat.

"Care if I join you?"

His eyes widened in surprise and his lip quivered slightly. He glanced around to see if she were alone.

"What are you doing here, stalking me?" A coat of tarter covered his crooked teeth.

"Why did you lie and pretend you didn't know me?"

"Sorry Vina, but honest to Pete, I didn't recognize you. It must be the hair color. I remember Jed's sis as a brunette, not a redhead."

She felt irritated when he called her by her nickname. "Don't call me Vina. My name's Davina; only my close friends call me Vina."

His smile collapsed into a smirk. "Then how about I call you *Bitch*?"

"Funny-so now you're a comedian?"

"I'm a scream and next week I'm gonna be on Saturday Night Live."

She leaned forward. "Now listen up, I know you're hiding something. My brother is dead and I want to know what happened."

23

A waitress wearing thick pancake makeup and iridescent eye shadow, with cantaloupe-sized breasts came to the table. Her hands held a coffee carafe and a platter of fried eggs, hash browns and sausages in farmer-sized portions which she set down in front of Keith.

She didn't look like anyone's grandma that Davina ever knew.

Thorne attacked a sausage with a fork and shoved it into his mouth.

The waitress looked at Davina. "Do you want to order anything, Hon?"

She was hungry but she refused to dine with this person she found disgusting. Information concerning her brother's death followed by a quick getaway to see her sister-in-law was what she wanted, not fried eggs.

"Nothing thanks," she said.

The waitress blinked her silvery eyelids.

"What's wrong, Honey? You seem sad and you look like you've been crying. Did this guy—"

"No, it's alright," Davina said.

"Can I have some O. J. Granny?" Keith asked, showing bits of egg yolk on his tartar covered teeth.

"Keith has a way of being obnoxious, doesn't he? You don't look old enough to be a grandmother."

"Thanks for the compliment, but I'm proud to be a grandma." Her eyes flashed false anger at Keith.

"Nobody but my grandbaby, Natasha is allowed to call me Granny. Now you call me June or I'll throw coffee on you." To show she was only kidding, she smiled broadly. "I wouldn't do that. You're one of my best customers. I'll get you the juice."

She turned and as she walked away her rubber soled shoes made a squeaky sound on the tiled floor.

Quickly, June returned and set the glass of orange juice on the table. Then she hurried off to attend to another customer.

"Number 8 on the menu is a winner. You really ought to try it, Davina," Thorne said. "It's the best deal on the menu."

He stopped chewing and removed the laminated menu stuck between the salt and pepper shakers, napkin holder and the wall. Flipping the menu open, he pointed with a grimy fingernail to a photo of twin egg yolks, sausage and hash browns.

"See that's how I like my eggs, over and—just like my women *easy*." Above his lips, the worm like mustache dripped crumbs.

"I'm not hungry," Davina said.

"Suit yourself."

Impatiently, Davina watched Thorne stream three packets of sugar into his mug.

"How can you talk about food? How can you eat like a hog, when Jed is dead? Didn't you sponge off him and get him to go bar hopping every night?"

Thorne stopped stirring his coffee and put down the spoon. "I didn't twist his arm. Sorry, *shit* happens."

Despite his glib talk Keith's eyes were wary and Davina for the first time sensed uneasiness and fear. He glanced around the restaurant and lowered his voice.

"Okay, here's what happened. Last night we were at Froggy's drinking beer, eating peanuts and Jed starts talking, bragging about how he's a scientist and he's invented this deer birth control drug and how it will control the deer population worldwide. You ever notice how many deer are running around this time of year? This guy sitting at the end of the bar speaks up and says he's a hunter and how all these animal rights people are trying to get rid of the sport of deer hunting."

"Go on, Davina said, "I'm listening."

"We had what you can say was a heated discussion. He said that nobody should mess around with Mother Nature. Hell, the guy acted a little odd, but finally everything was cool between us and he took off from Froggy's before Jed and me did. We stayed on until

25

closing time. Then we left in Jed's Corvette. Now Jed wasn't drunk mind you, just a little high and so was I. So we got to his place and he said I could sleep on the sofa and maybe we'd go fishin' later in the morning after we caught a few zs. He said that he could call in sick because he was due a day off work. He said if he got fired he didn't care."

"And then what? Did you hear any noises? I mean for Pete's sake, you must have heard something."

"I'm sorry, Vin- Davina. I thought I heard something in the middle of my sleep, but I thought I was dreaming."

He took a slurp of coffee and set the mug down. "The next thing I knew, it was morning and my back was hurting, not to mention my head. I got up to take a leak in the downstairs john. Then I went upstairs and knocked on Jed's bedroom door but there was no answer. I opened it and went in and saw his bed was empty. The bathroom door was shut and I couldn't open it. Then I got the feeling something bad had happened and I freaked out. I thought about my fingerprints being there all over the place so I began wiping off everything I thought I might have touched up there. But I didn't want to just leave, if he was unconscious, or worse. He might not be found for days. I remember how he talked about his sister and I know I met you once. I looked in his personal phone book and found your name and then I called you on my cell phone."

"The police can check the calls on a cell phone. You should have told the truth. You should have called the police."

"But-"

June, the waitress approached.

"Coffee is on the house," she said. She placed a mug on the table in front of Davina and filled it.

Although she would have preferred tea, and she didn't intend to waste anymore time, Davina thanked the waitress who then put a bill by Keith's plate.

"Thanks for stopping in," June said, and turned to take an order from a couple of elderly women seated at another booth.

"When you were upstairs at Jed's did you see a printed sheet of paper in the printer tray?"

"Nah, I don't know nothing about computers or printers, didn't notice anything." Thorne pulled a toothpick from his pocket and began picking between his incisors.

"Why did you lie to the police chief about calling me and then act like you didn't know me?"

"I'm on parole for a drug violation and I don't need no trouble. I really did plan to go outside and wait for you on the porch. Then I thought someone might see me so I took off. I jogged home as fast as I could and watched TV. I don't live too far from Jed's house. But then after a while I decided to get in my truck and drive back. I really wanted to know if he was okay, believe me."

"Somebody was hiding upstairs when I went up and I think it was you, Keith. You attacked me."

"I swear on my mother's rosary, it wasn't me." As he talked the toothpick almost fell out from between his teeth.

He seemed nervous and beads of sweat appeared on his forehead.

He looked at Davina intently.

"Jed told me your mom and dad are very rich."

"I don't believe he told you that."

"Not in so many words, but he said they owned a waterfront Florida condo, that they've been on an African safari and they're planning a cruise around the world. He told me that your dad trades Mercedes every two years. Living like that takes a thick wallet. Hell, your folks *are* rich. Now when they die, with Jed dead you won't have to share the inheritance with anyone. You'd better hope the police believe it's a suicide because they just might get the idea you knocked off your own brother for the future money you'd get. Davina, you look pretty strong for a woman. You coulda stabbed him with that arrow or you coulda shot him with the bow."

"I've had enough of this, you cretin!" Davina then noticed June standing behind a large leafy potted plant watching them.

"What a cretin?" Keith asked, with a sneer. "Anyway, I'll take that as a compliment. Like I said, you won't have to share your inheritance with Jed. I'd call that a motive."

To Davina the idea was crazy, but to police authorities, she feared the idea could seem plausible.

"You're a creep, and you're disgusting,"

A dribble of saliva ran down Keith's chin.

"Don't worry, I'm just foolin' but anything's possible. I got the idea when they were questioning me that the cops think Jed may have committed suicide. He had his reasons to check out." He pushed back his plate and glanced out the window.

"What reasons?"

"Shirlee wanted to bleed the man dry. She kept demanding more money than the alimony and child support they had agreed on. She wanted half of his 401K and his pension. That mother had a nasty temper. Jed said that when they were arguing, his wife threatened to kill him."

Keith Thorne got up and counted out some bills on the table. "You should go back over to the police station."

"Why?"

"You need to tell them the truth like you should have in the first place. And tell them you telephoned me while you were at Jed's house. You made the police chief and the detectives think I'm a liar."

"I'll think about it. Right now I've got work to do. You know I'm a taxidermy- well one of those people who stuff dead animals like deer heads."

"If Jed was your friend why wouldn't you want to

help the investigation of his death? Go back and tell a detective, or tell the police chief what you told me but leave out the false accusations about me. When the police check the phone records they'll see a phone call was made to me from Jed's phone or your cell phone."

"Nah, I don't think so. I don't own a cell phone. I lost it. I only use untraceable public phones."

As he talked, the toothpick wiggled back and forth between his yellowed teeth.

"Gotta go," he said. He waved to June and spit out his compliment to her cooking skills: "Good food, good food."

Davina watched him leave and aware of the task she still had to do, she quickly picked up her shoulder bag just as June arrived with the coffee carafe ready to refill the mug that Davina still hadn't touched.

A suspicious look strained across her face. "Would you like more coffee?"

"No thanks. I've got to go."

She left the café still angry at Keith's crazy rants and the shock of her brother's violent death heavy in her heart. Thorne couldn't fool Davina. He was the last one to see him alive. He *must* have had something to do with Jed's death.

She got into the Ford and headed to Peoria where she intended to deliver the news of Jed's death to her sister-in-law, *if* the police had not gotten there first.

As she drove well over the speed limit, she worried over being considered a suspect herself. Then Davina recalled that her neighbor, Cosmos Harris had seen her backing from her driveway that morning. The time of Jed's death had not yet been determined, but if by the implausible chance she needed an alibi, she feared Harris wouldn't support her story of the exact time she had left her house. Harris knew it was Davina who had led the neighbors into signing a petition of complaint against him for parading nude around in his back yard.

Momentarily, she held the idea of taking him a

peacemaking plate of cookies, or a pie, but quickly she dismissed the idea.

CHAPTER 2

Police Chief Leo Donovan sat at his desk, sipped black coffee from a Styrofoam cup and stared at the silver framed photograph of Helen, his late wife that he still displayed amid the clutter of his work space. Almost two years had passed since he had lost Helen in a car-train accident. While returning from her regular Tuesday night bingo game, her sedan stalled on railroad tracks. With the locomotive bearing down, she had waited too long before deciding to get out of the car. The engineer braked but failed to stop in time and slammed into the auto, instantly killing Helen.

Sometimes at night alone in the king size bed he once shared with Helen, he dreamed about his wife stuck there on the tracks, frantically unfastening the seat belt, fumbling with the door handle, the bright light of the approaching train glaring into her horrified eyes. Snapping awake, he would get out of bed and go to the kitchen for a shot of Jack Daniels to quiet the terror. He couldn't shake the guilt he felt for not being with her. If only he had been, she would still be alive.

With his wife's unfortunate death, Donovan abandoned his early retirement plans. Without Helen what would he do in retirement, turn lazy, watch television all day and half the night, overeat and get fatter? He had wanted to move to a warmer climate, perhaps Arkansas where he had once worked briefly as an eager, novice policeman. There he would use his law enforcement experience to open a private detective agency and the income would supplement his social security and pension. But that Tuesday, November night shattered those plans. No, he reasoned, it was better to keep working in Paxtonia for as long as he could. Now today for the first time since his wife's unexpected death, Leo Donovan felt attraction for another woman whose brother had died under mysterious circumstances, she being the one who had found his bloodied body.

Was it disloyal to sweet Helen's memory, or too soon he wondered, to feel attracted to another woman? Davina Reed was so different from Helen who had been quiet and shy. And that reddish hair enthralled him. Ms. Reed had told him that she was separated from her husband, so there was some hope for him. He took the last sip of coffee, now lukewarm. "Oh, forget it Donovan," he said aloud just as Police Lieutenant Caldwell poked his head inside the doorway.

"Forget what, Chief?"

A flustered Donovan squashed the cup and tossed it into the waste basket next to his desk. "There's something about Davina Reed that bothers me."

With a grin, he strolled on in. "Bothers, or *excites* you? She's not a bad looking chick- for a mature woman."

"Don't get smart with me, Caldwell. Ever since I decided not to take early retirement and wiped out your chance to replace me as police chief, you've had a bug up your ass. Get over it. I'm not going anywhere anytime soon. And what I mean by something about Ms. Reed bothers me, is I get the idea she wants to play detective in the investigation of her brother's death. It could be murder. It could be suicide. Did you see the size of the biceps on the Davidson body? His arms looked powerful enough to plunge an arrow into his own body."

"Yes, I did. By the way Chief, I was driving down Main Street in my patrol car and I saw Reed and Thorne sitting in a booth by the front window at Grandma's Koffee Kup." Caldwell rubbed his nose with his knuckle.

"Are you positive the woman you saw was Ms. Reed?"

"It was the red hair that made me take a good look. I'm sure-chatting away, looking real chummy." He helped himself to coffee from the coffee maker on the table in the corner. "That Reed woman is a busy body and seems determined to interfere in our investigation. I thought he didn't know her from *diddley squat*." He took a sip from his cup."Did Hansen make the coffee?"

"You know Pat did, and she resents it. She says we should take turns."

"What time did you see Ms. Reed and Thorne at June's cafe?"

"Not more than ten minutes ago. Just to confirm their identities when they came out, I drove by the cafe and parked down the street behind a van. I saw them leave separately, Keith first."

"Do you think those two whacked Jed Davidson? Oh, I forgot- you think it was a suicide." He made a face and emptied the coffee on a fern in a clay pot on top of the file cabinet.

"Don't pour your coffee on that plant. It was a birthday gift from Helen. And you should know it's too early to come to any conclusions. The deceased man was having serious marriage problems, maybe financial ones too. One of the officers found a pile of unpaid bills in a drawer and also inside the garage he discovered a bow and a quiver full of arrows."

"But Chief, did you ever hear of anyone stabbing himself with an arrow? Why not use a knife from the kitchen?"

"It's quite possible. I remember reading about

some guy who used his foot to pull a bow string and shoot the arrow into his chest. But we'll have to wait and see what the preliminary autopsy report reveals."

"I could sure swear Keith Thorne lied during questioning. He avoided looking me in the eyes."

Chief Leo Donovan leaned back in his chair. "I've been the police chief in Paxtonia for the last fifteen years, and before that I was a police officer here for five years. If turns out to be a murder, it's the first one in Paxtonia in twenty years."

"In the middle of a mild October night, his bathroom window wide open, no screen, someone could have shot him from outside, just like he was a deer. Weren't there some oak trees all around the house? With tree climbing spikes and a strap the killer could have climbed up a tree and then," (Caldwell pretended to shoot an arrow) "Whoosh!"

"If Davidson was drunk, or drugged out he still could have killed himself," the chief said.

"There were no prints on the computer keyboard, not even Jed's," Caldwell said. "If Davidson typed the note then why did he wipe off his prints?"

"That's something to consider."

Donovan shook his head. "It's a damn shame; his sister says he was a brilliant scientist with his name on several patents."

"I remember that I stopped Davidson's Corvette one night back in August. I was writing him a ticket for speeding and a DUI, but he said he knew the police chief of Paxtonia personally, so I ended up giving him a warning ticket instead. Did you know him like he claimed?"

"No, and let me tell you, if my mother was still alive and she drove under the influence and I stopped her, I'd ticket her. Now you tell Officer Hedges to drive over to Peoria Heights and officially inform Jed Davidson's wife that's she's a widow. There won't be any divorce now."

He scribbled on a note pad and handed it to

Caldwell. "Here's the address. Have Hedges ask Ms. Davidson if Jed was depressed, suicidal, and if he had any enemies."

"I'll get to it," Caldwell said, and added, "forget about my comments earlier about you and Ms. Reed. I was just joking around. You know how I am."

He left the room and the chief turned his chair and gazed out the window.

Caldwell's obvious desire to replace Leo as Paxtonia police chief irritated him. The guy's greed for his job was palpable.

"When hell freezes over," he muttered to a little bird fluttering just outside his window.

CHAPTER 3

It was almost 11 AM when Davina arrived at Jed's and Shirlee's spacious home located on a street of historic houses on the high bluffs above the Illinois River. Not a single dandelion or sprig of clover marred the beauty of the green carpet of lawn. A layer of asters and mums in hues of rose, lavender, pink and magenta made a colorful autumn display in front of evergreens that fronted the brick walls.

In the distance there was an amazing river view, and in the rear of the house a tennis court and a swimming pool. Davina recalled how excited Shirlee had always been in showing off the property and how she told all who would listen that it was a well known story that on a visit to Peoria in 1910 Theodore Roosevelt had called the view of the Illinois River from the bluffs on the two and a half mile stretch of road, the grandest view in the world.

Then in a hushed and reverent voice she would say Abraham Lincoln from time to time traveled the river by canoe.

Davina knew Jed had bought the home at the urging of Shirlee even though she suspected Jed could barely afford the monthly mortgage payments. There were five bedrooms and seven bathrooms, almost eight thousand square feet of living space and the lot was almost an acre, carefully and beautifully landscaped. It was too much space for a couple and one boy. Now the summer annuals were gone, pulled out while still in bloom by the hands of Javier, the gardener whose job was to deadhead flowers, trim shrubs and mow the vast lawn diagonally like Shirlee wanted so it would always be camera ready for those driving by, for those passing eyes to be astounded by the flora beauty accenting the Georgian mansion.

When there was no answer to the doorbell Davina followed the brick walk around the side of the house to the back where the autumn panorama had begun, the ashes and maples shifting purple and orange hues. Davina found her sister-in-law standing on a strip of lawn on the opposite side of the pool, dressed in a camouflage jumpsuit. The sight of the pattern momentarily unnerved Davina returning her thoughts to the earlier confrontation with the camouflage clad figure at Jed's rented house. Shirlee was engaged in shooting a bow and arrow at a three dimensional urethane foam deer decoy fifty feet away.

Years before when their marriage was new and the couple was still deeply in love, and before Jed's transition from avid deer hunter to enthusiastic conservationist, Jed had introduced Shirlee to archery. He had equipped her with a pink ladies bow, special lightweight arrows and a wrist brace. Back in those days, each autumn during deer hunting season they had gone deer hunting. Now Davina watched Shirlee release the bow string. Her eyes followed the twenty-eight inch arrow as it zoomed though the air and penetrated the buck's foam shoulder. Many spent arrows had chipped out jagged cavities in the fake deer.

"Hi, Shirlee," Davina called out. She dreaded delivering the tragic message that had brought her to this serene and elegant setting.

Shirlee pivoted. She had her ebony hair pulled back into a ponytail. "Vina!" At thirty-nine her body was lean and firm. To stay that fit Davina knew it was because Shirlee was obsessed in staying youthful in appearance. She followed a routine of swimming, jogging and frequent workouts at a health club.

"I rarely miss but if-my God! What happened to your hair?" She dropped the bow and walked around the pool toward Davina. "The color looks okay, a bit bold; it's just *unexpected*."

"My hairdresser got a little carried away but you'd better believe she's going to fix this or she'll never see me in her shop again." Davina wondered when she'd ever find time in her turbulent life to actually phone Flo and demand she fix her hair back to her usual color.

Shirlee's face with its deftly applied makeup, still divulged the fine lines of early aging surfacing around her eyes. "Why aren't you at your shop? I thought you were putting in lots of hours. I mean with Tom gone. Have you filed for divorce?"

"We're legally separated," Davina said. She detested being in the same marital situation as her sister-in-law.

"Isn't it ironic, within two months, both of us deserted by our husbands? I don't know what I'd do to pay the bills if it wasn't for the inheritance from Mom I got last February when bless her soul, she died from that horrible cancer. Jed's not giving me much money. Let's sit on the terrace. I'll get us something cool to drink." Davina didn't have to scrutinize Shirlee's face any longer. It was obvious she hadn't heard that she was now a widow, and that she would not be a divorcee after all.

"Meg is tending the shop today." How could she tell her? Back when Jed had first introduced Shirlee, Davina found her manner chilly and almost snooty, as if her extraordinary beauty could excuse her attitude. She came from Boston and Jed had met her through a colleague at Harvard. Shirlee claimed to be distantly related to Jackie Kennedy Onassis. Now the two women headed toward the terrace and Shirlee glanced at Davina.

"Vina, what's wrong with you? You look very pale. Don't you feel well?"

"Shirlee, I don't know how to say this-"

A back door opened and the youthful and sexy man Davina knew as Javier, the gardener came out carrying a wine bottle and two stemmed glasses. Dressed in a chambray shirt open at the throat and tight jeans, low slung on narrow hips, with his biceps bulging his shirt sleeves, he looked like a male model from a *J Crew* catalogue and Davina couldn't help wondering what the heck he was doing-filling in for Jed? He quickly strode toward them, surprised at Davina's appearance there, but welcoming her with a broad grin.

"Javier, have you met my sister-in-law, Davina?" She turned to Davina. "Javier Carrillo takes care of the landscaping." And Davina wondered what else? She couldn't miss the familiar glances they exchanged and the way Shirlee's face appeared flushed upon his arrival.

"We haven't been introduced but I think I've seen you somewhere; maybe it was here last fall or earlier this spring when I was busy spreading shredded mulch and getting Ms. Davidson's landscaping ready for the annual Good Earth Gardening Club tour. Anyway, it's a pleasure to meet you." He took Davina's hand and bent over and planted a moist kiss upon the back of her palm, unnerving Davina with the gesture.

"Yes," Shirlee said, "I was asked for the third time to open our grounds and allow people to come and walk around the yard admiring my garden displays. It's a charity event, a worthy cause, so I don't mind but it is a lot of work, a lot of it done by Javier." She ran her fingers over her forehead and into her ebony hair, a mannerism Davina had noticed before that occurred whenever Shirlee was upset or nervous.

"Would you beautiful ladies like some wine?" Javier proceeded to put the glasses on the Plexiglas table top.

"Sure we would," Shirlee said.

"So Javier, you're the gardener *and* the butler?" Davina asked, her voice taking on a sharp edge. It was obvious until he saw Davina, the wine had been meant for him and Shirlee.

"Oh, Javier is just like family and he's welcome to go into the kitchen anytime. It gets hot working in the yard, you know." She seemed a bit flustered as Javier proceeded to uncork the wine bottle with a corkscrew he pulled from his pocket. He streamed wine into the glasses and handed one to Shirlee and the other to Davina who read the label on the bottle, *Simi Rose of Cabernet*.

Suddenly the sight of this man angered Davina. Unexpected words tumbled from Davina's mouth in a rush: "I guess you and Javier don't care- but Jed is dead."

The wine glass slipped from Shirlee's hand and fell to the flagstones shattering into pieces, the liquid flowing like blood across the light grey stones.

"No! What happened?"

"Damn!" Javier exclaimed.

In a voice drained of emotion Davina related the details of the morning, all the time wondering if perhaps they already knew and were only pretending shock and surprise. Suddenly Javier swept Shirlee into his beefy arms, comforting her with his words, "Now, now; it will be alright, shhhh." Shirlee soon twisted out of his grasp and frowned.

"Forgive me for asking but Javier, did you have anything to do with Jed's death?" Davina asked in a steady voice.

Shirlee looked horrified. "How could you ask that of Javier?" She patted Javier's arm. "Excuse my sister-in-law, she's upset and doesn't mean it. But I think you should go, Javier."

Javier was instantly angry and offended. "Don't accuse me of shooting your brother with a bow and arrow. Look over there at that deer decoy stuck in the target zone with arrows. Shirlee's, er- Mrs. Davidson is the championship archer, not me. I am strictly an amateur."

Davina apologized profusely. "I'm so sorry, I think I'm losing it. I'm still in shock. Shirlee, where's Scott? He's got to hear about his dad's death from family, not the radio, or TV, or strangers."

"Scott moved out two weeks ago. He stays with different friends a few days at a time. It's hard to get in touch with him. He's angry about Jed and me breaking up." She tugged at a thread unraveling on the cuff of the sleeve of her camouflage outfit. "He's at school, unless he skipped."

"Do you want me to go with you to the high school and help tell Scottie?"

"No, Davina, I'm his mother, I should do it." She glanced at the gardener. "Javier and I will-"

Javier raised both hands in the air as if under arrest. "No, no, death, mourning and I don't get along too well, beside Scott hates me. And since the deer tracking outing Mrs. Davidson invited me to go to at sundown today is out, I think I should split. I've finished the mowing so my work here is done."

"Javier, don't you dare leave me," she ordered. She grasped his arm and looked woefully at Davina. "I'll need your helping planning the funeral. My God, what am I saying? Jed can't be dead."

Davina nodded. "Yes, I'll help."

"He always wanted to be cremated."

"What?" That was an eye-opener to Davina. But finding truth here was as improbable as finding dandelions in the midst of the flawless bluegrass and fescue grass. She glanced at her wrist watch where the replica of an endangered spotted owl pointed feather fingers to the time. "We should find Scott and tell him about Jed's death as soon as possible."

Shirlee bit her lower lip and leaned against Javier. "I can't tell him Jed's dead, I just can't. He'll hate me forever and blame me. He'll say it would never have happened if Jed had stayed here, if I hadn't made it impossible for his dad to live here. Davina, you've got to do it for me, *please*. And tell Scottie to come back home where he belongs and to quit acting like a homeless person."

"Okay, I'll do that," Davina said, "but you should phone the high school office right now and tell them who I am, and that I'm on my way. You must give your permission for me to speak on your behalf to Scott on this emergency family matter."

Shirlee quickly agreed. Davina walked back across the lawn and around to the front of the mansion her mission to bring the tragic news to Scott troubling her. Also bothersome images swirled in her head: The intimate way Shirlee and Javier exchanged glances, the fake deer stuck with all those arrows shot by Shirlee's hands, and there also was Keith Thorne's cocky, sneering demeanor. Did Javier, or Shirlee or Keith kill Jed? Could he have done the unthinkable and committed suicide?

While getting into the car Davina dropped her sunglasses and they slipped beneath the front seat. To retrieve them she reached down and her fingers searched the floor where in a happy surprise she found not only the aviator sunglasses, but rolled up and jammed in the floor track, the missing cell phone connector charger. She pulled the cell phone from her bag and attached it to the connector and plugged it in to the receptacle. Now once again she would have the convenience of a ready to use cell phone in her vehicle.

As she backed from the long driveway a Paxtonia city squad car pulled in, the young officer briefly turning his head to glance in her direction, unaware his message had already been delivered.

CHAPTER 4

With the hope that it was not a day when he had skipped classes, Davina headed toward the high school where Scott was enrolled. In her mind she rehearsed how she would tell him.

Upon arrival she parked in the school lot, put the recharged cell phone in her bag and entered the front door to Lincoln High School. She headed toward the front office where she told the lady behind the counter her name and relationship to Scott Davidson.

"Scott's mom, Shirlee should have phoned you," Davina said. "She wants me to talk to him at once." The woman nodded sympathetically as if she already knew the reason. Then Davina was told to wait in the sophomore counselor's office, and a student was sent to locate her nephew who was in Advanced Algebra, 3rd Period. Through the open door, she watched students going in and out of the main office. To Davina the kids looked significantly taller than classmates she remembered from her high school years. Many of the teenage boys hovered six feet in height and over, with some of the girls almost as tall.

Shortly a much younger version of Jed with a rhinestone stud imbedded in one ear lobe came in, on his face a look of surprise and wariness. "Aunt Vina what happened? Why are you here?"

The counselor, a kind faced middle-aged man with grey hair and wearing bifocals with a name tag, *Mr.*

Kuele clipped to his shirt pocket, followed Scott into the room. He closed the door and greeted Davina with a nod. "Have a seat, Son. "

"I'm sorry it's your dad-"

"Did he have a heart attack? I told him to quit smoking, but he wouldn't listen."

"No, it's worse," Davina said. "This morning I went to check on him and found him-" she took a deep breath and continued, "dead in his bathroom in his home in Paxtonia." The words hung horrific in the room where the usual discussions were less traumatic; such as deciding on a specific English, or Mathematics class to enroll in, or whether to take a second language class. Davina wanted to hug Scott but the look on his face, a mixture of disbelief, fear and anger suggested it better that she settle for a comforting touch to his shoulder. She watched his face go white.

"How? What happened?"

"Let me get you a glass of water," Mr. Kuele said.

"Yes, please get him some water." He hurried out the door.

"Oh, it's awful," Davina said, and fought to stay strong. She explained the events of the morning, beginning with the phone call from Keith Thorne and ending with finding Jed, and the struggle and knock down by the unknown person.

"Does- does Mom know?"

"Yes, she wanted to come and tell you herself but she was too upset. She was afraid you'd blame her. Your mom wants you to come back home. I'd like to go with you. I can drive you back there or if you feel like driving I'll follow your car."

The counselor returned and held out the water filled paper cup to Scott who shook his head, so he set it on the nearby table.

Scott cleared his throat and blinked back tears. Mr. Kuele's eyes misted up.

"Scott, it's okay to cry," he said. "I know what it's like to lose your dad when you're a kid. It happened to me too, years ago."

Scott pulled back from the counselor's hand patting Scott's arm and looked at Davina. "Is Javier Carrillo still there?"

"He was when I left, but he's probably gone by now."

Scott told Mr. Kuele that he wanted to talk to his aunt privately and asked if the counselor would leave them alone in the room for a few minutes.

"Sure," the counselor said. He handed Scott a box of tissues, left the room and closed the door.

"It wouldn't surprise me one bit if Javier and Mom killed Dad." Scott told his aunt he had been staying at his friend, Jason's house and that he kept a duffle bag with extra clothes inside his car trunk moving from one friend's house to another friend's house. "I'm not going back home. When Jason's mom gets tired of me, I'll find another place."

"Let's get out of here," she said, "and go and see your mom. When I told her about your dad's death she was very shocked." Davina had said the words she felt she should say, but she wasn't certain of the sincerity of Shirlee, especially since there seemed to be something going on between her sister-in-law and the gardener. In the hallway youthful sounds of laughter, untouched by the tragedy, engulfed them. The bell rang, marking the end of the 3rd period and the beginning of the 2nd lunch period.

"Let me treat you to lunch."

Scott shook his head, "Nah, I'm not hungry."

"Come on join me, my treat. Do you like tacos? I'm starving."

He smiled wanly. "I don't think so, oh sure, I guess I could. But I've got to go to my locker and get some books."

"First we'll get you signed out at the front desk," Davina said.

• • •

At *Paco's Hacienda* Scott's appetite was that of a typical teenage boy. He devoured four hard shelled tacos, a large order of fries and a refill of a jumbo cola. After missing her breakfast Davina's appetite wasn't skimpy either. She finished a large garden salad with Italian dressing, a soybean based enchilada, fries and a lemonade. Davina looked up from her empty paper plate.

"That was delicious. I'm glad you let me buy you your lunch."

"Thanks, Aunt Vina. I won't need any supper today."

"Me neither." She gazed thoughtfully at her nephew.

"By the way Scott, I think you should know that Police Chief Donovan over in Paxtonia will most likely want to talk to you, or one of his detectives will. It's nothing to worry about." His catsup smeared lower lip quivered slightly.

"Why does he want to talk to me? I don't know anything. Does he consider me a suspect?" The eye blinking mannerism Scott has suffered as a preteen resurfaced briefly. His long lashes agitated up and down until he rubbed his eyes, that little trick he had developed back then to stop the motion that had caused kids to make fun of him. Davina reached across the table and gently touched his hand.

"No, I don't think so. I'm sure it's routine, part of the investigation."

She doted on Scott for he was like the son she and Tom never had. She was fearful to ask, but desperately hoped Scott did have a solid alibi for his whereabouts the previous night. She wadded up the paper napkin imprinted with a little cartoon character in an oversized sombrero and placed it on the empty paper plate.

"The police chief suggested your dad may have committed suicide because of an unsigned note they found in the computer tray in his bedroom, but I think that's ridiculous. Somebody killed him and I intend to do all I can to find out who it was. I've already talked to the guy who was the last person to see Jed alive, a man named Keith Thorne."

She noticed a strange look flash across Scott's face but he didn't say anything.

"Chief Donovan has promised to keep me informed on the progress of the investigation. I'm just not convinced a small police force like the one in Paxtonia has all the resources needed to quickly find the one responsible.

"He's dead and nothing can bring him back."

"Can you think of anyone who would do this?"

"No, everybody as far as I know liked Dad—except Mom and Javier."

"Oh, Scottie, don't say that."

"I wouldn't doubt that they did it."

Scott went to the bathroom. Davina paid the bill and then phoned Meg at *Queen Anne's Lace*. S h e told her partner about Jed's death but skimmed over the details. Then she asked Meg to cover her shifts at the shop for the rest of the week.

"Sure I will," Meg said. "Things are slow here; we've only had two customers all morning. Oh Vina, I'm so sorry." Davina thanked her and flipped shut the cell phone. For her to have such an understanding person as a business partner, made her feel fortunate.

They left the restaurant with the understanding Davina would follow Scott as he drove back to his home where he would move back in and support his Mom while they planned the funeral. She had no trouble keeping up with Scott. He drove slowly as if he were an elderly and feeble person, five miles under the speed limit forcing her to continue braking to avoid rear ending his car. Halfway to the mansion Scott slowed down even more, put on the turn signal and pulled to the side of the street. Davina passed the Mustang, parked a few car lengths in front of it, got out and walked back to meet him. Against the background noise of traffic they faced each other. "I've decided I can't go back home," he said. Once more he thanked Davina for lunch and for coming to Lincoln High School to tell him about his dad's death. He hunched his shoulders and at that moment looked so much like Jed that Davina's eyes filled up again.

"It doesn't seem like it's my home anymore. I'm certain Mom is fooling around with the gardener. I've caught them wrapped up in each other's arms and hugging each other right there behind one of her fancy evergreens. Don't try to talk me into it, Aunt Vina; I've made up my mind." In a small notebook he scribbled on a sheet of paper, tore it out and handed it to Davina. "That's Jason's cell phone number. You can give it to the police chief too, if you want; I've got nothing to hide."

"Of course you don't. But come and stay at my house. You should stay with family now, if not with your mom, then with me."

"But it's too far for me to drive to school from Midville. I'd always be late."

"You *are* coming to the funeral right?"

"Yes, let me know when and where it will be and I'll be there." Davina twisted the house key off her key chain and handed it to Scott, who reluctantly took it and put it in his pocket.

"Don't you need it? How will you get back in your house?"

"Through the attached garage, besides I have an extra key at home. If you change your mind no need to call, just come on over and help yourself to anything in the fridge or freezer, *me casa, su casa*."

Scott smiled faintly. "It always was open house at Aunt Vina's."

"You can have Sun's old room. When she got married I turned her bedroom into the guest bedroom. You know which one it is."

He mumbled his thanks. "I'll keep the key for now but I think staying with you would make for a too long commute to Lincoln School. I'd probably get a speeding ticket."

"Just think about it. I could wake you up early and get you going. Whatever you hear on TV or read about in the newspapers about your dad, remember he loved you very much and was really, really proud of you."

"I know," he said. He gazed at something past her shoulder and she knew it was time to leave him.

"Bye, Scott. Take care and keep in touch."

"I will and thanks again for everything," he replied. Then he turned, walked back and got back in his car. She watched him execute a U-turn and become a silver dot disappearing into the traffic.

CHAPTER 5

In 1964 Midwestern flower child Davina Davidson
wore a headband around her forehead and a single
long auburn braid swinging between her shoulder
blades. Her head swirled with idealistic thoughts and
as she walked, skipped and ran, East Indian beads
bobbed against the bodice of her granny dress. A
vegetarian, she drove a yellow *Volkswagen* bug with a
bumper sticker that proclaimed: *Meat Stinks!* She was
thinking of dropping out of college and joining a
commune in Mississippi when she met Tom Reed, an
English assistant professor at Illinois State University.
On campus his classes were popular. He had a laissez-
faire attitude, and in the hopes of snagging an easy A,
Davina had enrolled in the class he taught,
Comparative Literature 201.

Assistant Professor Reed favored tweed jackets
with suede patches on the elbows and outside the
classroom he smoked a pipe from which aromatic

smoke curled like incense and sometimes floated into the pretty nose of Davina when she frequently stopped into his office with any question she could think of to ask him for she was hopelessly infatuated with him. His hair was prematurely grey which gave him a distinguished look and Davina found him intriguing.

He liked to joke with the students especially the pretty girls and there wasn't a hint of anything inappropriate on his part. But he didn't discourage Davina. He told her she was cute and fun to be around. He confided to her the literary dreams he held, and how in his spare time he wrote poetry and literary short stories and that someday he would write a great novel. She loved him instantly.

One day she stopped in his office with a potted plant and set it on his desk next to a mug of pens and pencils.

"It will bring favorable *karma* to you," she said.

He thanked her, shut the door, locked it and embraced her with enthusiasm, also planting a kiss upon her surprised lips. The window faced a brick wall and except for a Monarch butterfly resting outside on the window ledge, no eyes could see them in their first sexual encounter.

Later he said they should keep their relationship secret. As their relationship developed and deepened she began to dream of a life with him in a cozy home with his baby.

Tom Reed, born and raised in Oklahoma was also a deer hunter. Davina found this aspect of him distressing, but it didn't stop the progression from being his student, his lover, (Their song was *I'll Be Yours My Love*, by The Dave Clark Five) and then his wife.

With his acceptance to fill a vacancy as an assistant professor, non-tenure track, at a college in Saint Louis, they eloped, and he turned in his resignation.

As new arrivals to Saint Louis, the newlyweds quickly settled into their rented apartment, furnishing it with used furniture and cheap bookcases to hold Tom's many books. In their spare time they explored the city. They were busy, happy and in love. But when hunting season arrived, sometimes on weekends Tom went deer hunting with a colleague who held a similar interest in the sport. Then Davina busied herself at home and tried not to sulk.

In their love and passion for each other they compromised on the deer hunting issue. Since he wouldn't give up hunting deer, at Davina's urging he switched from hunting with a rifle to a bow and arrow, for she thought the odds would be more in favor of the deer. Later she found out the type of weapon used didn't really make that much difference to the prey.

Eventually he decided the best and least tiring way to shoot a deer was in a tree stand because he told Davina the deer never looked up. She forgave him his love of the sport but secretly she felt deer hunting was a cowardly endeavor, that the deer didn't have a chance and were merely innocent, sad eyed victims. She told him the only way she'd shoot a deer was with a 35 millimeter camera, a comment that didn't sway him in the least.

Desire and love, and later the birth of their daughter fused their lives. Davina insisted on naming their baby, Sunshine Marie.

"At least it's a more acceptable name than Moonbeam," Tom said. Her nickname morphed into Sunny and when she became a teenager, Sunny would insist everyone call her by Marie, her middle name. After a few attempts both parents gave up. To Tom she was Sunny. To Davina she was Sunshine, sometimes Sun. Many times she would ask, what were you thinking, giving me such a stupid name?

Because Davina was a vegetarian she never ate the deer meat Tom brought home from his hunting trips. Mostly they gave it away to friends and sometimes to a food bank. Davina's happiness at that time was such that she wished it possible to freeze time, knowing she would never again feel quite as satisfied with her life. While they lived in Saint Louis, she encouraged him to take up the game of golf to relieve the job stress he was beginning to feel.

Davina worked on finishing up the credits she needed for graduation, but when her pregnancy proved to be a difficult one she dropped out. In addition to the duties of a faculty wife and mother, she busied herself by joining the American Civil Liberties Union and the National Organization of Woman and kept current her subscription to MS Magazine. For a while she was a volunteer tutor at a local library in an adult literacy program and found great satisfaction in teaching adults to read, thereby improving their lives.

Then in 1970 they moved to Midville, a small town in central Illinois and Tom commuted to his new job with a significant increase in pay at a private college. Once again he was an assistant professor, but was now on tenure track. He told Davina this was where he wanted to spend the rest of his career. Midville was a typical small town where the kids engaged in seasonal sports and their mothers played bridge, gossiped, baked cookies and attended PTA meetings. It was a pleasant life and as Davina grew older those crazy, dizzy altruist days of the 1960s disappeared along with the long braid and the granny dresses, but in her mind and spirit she still held on to remnants of nonconformity.

While living in a subdivision on the edge of Midville, Davina renewed her interest in handicrafts, a legacy from her mother who could take an empty gallon plastic milk jug and turn it into a turkey container to hold an autumn flower arrangement, or a bird feeder to fill with sunflower seeds to hang from a tree limb.

One day six year old Sunshine came running inside.

Her hands clutched a bunch of wildflowers. With pride and a smile, she handed the bouquet to her mom.

"Thank you so much, Sunny. How pretty it is!" She put the commonly found *Queen Anne's Lace* in a vase and inhaled the carroty scent.

Later in the day she stopped vacuuming the carpet and went over to study the flat disks of creamy white, each one centered with a fleck of purple, and a dream surfaced in her mind. She would one day open a gift shop with the name, *Queen Anne's Lace.*

When Davina realized Sunny had gone into the ravine to pick the wildflowers, she scolded her. Occasionally all sorts of wild animals, raccoons, possums, ground hogs and deer would come up from the ravine and into the back yard and she knew there was danger down there. Once Davina even saw a red fox run from the ravine, across the yard and into the front of the house where it turned down the street and headed toward the highway.

A wild animal in the back yard was not an everyday occurrence but it happened enough times that the couple took notice. She and Tom had thought of fencing the back yard but finally agreed it would spoil the view and decided they would carefully monitor Sunshine whenever she played in the back yard. They told the child that if she saw any animal other than a dog or cat coming into the yard to run into the house right away.

• • •

Now Davina watched her nephew, Scott drive away. She got in her Ford Escort and turned the ignition key uncertain of where to head. She didn't want to go back to Shirlee's mansion without Scott and she didn't want to go home. She would phone Sunny, and also Shirlee later that night. And how could she tell her parents down in Florida that their son was dead? It would break their hearts.

The sky clouded over and it looked like rain, on the day her life was torn apart by Jed's untimely and violent death. For awhile she drove aimlessly. Soon she found herself on Highway 29 headed into the countryside toward the town of Silver Bay with a desperate need to talk to the man with whom she had shared the most important part of her life. Davina knew Tom's work schedule and today he didn't have any classes to teach. She was almost certain she'd find him in his cabin. With only a lone vehicle following a quarter of a mile behind her auto, her head still aching, Davina drove, enveloped in her thoughts.

After trading stocks online for a few years Tom had made a large profit and decided on his own that he needed a place to get away on weekends so that he could think and have the solitude to write poetry, short stories and especially that novel he had put off writing for so long. He didn't ask Davina her thoughts about the idea but one day he just announced to her that he had bought a little cabin by the river.

"It's very primitive and I don't think you'd like to stay there, but of course if you want to, you can."

She was a bit miffed that he hadn't consulted with her before buying the place and complained so much that he made a show of wanting her to stay there with him on the weekends she wasn't working at the gift shop. For her first visit he picked a summer weekend that turned out extremely hot and humid. Since there was no air conditioning in the cabin and it was small and confining, she felt miserable. Later, she would come to the conclusion that he had chosen that particular hot weekend for her to stay so that she would decide it wasn't for her and that she'd leave him alone when he went to the cabin.

So in that riverside cabin near Silver Bay, Tom now lived with his mid-life crisis and (Davina assumed) had overnight visits of one of his English students, Nikki whose frail and youthful beauty was displayed in a dark, gothic manner. The few times Davina had seen Nikki, the young woman wore all black clothing and her hair was dyed jet black. Davina wondered how her life had come to this weird situation with her husband involved with such a creature, (he insisted he wasn't) not admitting that she and Tom had grown apart.

As she drove to the cabin she hoped Nikki was not there for she wanted to talk to Tom privately and tell him of Jed's death and if only for a moment weep on his strong shoulders.

It had been in late April that she had first seen Nikki and stumbled upon what she thought was an affair in progress. Tom had organized a poetry reading for his students at a coffee house bookstore and when he mentioned the time and place he didn't invite Davina to attend. It could have been an oversight on his part, but Davina became suspicious for he had always included her whenever he read his poetry publically. Tom said he had a new sonnet he had written and would read it for the students at the event, but before she could think to ask if he wanted her to attend the event he had said he was going to do some errands and slipped out of the house. At the beginning of their relationship all those years ago Tom told Davina she was fun, unpredictable and full of playful tricks, an aspect of her personality he definitely liked. Could she be that way again? She decided to attend the poetry reading in disguise. Carefully she had made her plans involving the use of a blond wig, tinted glasses, a dull outfit of grey Tom had never seen, and a color she would never under any other circumstance ever wear. In her concealing outfit she had gone to the reading and had sat in a chair in back, by the wall where she sipped punch from a paper cup and ate a grocery store cookie and imagined a successful reconnection with her distracted husband. In the crowded room, she felt certain he was totally ignorant of her presence.

But things turned out differently than what she expected. Right before her eyes Davina watched Nikki pilfer Tom from her. Dressed in black denim and leather and perched on a stool with her fingernails gnawed-to-the-quick, Nikki in a breathy voice recited her poem from memory. Simultaneously, she plucked petals from a red rose, dropping petal after petal to the floor.

In Davina's opinion Nikki's poem wasn't like Plath or Yeats, but more like Dr. Seuss. But when Nikki finished speaking and dropped the final petal from the rose, the audience erupted in wild applause, some shouting "Cool! Way to go, Nik!" Davina knew something in her marriage was definitely amiss when Tom shouted out, "Bravo! Bravo!" Davina fled the poetry reading before Tom had begun to read his newly penned sonnet. She didn't want to sit and listen to a poem he had written that may have been inspired by Nikki.

● ● ●

Now halfway to Tom's cabin on a winding road that aligned itself through irregular patches of drying cornfields with the eastern side of the Illinois River, the rain drops began falling on the windshield. It was then Davina finally noticed the dark blue sedan following her. In the rearview mirror with the rain falling she couldn't tell if the figure behind the wheel was male or female. She turned on the wipers and so did the figure following. Through the rearview mirror Davina saw the shoulder length dark hair, sunglasses although it was cloudy and raining and a baseball cap pulled low on the forehead. With rain pelting the rear window, Davina couldn't make out a recognizable face.

She sped ahead putting distance between the two

vehicles and the person in the sedan dropped back apparently losing interest in pursuing her further. She drove on and checked the rearview mirror and the side mirror. The sedan was gone. That was crazy, she thought. Davina turned onto the gravel driveway leading to Tom's bungalow.

She saw a light was on inside the cabin and got a queasy feeling and wondered if he would be happy, or disappointed to see her. And what if he wasn't alone? She thought of fleeing but instead jumped from the car and ran through the pummeling rain and up the steps to the minuscule porch. Faint sounds of Mozart seeped through the door, counterpoint to the battering rain that also blew across the porch.

Shivering she knocked on the door, and then stood hugging herself for warmth. The music stopped and seconds later the door opened. It had been months since they had last seen each other and now there he stood before her, his eyes studying her, still handsome and princely, his face barely etched with lines, aging in a slow and subtle way.

"Come on in Vina," Tom said in a spirited voice, as if her appearance at the door of his dumpy little hideaway was wonderful and expected. "Let me get you a towel to dry off."

He wore a maroon flannel shirt, khakis and his scuffed penny loafers bearing his lucky Czechoslovakia coins from that trip he took before they had ever met. She wanted to both hug and slap his face.

She stepped inside and he went to find a towel. Always a pack rat, Tom's cabin looked like a hoarder's heaven, albeit a small one with books, magazines and other clutter.

"Something awful has happened," she said as he brought a thick towel from the bathroom. She told him of finding Jed's body. A shocked look came on his face.

"Ah, Davina I'm so sorry, I know how close you two were." He wrapped the towel around her, giving a bear hug that surprisingly felt comforting, bringing back memories of when they were together and she thought things were fine, even when it turned out that things were not so fine. She could smell the wood and pine scented aftershave she had given him on his last birthday when they were still together. He let her go and stepped back.

Davina dried herself with the towel. Except for a ticking clock on the wall, the room was quiet.

She told Tom of the police chief's suggestion Jed's death may have been a suicide.

"I never figured Jed to be the type to commit suicide. But who would want him dead?"

"I don't know. Jed would never commit suicide, he just wouldn't. Someone either shot him with a bow and arrow or stabbed him with the arrow. Tom, I'll never forget the sight of him. I don't know if I can even sleep tonight. I just keep seeing him lying there on the floor, all bloody. And then someone disguised in camouflage clothes attacked me."

"Are you alright?"

"Yes, except for this bump on my head."

"It looks painful. I'll get some ice."

"That's okay, by now ice may not help." Beginning with the morning cell phone call from Keith, she told Tom everything that had happened. Then she stopped speaking and stared at him intently.

"Why are you looking at me like that?"

"It could have been anybody, even *you*, for you know how to handle a bow and arrow. Remember that Thanksgiving Day last year when the two of you almost came to blows over some silly argument? I was so embarrassed. You've never really liked Jed, you've always been jealous of him."

"Me, jealous of what-his ability to get falling down drunk?" His face sagged and Davina at once regretted her accusing words.

About the jealousy, there was some, she thought, but she need not have said so. Where Tom had plodded along for years before finally heading up an English department and getting tenure, Jed had in spite of a drinking problem and depression that periodically surfaced, been very successful as a scientist. At first Davina had thought Tom, too would find success as a writer, perhaps becoming hailed as a second Hemingway, but so far he had only published two chapbooks of poetry and one short story and the novel had never materialized.

Tom seemed content with his life until the day he had walked out on her in May, she shouting for him to "Go, just go, I don't want you here anymore!"

"I'm sorry," she said, "I'm so upset. Jed's dead and since I found his body even I may be a suspect."

"I wasn't jealous of Jed's work and his accomplishments, only your devotion to him."

"I think you know very well that he had a hard time as a kid. He was introverted but his IQ was near genius and he skipped two grades. His birth was unplanned and Mom didn't give him the attention that she gave me. I was ten years old when he was born and he was like one of the baby dolls I had out grown, but only better. Jed always felt unloved, a bit unwanted and with those thick glasses he wore the kids made fun of him, so I guess I tried to make up for it."

Now Jed was dead and here they were, arguing with Jed at the center of it all.

"I know he was gifted, I won't argue with you over that," Tom said. "Did you know a month ago there was a feature story about Jed in the Chicago Tribune?"

"No, I didn't see it, what was it about?" That he had neglected to brag about the major news coverage was typical of Jed. About his work he was usually quite modest.

"In the article Dr. James Eliot Davidson was named, along with two other research scientists who had perfected a birth control serum to control the deer population."

"Do you still have the newspaper with the article?"

"It's probably here somewhere. I was saving it for you in case you'd missed it. Scott might like to have it now as a memento of his dad." He came close to Davina and with him the faint scent of the aftershave lotion she had given him. There was a bourbon scent too and she wondered if his relationship with the much younger Nikki was causing Tom to drink. He nuzzled her cheek. "I've missed you so much," he whispered.

"What about Nikki?"

"She's gone." He nibbled on her ear very gently.

"Gone where?"

She felt like a snowflake melting from the heat of his breath in her ear as he began maneuvering her toward the bedroom.

"I sent her away. I realized it was silly of me to let her hang around. I told you there was nothing between us; I've always been faithful to you. Come on Davina."

She felt her body yielding and their mouths opened to familiar territory, home, she was almost home, but something halted her and she lodged herself in the bedroom doorway.

"Stop it!" Breathless, she wouldn't let a return to her be this easy. He pressed forward but she pulled back.

A hurt look appeared on his face. "Why did you really come here, Vina? It's more than Jed's death. You miss me, say it's so, and I miss you so much. I want us back together. I'll do ANYTHING to make up for whatever you think I may have done although I'm innocent of adultery and you just won't believe me." He pulled her back into his arms and began kissing her.

"Please stop! I've decided to be celibate."

"Oh, wasn't that what you were the past year before I left?" His voice had a sudden sarcastic edge. Her sexual desire had never matched his.

"I shouldn't have come here," she said. "It's been a horrible day. I feel like someone's tap dancing on my head. I really need to get back home. Now just where is that newspaper?"

Then she twisted out of his grasp and walked to the nearest stack of newspapers and picked up one.

"Do you think you can find that article about Jed and the other scientists? I'd like to have it for Scottie, and then I'll go. It's getting dark and I don't like to drive at night. I want to go home and think about how I can help find out who killed Jed."

"Isn't that what we pay the police to do?"

"They are suggesting he may have committed suicide. I know he would never do that. He loved Scottie too much to leave him without a father. This isn't a Hemingway scenario. No one in our family has ever killed themselves. Someone murdered Jed." She began sorting through the newspapers.

"You won't let me show you how much I still care for you, so I'll help you find it." He joined her and shuffled the papers until he found the one with the article. "Here it is. Take the whole section. It continues on another page. Interesting piece, it was." Then he reached out and touched her hair.

"What's with the red tint? I like your hair the way it was before. This doesn't suit you, but that's just my opinion of course if-"

"My hairdresser goofed up, but you have a knack for saying the wrong thing at what could have been the right time." Why ever did she say that? She folded the newspaper and put it inside her roomy shoulder bag. Suddenly she thought of the police chief and his comment. "Some people, some *men* like my new hair color even though it was accidental."

"Calm down Vina. It doesn't really look horrible, it's just takes some getting used to. Let me make some fresh coffee before you go. It'll perk you up for the drive home. Would you like Colombian, Vanilla Almond, or Mocha? The Mocha is my favorite."

"No thanks, I've switched to drinking herbal tea. You know it's strange but on my way driving here I noticed that someone was following me. Once I almost got run off the road. I thought maybe it was your weird, child girlfriend, Nikki."

"She's not my girlfriend." Tom listened as Davina related how she couldn't tell who it was, only that the person had on dark clothing and wore a baseball cap.

"It wasn't Nikki, she's a bit strange but not that reckless. Do you want me to follow you home in my car and make sure you get home safely? I could stay a few days, sleep on the sofa. I won't bother you."

This was a moment she had thought about many times since that day in May when he had driven off with only a brief case, a garment bag and an angry look on his face. But she tilted her chin in confidence, "No," she said, "I'm learning to get by all by myself."

"Vina, think it over." He followed her to the front door. "I made a colossal mistake leaving you but you were insistent and yelling for me to go and so I did."

"Bye, Tom, see you at the funeral."

She stepped outside and into the blowing wind, the rain now slackened to a drizzle. Inside the car, Davina started the engine, turned on the wipers and headed down the driveway, glancing once into the rearview mirror. Tom still stood in the doorway of his cabin watching her. She gunned the motor, and the tires spit a gravelly goodbye.

CHAPTER 6

Back home the lump on Davina's head still drummed pain so she took a pain pill. She fretted about how to tell her parents in Florida about Jed's violent death. After she had left a phone message for Shirlee, she phoned Sun who was so shocked to hear of Jed's violent death she dropped the phone receiver, then her voice came back and she asked if there was *anything* she could do.

"Nothing," Davina said, "just come for the visitation and funeral. I'll let you know when Shirlee has finalized the arrangements. I don't know what she's doing. She didn't answer the phone." At 27, Sunshine was doing well as an assistant office manager, married to Gary, an ambitious lawyer and they lived a short drive away in Bloomington, Illinois. Then Davina thought about her mom and dad and how to break the tragic news to the couple, now in their mid-eighties, still healthy and active with minor heath issues but with their advanced ages, each year growing more frail.

Anna Simmons who was a registered nurse and an

old friend of Davina's had relocated to Florida the previous year. She lived in Tampa in the vicinity of Davina's parents and sometimes they met for lunch. Eliot and Gretchen Davidson enjoyed the company of her congenial friend. Davina decided in her absence, Anna should tell them of Jed's death and then Davina would follow up with a phone call to them. Davina phoned Anna who quickly agreed. Anna also offered to help her parents make flight arrangements if they wanted, although they were entirely capable of doing so themselves. But one never knew, it was better to be prepared, she reasoned. The phone call from Davina to her mom and dad was sad and tearful and they talked until there was no more to say. Finally they said their goodbyes, their minds grief burdened, remaining linked by sadness over the miles of distance from warm and sunny Florida to the chilly landscape of Illinois. Weary, tired and hungry Davina popped popcorn in the microwave. Not caring that it was a diet defeating action, preparing comfort food deluxe, she melted a half stick of butter and drizzled it over the popcorn. Then she got the newspaper article about Jed and the birth control vaccine and went into the family room and turned on the television set, where a 40's era black and white movie played.

She watched Victor Mature pour himself a drink and begin to pace a room. But she was not in a mood for film noir and its dark melodrama and cynicism so she clicked the remote to a cartoon channel and let it play on mute, just something to make her feel not so alone. She sat down on the sofa and unfolded the newspaper. While munching buttered popcorn and sipping a cola she read the article, carefully and with lots of paper napkins handy so as not to smear any grease on the newspaper. FIGHTING DEER OVER POPULATION, the headline stated above a photo of a deer herd in a field.

A sidebar diagram of a birth control dart explained

how from a rifle fifty yards away the dart was fired. The firing pin ignited the powder charge and the resulting explosion propelled the plunger forward to inject the birth control vaccine into the targeted doe. Then the dart fell to the ground leaving the doe infertile for four years. Davina's eyes lingered over the photo of Jed. He was wearing a laboratory coat, his hands displaying a dart. He looked distinguished.

After reading the article further, Davina discovered two other scientists were testing the same birth control vaccine, Pro310, in different areas of the country, Benton Cooper at CSS Research Institute in Tucson and Andy Foley at Dixie Laboratory in Huntsville, Alabama. Davina set aside the popcorn, wiped her hands on a napkin and got up with the intention of calling Directory Assistance for the phone numbers of the listed companies. She supposed she could have turned on the desktop computer and done a web search but she was tired, her head hurt and she wanted a quick response. She glanced at the clock on the fireplace mantle and wondered about the time zones and if it was too late to make the calls. She decided she had to try so she got the numbers. Maybe Jed had an enemy in the scientific community. She tried both numbers but got recorded messages.

Davina paced from the family room through the kitchen, down the hall to the master bedroom and back circling through the dining room and stopping once in the living room to feed the tropical fish in the aquarium. At ten o'clock she watched the local news on WMBD. A reporter stood before Jed's rented house relating news of his death: "A prominent local scientist James Eliot Davidson, known also as Jed, was found dead in an upstairs bathroom of his home in Paxtonia. The cause of his death was still being determined by authorities. It appeared he had been shot with an arrow, but suicide has not been ruled out." Crazily, she wondered if Jed hopelessly depressed and drunk had indeed committed suicide.

Davina took another pain pill with tap water, undressed, put on a night shirt and went to bed. She lay awake for a long time feeling alone and utterly depleted of energy. In her mind she replayed the events of the day, cried into her pillow, and finally went to sleep.

Bad dreams she did not remember upon awaking, caused her to toss and turn leaving the covers tangled. Going to bed on her portion of the bed, she opened her eyes to find herself lying on the other side, as if she had an instinctive urge to fill Tom's body imprint in the mattress with her own. Sunlight streaming between the slats of the mini blinds brightened the room. She unwrapped herself, threw back the comforter and got up with the burden of her brother's death heavy on her mind. Whoever the person was who had killed him must pay. She vowed to do everything in her power to see justice done. Davina dressed in sweats and lifted a slat of the blinds. She saw frost on the lawn and decided to exercise on the deck.

Outside on the back deck she pushed back chairs making room to do her Tai Chi routine. As she moved, the crisp, fresh air filled her lungs, while across the yard sunlight filtered through the trees, and the squirrels scampered and buried acorns. Twenty minutes later back in the kitchen, Davina prepared a mug of herbal tea. She took a sip and parked the mug on the table, then lifted the receiver of the wall phone and punched the number for Dixie Laboratory. When a woman answered, Davina asked to speak to Mr. Andy Foley.

The woman hesitated. "He's no longer with us," she said.

"But it's urgent that I talk to Mr. Foley. Do you have a phone number where I can reach him?" Davina picked up a pen and held it above a pad of paper.

Silence, a throat clearing, "I'm sorry but when I say he's no longer with us, I mean he's deceased. A week ago Mr. Foley was mowing his yard and a stray arrow shot by a hunter hit and killed him." The pen slipped from Davina's fingers.

"How could that happen if he was in his own back yard?"

"He lives in a rural area next to farmland and even though No Trespassing signs are posted, they are often ignored. Police are still looking for the hunter."

"It could have been a deliberate shot," Davina said.

"I really don't think anyone down here would deliberately shoot a bow and arrow at someone. It likely came from someone trespassing on land he should not have been hunting on. Mr. Foley had complained to authorities several times. He told me that he hoped he never got shot while out in his yard. Whoever shot the arrow that killed him is probably way too scared to come forward."

"Do you know if it was dark outside when he got hit by the arrow?"

"It was still daylight, late afternoon. Who am I talking to? You've called at an inconvenient time."

"I'm sorry, my name is Davina Reed and only yesterday my brother was"—*CLICK*

"Hello, Hello!"

Davina hung up the receiver, angry and a bit shaken. The sip of hot tea she took did not warm the chill she felt deep inside. She thought for a moment and again picked up the receiver, this time punching in the number for CSS Research Institute in Tucson, Arizona. She asked the person who answered if she could speak to Benton Cooper. Impatiently, Davina waited as the call was transferred.

"Hello, Benton Cooper speaking." His voice was a confident baritone.

She introduced herself. "You don't know me but I think you may be in danger, Mr. Cooper. Yesterday, my brother Jed- you may know him as James Eliot Davidson, was murdered."

"Do you mean Jed Davidson of BioChem

69

Corporation in Peoria, Illinois?"

"Yes, I'm afraid it is actually true although I'm still finding it hard to believe."

"I am so sorry," he said in a shocked voice. "Tell me what happened."

And she did, her voice filled with so much emotion she had to stop now and again to regain her composure so she could continue.

"The police did say that because of the suicide note found in the computer tray, Jed may have killed himself, but I don't believe it."

He was silent a moment. "I don't want to jump to conclusions but the last time we spoke by telephone- must have been about two weeks ago- Jed sounded depressed and it was obvious he was under the influence of alcohol or drugs-sorry forgive me, he was a fine man."

"My brother would never harm himself. I think someone is stalking the scientists who developed the deer birth control drug, Pro310. Did you know that Andy Foley of Dixie Laboratory in Huntsville was also shot and killed by a bow and arrow? He was at home mowing his yard where he should have been safe."

"Yes, I heard about his death," Cooper said, "but I understand it was an accident, that a deer hunter ignored no hunting signs posted on the farm next door."

"I think you should watch your back, Mr. Cooper. I think Mr. Foley may have been deliberately killed. Look at the facts. Two out of the three scientists who developed Pro310, are dead within a week of each other. You may be the next targeted victim because of your work on the serum."

"The newspaper article garbled some of the facts," Cooper said. "Although Foley and I tested the serum on female deer at wildlife refuge parks, Jed actually developed the serum. Anyway, considering chance, coincidence and predictability, the odds are the two

70

deaths aren't connected."

"But just think, Andy Foley was hit in broad daylight while mowing his yard, and the hunter who did it hasn't been found, and may never be found. Jed's death is even more suspicious."

"I'll think about that. I appreciate you called me and thanks for your concern. Now let me say something Mrs. Reed, or is it Ms. Reed?"

"Ms. is fine, my husband and I are separated."

"Jed and I go back a long way and he has mentioned you many times. He said you were a terrific sister and he was a nerd and once you scared off a kid who routinely beat him up as he walked home from school. As an only child and a geek myself, I was extremely jealous. I'm sorry for your loss. In the scientific community Jed had many friends and will be greatly missed."

"You're kind to say that."

"Because of my heavy work schedule, I may not be able to attend the funeral but my thoughts will be with you. And anytime you're in Tucson, please stop in. I'd be honored to treat you to lunch."

"Thanks," Davina said, "that is a possibility, because sometimes I travel on business for the gift shop I co-own. But Mr. Cooper, please be careful. I feel strongly that Foley's and Jed's deaths are related."

Cooper told her the two deaths were horrific and a great loss to the scientific community. "Both men were first rate scientists, and good friends. Thanks for the warning. I'll keep my eyes open although I'm just not sure they were homicides."

They exchanged phone numbers and addresses and promised each other to keep in touch. Davina hung up the receiver feeling like she had found a new friend. If they ever met in person, Davina just *knew* she'd like Benton Cooper.

The continuing headaches and memory loss of some events preceding Jed's death convinced Davina to phone her doctor's office for an emergency appointment. Dr. Reeves was out of town, but Lucille Patterson, APNP, agreed to see her.

Once there Davina explained what happened to cause the bump on her head. "Before I was attacked and fell I had an excellent memory. I could tell you what I ate at a certain restaurant in Milwaukee ten years ago, or who won the female best actress academy award in 1982, but now I can't recall if I fertilized my lawn yet this year, or remember what, if anything I ate for breakfast yesterday. It's scary."

Nurse practitioner, Patterson asked questions, examined the bump, took Davina's vitals and sent her down the hall for an x-ray of her cranium.

Afterwards Davina read a magazine while she waited for the results. Later, Ms. Patterson came with the news that Davina had suffered a mild concussion and handed her a prescription for pain pills to take as needed.

" Please no jumping and no jarring of your head and get some rest."

She told Davina to call again if she had further concerns and advised that she make a follow up appointment with Dr. Reeves in two weeks. Davina walked out of the clinic with a sense of relief.

CHAPTER 7

Davina stopped at a service station and filled up the gas tank, then continued driving toward Paxtonia. Occasionally, the border of bushes and trees parted their autumn beauty to reveal the unfurled grey ribbon of river. Just before the city limits sign she saw what she was looking for, the sign that advertised Froggy's Bar and Grill in green letters with a pointing arrow. She steered the Ford Escort off the highway and onto the access road where she continued past a marina, then a boat repair shop where a yacht dangled from a large pulley like a wounded whale.

She pulled into Froggy's gravel parking lot and shut off the engine. As part of her personal investigation into Jed's murder, she decided she would pretend to be an insurance investigator; a deception she felt would increase the likelihood of getting answers from the bartender and keep secret that Jed's sister was interfering anyway in the Paxtonia police investigation of his death. A black beret hid her hair and from her earlobes hung modest disks of gold. To complete her insurance investigator look she had added a pair of black rimmed glasses of low magnification bifocals she bought from a drug store.

She glanced in the rearview mirror and with a tissue blotted her lipstick into a faint stain, confident that she now looked properly professional and unrecognizable.

The afternoon sunlight filtered through the clouds and she noticed the only other vehicle in the parking lot was a pickup truck. A greasy odor emanating from Froggy's overlapped the wet scent of the river and invaded her nostrils. She walked toward Froggy's the rough gravel pressing through the soles of her low heeled shoes. Handrails of thick rope ran along each side of the plank walkway leading to the entrance of Froggy's. Davina stepped past a cement frog seated in a bed of pebbles, pushed open the door and passed an entryway display of a draped net ensnared with crusty starfish. No one was behind the bar with the bottles of *Johnny Walker* and *Jim Bean* and stacked tumblers. Inside a glass case and on sale were T-shirts with the logo, a bullfrog smoking a fat cigar emblazoned with Froggy's. She continued pass the sign clipped to a metal stand that stated, *Please seat yourself,* and called out, "Hello!" Her voice traveled past tables and chairs, the jukebox that dominated the wall like a fat lady in a carnival show, a pool table where now beneath a lone light she saw a man put down the pool cue and turn in her direction.

"What can I do for you? Want to see a menu?"As he approached she noticed above the grin, a mustache as thick as the straws of a whisk broom. His gargantuan belly reflected the hazards of his job. He wore a T-shirt like the ones for sale in the case and it strained across his chest and belly like a too small girdle.

"No thank you. I'm Emily Jones, an insurance investigator."

"Pleased to meetcha, I'm Travis, the bartender and sometimes cook." His front teeth were separated by a wide space with the right one bearing a corner chip.

"I'd like you to take a look at this photo," Davina

said and handed him a photo of Jed. "Did this man come in here last Monday night?"

He looked at the photo, and then studied Davina's face. "I heard about this man on the ten o'clock news last night. That's Davidson, the guy who was found dead inside his house in Paxtonia. The TV newscaster said the police found an arrow stuck in his chest and they can't decide if it's murder or suicide."

Davina's smile faded. "I'm trying to find out the truth."

He stared at her. "You say you are an insurance investigator so please show me some identification."

She pretended to search inside her deep shoulder bag, and then looked up. "I must have forgotten to bring my billfold with my identification. This is embarrassing. You'll help me, won't you?"

He observed her intently and Davina feared he would tell her to get out, but he didn't. "Yeah, he was in here with that guy who works at the taxidermy place on the corner of Wilson Avenue and Peabody Street- Keith Thorne."

"Did Jed seem depressed to you?"

"Not a bit. He and Keith got into an argument with a stranger sitting at the bar but nothing serious happened. The guy left and Jed and Keith stayed on until closing time. They were feeling pretty happy."

"What did the man they argued with look like?"

Travis scratched his armpit. " He was average height and build. He had a mustache and messy beard with a mean look in the eyes."

"And about how old do you think he was?"

"I'd say maybe in the fifties, hard to tell, half of his face hidden under that hair."

"Had he ever been in Froggy's before?"

"It's possible, but not while I was working. Jim, the part time bartender might have seen him. I can't figure why a smart man like Jed would hang around with a creepy guy like Keith."

"They shared an addiction to booze," Davina said.

"How would you know that? Who are you *really*?"

Davina sighed. "I'm Jed's sister, Davina but please don't tell anyone I was here asking questions."

"Why didn't you say so?"

"I'm sorry, I thought if I told you who I was you wouldn't talk to me."

"It looks to me like you could use a drink. On the house, what's your pleasure? I make a mean Mojito, using fresh mint leaves my sister keeps me supplied with."

"Thanks, but I don't really drink all that much."

"Okay and uh, one more thing," Travis said. "Jed's son, Shawn-or is it Scott, came in after the bearded man left. He's punky looking and wears an earring, like a girl."

"How long was Scott here Monday night?"

"Probably about five minutes. He bummed some money off his old man and left. If my son wore a rhinestone earring, I'd kick his butt from here to St. Louis."

Davina thanked Travis again and headed for the exit with the sound of his voice calling out after her: "Hey, Davina shouldn't you let the Paxtonia police department handle this?"

It was quite odd, she thought, that Scottie hadn't mentioned being with his dad the night before his death. As long as she was in the area Davina decided to drive to Jed's house. Approaching his rental house she saw that the crime scene tape still remained where it crossed the driveway. There were no squad cars on the scene. Davina recognized the kid wearing sunglasses standing on the driveway with a pot bellied pig as the boy she had seen the previous day. She stopped the car and got out. She lifted the yellow tape and stepped underneath.

"Hi," she said, "That's a cute pig, what's his name?"

The boy seemed to stare past Davina. He pulled the leash and the pig squealed in protest. "Don't come

76

near me or I'll order Marvin to bite you," he said.

"Okay, relax. I'll stop right here." Davina. said. "I've been thinking to get a pot bellied pig for a pet, myself."

"I don't believe you. You're just saying that."

"Okay, maybe I am. I prefer tropical fish as a pet for easy maintenance but Marvin is awfully cute and I might want to get one just like him. Is he lots of trouble?"

"Nope. "

"I'm Davina. What's your name?"

"Alvin."

"I was wondering, Alvin, did you see or hear anything unusual going on here at this house Monday night, or very early Tuesday morning?"

"I didn't see anything; I'm legally blind."

"Oh, I'm sorry." She wondered to what degree he was blind for she had heard that some people who were considered legally blind had very limited vision but could see fuzzy shapes and colors.

"But I did *hear* something," Alvin said.

"What?"

"There was something out in back of Mr. Davidson's house. I bet you don't believe me. Nobody believes anything I say."

"I believe you."

"Did you see the green house? That's where I live. Sometimes I sneak out at night. Since Dad took off, Mom never lets me do anything. She treats me like I'm a girl, so sometimes at night I go out and walk around just to prove to myself I can." He stepped closed to Davina, and started sniffing. "What kind of perfume are you wearing? It stinks."

"It does? That is a fifty dollars a bottle stink," she said chuckling to herself.

"It smells like a men's john. You should go and wash it off."

"I may have to change my perfume. So you were hiding in some bushes?"

"I gotta go. If you tell my mom I was out at night

when she thought I was in bed sleeping I'll say you are a rotten liar."

He yanked the leash and the pig let out a squeal.

"Don't you dare follow me Lady, or I'll scream and say you were molesting me."

He turned and began walking in the opposite direction from Davina.

"Wait, a minute Alvin. Did you hear anything unusual or suspicious that night?"

"I heard some animal. It sounded sort of like a cow mooing, but not *really*- then I ran off. I gotta go."

"Thanks for talking to me, Alvin." She lifted the yellow tape barrier and stepped beneath it, and hurried to her car. As she headed back she saw in the distance an SUV turning the corner and coming in her direction. She looked for a way to escape the possibility of being seen and recognized. Just ahead she saw an unmarked street that looked like a little used lane.

She took a right turn down the lane. Maybe it would lead her away from the area.

Soon Davina emerged from the narrow lane, happy with her successful dodge.

S h e drove until she found Wilson and Peabody and spotted the taxidermy shop. There was a sign in the window: *CLOSED*.

• • •

Tired and hungry, Davina drove back to Midville. She stopped at the local supermarket to buy a few groceries. Inside, she tugged a cart from the mass of jammed carts and reflected on events of the past two days. She pushed her cart past a center aisle counter heaped with green tinged bananas and jugs of cider immersed in crushed ice, and a hill of apples doubled in number by the reflection of the overhead mirror.

Deep in thought Davina's eyes didn't stray to the seasonal pumpkins and potted chrysanthemums.

So many things surrounding Jed's death seemed askew, like Scott, her nephew who neglected to tell her about seeing his father the night before she found Jed dead. She wondered just how blind Alvin, the kid with a pot bellied pig really was, and if he had been truthful or just making up things to say to a woman who in his opinion wore stinky perfume.

Davina paused by the lettuce section and absentmindedly examined some escarole. She couldn't shake from her mind the image of her brother on the bathroom floor, his hands clutching the shaft of the arrow, blood oozing scarlet against the white T-shirt. However depressed Jed was in her heart she knew he would never hurt his own son by killing himself. It didn't matter what Police Chief Leo Donovan thought. And what about Shirlee and Javier? Shirlee's tears and shock had seemed genuine. And on the trip to Tom's cabin, who could have been following her, and why? Did Jed's involvement with Keith Thorne get him killed, or what about his work on the deer control serum? The automatic misting machine sprayed her hand and roused her from her deep musings. Deciding on the red leaf lettuce, she then tore off a plastic produce bag from the suspended roll and filled it. After selecting carrots and radishes, Davina recalled she was out of herbal tea and headed toward that aisle.

While Davina studied the array of boxed teas at the end of the aisle, the sound of a loud, squeaky wheeled grocery cart approaching caused her to look up. Although there was something off kilter in his appearance, she recognized at once her peculiar neighbor, Cosmos Harris whose gaze was fixed on the shelves of coffee. She didn't want to contend with him and his animosity toward her so she tossed a box of herbal tea in her cart and wheeled off in the opposite direction so quickly she almost knocked over a pyramid of raisin bran cereal as she rounded the corner. Hurriedly, she plucked a few more items from grocery shelves and headed toward the frozen pizza section where she opened the freezer door and quickly pulled out a vegetarian pizza and tossed it in her cart. In her quick glance, her neighbor's appearance had seemed changed, different in some way, but how?

She reached a checkout counter and quickly transferred the items from the cart to the conveyer belt. She stepped forward to swipe her credit card and then she saw him again. Davina was surprised to see the lean frame of Cosmos Harris already outside the plate glass windows of the supermarket. He must have gone ahead of her through the express lane. Davina watched him hurry into the parking lot, realizing then why he looked so different. He had shaved off his beard and mustache.

When she arrived home Davina parked the car and took her groceries to the kitchen, put them away, then went out to check the mailbox at the end of the driveway. Inside was a thickly filled manila envelope addressed to her, on top of a magazine. She went back into her house and with curiosity, opened the manila envelope. There was a folded sheet of paper and another smaller manila envelope sealed and with her name on it.

Davina,

Please keep the enclosed envelope in a very safe place for me. You know I don't like bank safe deposit boxes. Don't tell anyone about it. It's IMPORTANT.
Jed

Davina walked around all the rooms and tried to think of a safe place and where a burglar would never think to look. She lived alone in the house and if she never again lit a fire in the fireplace she decided the perfect spot to stash the envelope was inside the chimney. She decided to open the envelope and carefully unsealed it. Inside she found a disk, and papers with mathematical formulas which held no meaning to her. She reclosed the envelope and placed it in a plastic freezer bag.

Then she walked to the fireplace, pushed back the metal mesh curtain covering the opening, reached in, and pulled the damper chain. The damper popped open. Carefully, Davina placed the envelope in the interior of the chimney against the metal wall, taped it securely and closed the damper. She slid shut the metal curtain. While washing the soot off her hands Davina felt confident that she had put the manila envelope in a safe place.

CHAPTER 8

Pudgy, sandy haired Police Lieutenant Jerry Caldwell 34, drove a squad car around the streets of Paxtonia, sometimes accompanied by a German Shepherd dog After he had rescued the dog from an animal shelter, he named him Sherlock and spent weeks training him to sniff out drugs, track human scents, and attack on command. Caldwell referred to him as his partner.

By stopping vehicles with teenage drivers for petty causes (such as driving five miles over the speed limit, a broken light tail cover, or a tire that looked like it was low on air) and using Sherlock with his keen nose, Caldwell hoped to halt the creep of any marijuana into town. To the students of Paxtonia-Lena Consolidated High School, he was a major pest. If the teen driver he stopped was male, he'd get a ticket, but if it was a pretty female, he instead flirted and made bumbling jokes. While Caldwell tried to act cool, the girl behind the wheel would say, "Yes officer," and "I'm so sorry, officer," and mumble an excuse she hoped he would accept so she wouldn't get a ticket.

His job as a Paxtonia police officer offered Caldwell security, a decent salary, health care, and a generous pension plan. He wanted two events to happen in his life: marriage to a pretty woman, and a job promotion to Police Chief of Paxtonia. Only then would Caldwell be satisfied and truly happy.

For five years Caldwell had worked hard as Chief Donovan's subordinate, patiently awaiting the opportunity to fill the position he desperately craved. From the moment he heard of Police Chief Donovan's early retirement plans, he resolved to become his replacement. However, with Mrs. Donovan's unexpected death, the chief had cancelled those plans. While he stewed over his awful luck, Caldwell became moody and increased the time he spent indulging himself with glazed donuts and sugared coffee.

One day while bending down to pet Sherlock, his pants split open, prompting him to step on the bathroom scale and watch his weight now registering two hundred and twenty pounds. He had always been what he considered pleasingly plump, but now he had to admit to himself that he was obese. He stepped off the scale with a new attitude. He promised himself to cut his food intake and get more exercise. He vowed to give up all sweets including his beloved donuts. He'd change his life, lose weight, get fit and prove his merit to be the town police chief. Now with the occurrence of the unexplained death of Jed Davidson in Paxtonia, came the possibility for Caldwell to prove to the members of the town council of his worthiness for the position. He could do that, if he could solve the mystery of Jed Davidson's death.

•   •   •

Holding a hand over his mouth, Lt. Caldwell's stomach felt queasy as he watched Mike Appoloni, a doctor with pathology training from the McLean County coroner's office as he did a visual examination of the body of the deceased. Caldwell cleared his throat and as much as possible avoided looking at the body on the steel table. He busied himself by scribbling on a pad on his clipboard. "Try to touch the arrow shaft as little as possible as I have to dust it for fingerprints," he said.

Dr. Appoloni peered over his bifocals with a steely stare at the officer. "You don't need to tell me how to do my job. I've been doing this for over twelve years." He wore a lab coat and surgical gloves and a paper mask covered his nose and mouth. Carefully, he removed the razor sharp arrow from the body of Jed Davidson and examined it.

"Sorry, I don't mean to criticize you. Here's the cardboard evidence box for you to put it in. I'll set it here on top of this cabinet. Excuse me; I'll be back in a minute. I got to go and get a drink of water," Caldwell said. He left the room and walked down the hallway to a water faucet where he pushed the lever and let the water spray his forehead. He knew it was irrational, but he couldn't bring himself to drink the water here. He paced back and forth and to escape the death smell clinging to him, stepped outside for some fresh air. Ten minutes later he returned to the autopsy room with the hope he could pick up the packaged arrow, seal it and leave. Appolini heard him come in and glanced up, scalpel in his hand.

"Where did you go for that drink of water, Springfield?" Blood dripped from his gloved hands.

Caldwell grinned sheepishly. "I think I'm coming down with something, I've been feeling a little headachy. What'd you find out?"

"I'm in the midst of this autopsy which will take at least a couple of hours more and I don't yet know. I can make a preliminary report in forty-eight hours. The weapon entered the decedent's T-shirt and chest right here. Come take a look if you like. You can see where it entered, just between these ribs and then it lacerated the heart and he bled to death."

Caldwell crept forward and took a quick look, almost gagging at the sight. Again the odor of death invaded his sinuses and the sight of blood further sickened him. Quickly he stepped back.

"I guess it's too early to know if drugs are in his system."

"I won't know for certain until I send the samples to the state crime lab and get the results. Are you sure you're okay? You look really pale."

"I'm alright. What's your gut instinct, was it murder or suicide?"

"If it was a suicide, statistics have shown that he would have lifted the T-shirt to stab or shoot himself. There were no defensive cuts or bruises to suggest a struggle. And I didn't find any hesitation marks like he was getting up the courage to stab himself by pricking his skin with the arrow."

"So off the record do you think it was murder?"

"You can draw your own conclusions."

Dr. Appolini peeled off his gloves and went to a cabinet and removed a paper bag. "Here are the clothes Davidson was wearing," he said and handed the bag to Caldwell. Caldwell asked for the arrow and Dr. Appolini reached back in the cabinet and removed the box containing the arrow. "The brand name on the shaft of the arrow is Hamilton Carbon," he said. He handed the box to Caldwell. "Aren't you sending it to the state crime lab?"

"No, I don't want to wait. I will dust for prints back at the police station lab." Dr. Appolini handed him the cardboard evidence box containing the arrow. With package mailing tape he pulled from his pocket, Caldwell carefully sealed the box. "Thanks Doc, I'd say for you to have a good one, but considering what you're doing right now with the body, I don't think it'll be a good day for you, just a bloody one."

Caldwell headed for the door and his escape with Dr. Appolini's response tailing him.

"You're wrong about that, Officer. I enjoy my

work and I assure you after you've left this room I will once again have a good one, as you put it."

Outside Caldwell found the day sunny, the sky cloudless, and the air fresh. He couldn't understand the cold detachment that Appolini seemed to hold as he cut into human flesh. Caldwell felt happy for the change in his surroundings. He stashed the two evidence containers in the trunk of the squad car, and then he drove to the nearest service station, not to gas up the tank but to make a trip to the men's rest room. At the sink he filled his palms with green liquid soap from a wall mounted dispenser. He scrubbed and scrubbed his hands until he was satisfied all the germs from the autopsy room had vanished down the drain. On his drive back to Paxtonia he stopped for a carry out hamburger and diet cola which he ate as he drove.

When he arrived back at the police station Caldwell stuffed the half eaten burger and empty paper cup into a trash container outside the entrance. Then he went inside and to the Police Chief's office.

Donovan was seated at his desk and on the telephone.

"Thanks, June Bug," he said, and hung up the receiver.

"Good afternoon Chief," Caldwell politely greeted his superior. "Dr. Appoloni said the victim, Davidson didn't commit suicide. I'm on my way to the lab room now to test for latent prints on the murder weapon."

"Hold on, that was June who runs Grandma's Koffee Kup on the phone. She overheard a bit of the conversation that took place between Keith Thorne and Davina Reed."

"Is that so?" Caldwell removed the wrapper and foil from a stick of chewing gum and folded it into his mouth.

"June Bug is what I call her sometimes. We kid around a lot when I go in for a donut and coffee. Anyway, she said Thorne admitted to Davina Reed that he was inside Davidson's house and that he slept overnight on the sofa the night Jed died."

"Was *murdered*," Caldwell mumbled.

"Thorne went upstairs, found the bed empty and the bathroom door locked. He banged on the door and yelled and when there was no answer he freaked out and left."

"What else?"

"That's it, except June heard the punk also say he'd deny everything if Da--that is Ms. Reed repeated his story to the police."

Caldwell held up a long cardboard box. "I'm on my way to the lab to check for prints on this arrow Dr. Appoloni pulled from Davidson chest."

"No, go put it in the evidence locker. You can do that later. Right now I want you to question Keith Thorne about what he told Ms. Reed."

"But I want to-"

"That's an order; *I'm* still the police chief here."

"Don't I know it," Caldwell muttered. He stomped from the room with such force that a framed photo of Chief Donovan with other Paxtonia dignitaries at a ribbon cutting ceremony hanging on the wall tilted sideways.

Chief Leo Donovan twirled a pencil between his finger and thumb, satisfied he had temporarily diverted Caldwell. Davina Reed couldn't possibly have had anything to do with the death of her brother Jed. But what if her finger print *was* there?

Police Officer Patricia Hansen breezed into Donovan's office with her heavy lily scented perfume cloud surrounding her body, and interrupted the chief's musing. "Guess what, Chief?"

He dropped the pencil on his desk top. "You want the rest of the day off so you can go river boat gambling?"

"Very funny."

"Then I give up."

"While you were out of your office, Officer Hedges

87

tossed his badge on my desk and said tell Leo Donovan to shove it up-well never you mind, use your imagination." Hansen blushed and dropped the badge on Donovan's desk. " I guess Ron didn't want to tell you to your face."

"That *would* be like that chili pepper to quit without giving a two week notice- not that I intend to replace him."

From the beginning Donovan felt it had been a mistake to add Hedges to the police force. Hedges had aced the psychological tests, hiding his true temperament. Hired before Donovan's wife's accidental death on the railroad tracks, the novice officer had only been on the force for two weeks when he got married to Jennifer Flatts, the unwed mother of an eighteen-month-old baby girl. She was also a manic-depressive person. Coupled with the problems of dealing with an erratic wife, and the demands of his police duties, the true character of Ron Hedges emerged. Under pressure he became like a volcano, erupting his fury on anyone in his presence.

"Hedges said he's leaving tonight for Cincinnati, or was it Cleveland? Anyway, he's gone- thought you'd like to know. I guess you're real sorry to see him go, huh?"

"Yeah, and I guess we won't get to throw him a good-bye bash," Donovan said to Hansen's departing back side. With a bit of glee he tossed the badge into a desk drawer.

Then an idea entered his newly love struck mind. The day Davina gave her statement she had asked for a drink of water and Donovan had filled a tumbler and brought it to her. He still had that glass in his possession. Later in the day, he lifted her prints from the glass, telling no one in the office. He found a match to the print on the doorknob of Jed's bathroom door-no surprise there.

As soon as the evidence locker room was deserted

and no one was around to see, Donovan would test that arrow shaft for prints. He would tell Caldwell about the testing only if the results if any, didn't implicate Davina Reed with whom he was now obsessed. But if Davina's print, or prints were found there, then Donovan would have to rethink the situation.

CHAPTER 9

The autopsy had been completed and all the family members had persuaded Shirlee not to proceed with the cremation of Jed's body. In the morning on Friday, the day of the visitation, and with Paxtonia police on duty to protect the death scene, Davina and Shirlee entered Jed's house to pick out his burial clothes. Davina assumed Shirlee would accompany her upstairs. Still suspicious of Shirlee and Javier, Davina wanted to see for herself the look on the face of the new widow while standing in Jed's bedroom next to the bloody bathroom floor. Would she see on her sister-in-law's face genuine sadness and grief, or fake tears? But at the last moment, Shirlee balked at the idea of climbing the stairs. Her face turned white and agitation erupted. She turned around and walked back to the front door.

"I can't go up there. Please you do it," Shirlee said. "Get his navy suit, shirt, a yellow tie, Jed liked yellow ties. Does he need shoes?"

"I don't think so. I really think you should help me pick out the clothes. Don't you want him to look decent at the visitation?"

"I can't go up there."

"If you're not going upstairs, then you'll have to

wait outside," the police officer said in a stern voice to Shirlee. From his eyes no sympathy emanated, only a look that Davina read as suspicious, or maybe the cop was merely impatient.

"Yes, officer, I'll wait in the car."

"Let's go," the cop said to Davina and he headed up the creaking stairs. "You've got five minutes to get clothes from the bedroom closet. Don't touch anything else."

Under the watchful eyes of the police officer, from the closet Davina gathered up Jed's attire, a navy suit, white shirt, yellow tie, underwear, socks and a pair of leather house slippers. The policeman helped Davina carry the clothes and slippers back downstairs and to her car.

As they were heading to the funeral home, Shirlee turned to Davina who was driving and said, "I want to hire someone to clean up the bathroom. You said Jed's blood is all over the floor. People talk and someone may start gossiping about the bathroom and how it looked with all the blood and then it will get all around and everyone including my gardening friends will hear and start gossiping, and all those who have come on the tours through my yard, *our* yard."

Davina gripped the steering wheel and fought to suppress her rising anger as Shirlee rambled on. "He was renting that house and didn't own it, but I want someone to wash the floors before the landlord hears anything. Will you get someone to clean it, Davina? Of course, I'll pay you back."

Davina braked and pulled off to the shoulder and looked at her sister-in-law. "Shut up, just shut up, Shirlee! All you care about is yourself and your reputation and image. I don't think you ever loved Jed and now you're carrying on with Javier -"

"That's not true," Shirlee said. She then began to cry and Davina looked for real tears. It surprised her to see a tear, and then another spill over Shirlee's eyelids. She watched them roll down the carefully made up face. Davina took a gulp of air, said she was sorry and didn't really mean the words she had just uttered and tried to comfort her.

"Okay, I'll do what you want," she said. "I'll call a cleaning service." Then she clicked the turn signal, steered back onto the highway, accelerated and wished she could skip the next two sad days and immediately begin the search for Jed's killer.

Shirlee dabbed her eyes with a tissue and thanked Davina and reached over and turned on the car radio. "Is it okay to listen to some music?" She adjusted the volume.

"Go ahead."

Outside the moving auto the Illinois prairie interspersed with fast food joints, telephone poles and gas stations slipped by as on the radio the Cardigans sang *Lovefool.*

● ● ●

Later at the 5 PM to 7 PM visitation, the line of people entering the front doors of Sloan and Mitchell's Mortuary extended down the front steps and to the sidewalk then continued all the way to the end of the block, the crowd a confirmation of the prominence of the deceased, James Eliot Davidson, PhD.

If a man's worth is measured by the number of mourners at his visitation, then Jed died quite rich, Davina thought as she observed the many somber faces approaching the receiving line where she stood in front of the coffin. Jed reposed in a navy business suit with folded hands, a rosebud in his lapel, serenity frozen on his face.

Davina rarely wore black but now dressed in a high necked black sheath she had pulled from the back of her closet and hastily pressed, Davina stood in the receiving line, her headache eased by the effects of a pain pill.

Gretchen and Eliot Davidson, Davina's and Jed's octogenarian parents had flown up from Tampa for the visitation and funeral. They were standing in the receiving line to one side of Jed's casket next to Jed's widow, Shirlee and their grandson, Scott.

When Davina had suggested to her parents that they would be more comfortable if they sat in chairs in the front row instead of standing in line, they said no, they wanted to stand, too. Davina could see how saddened they were to lose their son in the prime of his life by an act of violence by unknown hands.

Sometimes in brief moments between shaking hands and accepting condolences and hugs, Davina would sneak a peek at her father's grief imprinted face. Eliot had toiled his way to success, working long hours and succeeded in becoming vice president of a Peoria distillery. Then when the plant moved to a southern state he retired under a golden parachute and lived a luxurious life with Gretchen in Florida. Davina wondered if her father felt any regrets or guilt now for leaning so hard on the youthful Jed.

Had that pressure contributed to Jed's turning to alcohol? Quickly she dismissed the thought. Jed was responsible for his own actions, his success and his failures. In spite of his awkwardness and his inferior eyesight, he was blessed with a high IQ that he made the most of, overcoming his deficiencies, marrying a beautiful, if greedy woman and becoming the father of Scott.

Those paying their respects included co-workers of Jed's, scientists, researchers, laboratory technicians and secretaries. Also in the slowing moving line were several locally renowned people, including Mark Levin, builder and developer, along with the mayor, Frank Armour. She also noticed a man in line wearing a long white robe with a colorful Arab headdress and wondered how Jed had made his acquaintance. With words of sympathy, they all shook Shirlee's hand, or patted her arm, some giving her a comforting hug. In a time when it was no longer expected the widow wore head-to-toe black and a veiled hat and Davina saw Shirlee weep for Jed and she wondered if she had misjudged her sister-in-law. But then she saw Javier, who had not come through the line, sitting on a folding chair in back, looking bored. She suppressed her anger and stole a glance at her nephew, Scott who looked almost comatose. Davina noticed the rhinestone stud was missing from Scott's ear lobe. Her nephew's stoic face revealed little and there was only a sporadic blink of his eyes as he tried to contain the tears forming. That Scott hadn't told Davina he was at Froggy's the night before his father's death, still troubled her.

At the right moment and at the earliest opportunity she would ask him why he had not mentioned it to her. The line seemed never ending and after an hour and a half, her parents gave into their weariness and went and sat down in the front row so the people could come to them, and they could rest. Davina noticed Tom approaching the receiving line accompanied by Sunshine and Gary. She knew Tom would come, but he didn't say much, just gave her a quick hug, continued through the line and left the funeral home. Seated next to Gretchen and Eliot, Sunshine and Gary lingered, and then they too left. Sunshine caught Davina's attention, waved and mouthed, "See you tomorrow."

Davina shook more hands and received additional hugs and her feet began to hurt from standing in the high heels she was unaccustomed to wearing. Then she was startled to see Jed's drinking buddy, Keith approaching in the line.

When he stood in front of her, he said "Sorry," and shook her hand then moved and stood briefly in front of the casket, where she heard him mutter, "Oh, Man," then walk away, one fist rubbing an eye and she considered the possibility that maybe he had nothing to do with Jed's death. Next in line was Davina's neighbor Margie Jager, who lived across the street from her in Midville. Even though Margie was middle-aged she had newly attached braces on her teeth. They hugged. Margie expressed her condolences and then promised to come over and help Davina rake the leaves in her yard and bag them up whenever she wanted her help.

Davina thanked Margie and then looked up to see a tall, thin black man, middle-aged and impeccably dressed. He peered at her through round, rimless lens. "You're Jed's sister, aren't you?" She nodded. "I can see the resemblance in the eyes. I'm Maurice Wingate, a vice-president at BioChem where Jed worked," he said. "And I'm so very sorry for your loss."

"Thanks for coming. I remember Jed spoke highly of you."

"He was a smart and very kind man." Then Mr. Wingate leaned forward and so close she could smell his mint-scented breath. "I've got to talk to you," he whispered. "Call me after the funeral. It's important."

He shook her hand, pressed something into her palm and quickly walked away and toward the exit. She looked down and in her hand she saw his business card which she proceeded to slip into her pocket, a curiosity rising as to the matter he wanted to discuss with her. And then Paxtonia Police Chief Leo Donovan stepped in front of Davina, startling her with his unexpected presence.

S h e stepped back bumping the stand holding a sympathy wreath of carnations and gladioli. To her relief it shook but didn't fall. She had a sudden vision of the police chief fastening handcuffs around her wrists. "Hello, Chief Donovan."

"It's very sad to lose your brother in the prime of his life, I'm so sorry," he said. "Please accept my sympathy." Then, like a bulldozer he rolled forward and gave her a hug so exuberant that she feared the force might break a rib. "This may not be the best time to ask and I mean no disrespect, but may I take you out to a nice restaurant sometime?" He drew back and smiled expectantly.

"I don't know-I'm really busy."

"How about I pick you up around six-thirty, day after tomorrow, Sunday night?" He stared at her as if she'd better not decline his invitation. Then he was gone before she could get the courage to say no. Davina's mother noticed the awkward encounter and got up and when there was a pause in the line of mourners, she walked over to her.

"Who was that man?"

"He's the police chief of the city of Paxtonia," she said. Davina then related the exchange of words between her and the chief.

"Why does the police chief want to take you out to eat? Didn't he see your wedding ring? It seems highly irregular to me."

"I don't know. I think I'd better go out with him. Maybe he'll work harder to solve Jed's case."

"Don't do it, Vina. Tell him you're a married woman which you *still* are." She glanced at Davina's left hand. "Where's your wedding ring?"

"I took it off; it was giving me a rash."

"So after all these years, suddenly it gives your finger a rash?" She frowned. "I wish you and Tom would get back together. Why are so many couples getting divorced these days?"

"Oh, Mom let's talk about this later, okay? Besides, maybe Chief Donovan won't show up Sunday. But if he does, I'll talk my way out of it." Her mother was beginning to irritate her, transporting her back to those difficult teenage years so long ago.

• • •

The next morning Davina scanned the local area yellow pages and partly because of the cute advertisement of a cartoon maid with a frilly apron, chose Heartland Mini-Maid Cleaning Service to phone for a quote. She spoke to a cheery voiced woman named Rhonda, who appeared to be the lone maid employee and arranged for Jed's house to be cleaned the following Monday.

"I'll meet you in front of the house around 7 AM," Davina said, then went on, "I hope that's not too early for you." No need to tell her the cleaning included a bloody floor, she reasoned. She put down the receiver and then went to the bedroom and put on the same black dress she had worn the previous night to the visitation, adding around her neck a silk scarf with a geometric black and white pattern. The funeral of James Elliot Davidson, PhD. took place at 11 AM at the mortuary with the number of attendees significantly less than those who had attended the visitation the previous night. The service ended with a soloist who sang Amazing Grace and then the Reverend Brian Browne invited all in attendance to a lunch that would begin a half hour later at a banquet hall. The grave site ceremony was brief and attended by only a few, including Davina, her parents, Shirlee and Scott, who had been convinced by Davina to move back home. Although Davina had invited her parents upon their arrival, to stay a few days at her house in Midville, they had opted to stay with Shirlee who before the funeral had helped them put their suitcases in Davina's car trunk. After the luncheon Davina drove her parents to the airport for their late afternoon flight back to Florida.

• • •

While the funeral was taking place, meanwhile over in Paxtonia, Lt. Jerry Caldwell found Keith Thorne working in a taxidermy shop located on the north side of Paxtonia. When Caldwell stepped inside the shop a mixture of fur, hide and glue odors greeted him. On a shelf a radio boomed country music as Tammy Wynette implored women to *stand by your man*. On the wall a buck deer head mount with massive antlers gazed into space next to a sword fish mount and a bear head mount. All were fine animal specimens.

"M r .   T h o r n e ,   p lease turn down that radio. Remember me? I'm Officer Caldwell from the Paxtonia Police Department. I'd like you to answer a few more questions." He pulled from his pocket a ballpoint pen and notebook.

"I'm really busy," Thorne said. He was doing something with a slab of foam. He wiped his hands on a rag and reached up and shut off the radio. "I've told you everything before, in the station." Behind him a big eyed deer head awaited mounting.

"Let me get this straight. You said that you felt Davidson killed himself because he was depressed over the split up with his wife, right?"

"That's what I said."

"The pathologist, who did the autopsy on his body, thinks it was murder and not suicide."

"I don't know nothin' except what I told you in my statement."

"Very soon I'm dusting for fingerprints on the shaft of the arrow and you'd better hope you didn't leave any prints."

"You won't find any of mine on it, that's for sure."

"We'll see. You were in his house the night he died and it is strange that you didn't hear anything."

He stopped working and wiped his hands on a rag. "I was drunk, sleeping on a sofa downstairs. Anyway, why'd I want to hurt my buddy, Jed?"

"Jed was an educated man, a respected scientist and a PhD. with several patents to his name. I don't mean any offense when I say this, but why would he hang around with a nobody like you?"

Thorne's cheeks flamed red and he glared at the policeman. "Who you calling names?"

"Sorry, but it just doesn't make sense to me. What did you two talk about?"

"Women."

"Who? What women?"

"Babes and his wife. He was real sad and upset about the breakup."

"Hey, Keith you mount deer heads, do you also hunt deer, yourself?"

"Nah, I fish-crappie, catfish-you writin' that down?"

"I'm just taking a few notes so I don't forget." He turned a page in the notebook.

"What can you tell me about Jed's family, especially his sister, Davina?"

"Look, I mind my own business. I've got to get back to work. I've got a deer head to work on."

"Davina Reed thinks you hid in her brother's bedroom closet and when she came upstairs you struggled with her. You chloroformed her, and then printed a fake suicide note on the computer, or maybe you had already printed it."

"You're makin' me mad with all these lies."

"Are you willing to take a polygraph test to clear your name?"

"Nah, I don't think so. Any moron knows lie detector tests ain't admissible in a court of law."

Caldwell put away his notebook and pen. "Thanks for talking to me. I'll let you get back to your animal stuffing work. If later, you think of anything that might help to solve the murder of your friend, call me." He handed him a card. "My number." Caldwell started walking to the door.

"There was one thing," Keith said.

Caldwell stopped and turned to face Keith. "What's that?"

"One day when Jed was pretty plastered he said someday he and his sister would inherit a small fortune when their parents died. And with Jed dead, I got to thinkin' his sister would get all that money and property and not have to share it with him. Might sound mind-boggling but hey it's a crazy world."

"Do you really think Davina Reed killed her own brother?"

"No, I'm telling you what Jed said one night when he was plastered. You figure it out."

"Okay, but a little friendly advice, Thorne-check in with your parole officer. He says you missed your last appointment."

● ● ●

Back at the Paxtonia Police Station, Caldwell unlocked the evidence locker where earlier he had placed the arrow, along with Jed Davidson's clothing given to him by Dr. Appoloni. T h e c l o t h i n g was still inside, but the box that had contained the arrow Appoloni had pulled from Jed Davidson's chest was empty.

.

CHAPTER 10

On Sunday Davina slept later than usual, letting her body rest and replenish from the ordeal and exhaustion of Jed's Saturday morning funeral. She had got out of the habit of attending church services on a regular basis and today she would stay home. Also, there would be no morning exercising among the pines or on the deck for the previous night the TV meteorologist on WMBD had given a forecast of overnight temperatures in the low thirties with a frost warning. She yawned then walked into the living room and gazed out the bay window at the picturesque back yard where the grass wore a glaze of frost. Two squirrels scampered over oak leaves and pine needles, gathering and burying acorns. Davina lay down on the carpeted floor.

She rolled onto her back, clasped her hands behind her neck and did twenty modified sit ups. Then she did ten leg lifts on each side. As Davina got up from the floor her left leg creaked loudly. Frowning at the reminder that time was passing, she then assumed the Tai Chi stance in an area of the room where there was adequate space to move around. As a novice in the practice of Tai Chi, while engaged in the slow, controlled movements, Davina felt she was improving her flexibility daily. Seventy per cent of her body weight she shifted to her right foot, leaving the balance of her weight on the left foot. She held an imaginary globe in her hands, moving and turning gracefully and feeling the tension slip away. All the disturbing thoughts from the previous tragic days that had been lingering in her head evaporated temporarily.

Her exercises completed, Davina took a shower then dressed for work in a long, patterned skirt, a black, ribbed turtleneck and boots. She didn't have to hurry for the shop didn't open on Sundays until noon. She felt no eagerness in returning to work after the hiatus, for although she hated to admit it, *Queen Anne's Lace* wasn't making much of a profit. Business was slow and some days only two or three people came into the shop. Shoppers had fled to discount malls, or ordered from web sites on the internet. Davina felt that some crafters who came into the shop were snooping, checking out the handcrafted merchandise, apparently with the intention of copying the objects themselves and thus depriving *Queen Anne's Lace* of sales.

She and Meg would not allow anyone to take photographs of the items as some coming into the shop were inclined to do. Although the crafts from Appalachia sold well, there was little market for the pricey items Meg had insisted on adding to the shelves, like the cloisonné and Ming vases or the hand carved screens from India. She was aware that eighty per cent of new businesses fail, but did *their shop* have to be one of them?

Davina went into the kitchen, heated a mug of water in the microwave oven and submerged a chamomile tea bag. Into the toaster she slipped a slice of seven grain bread, moments later spread it with a smidgen of butter then sat at the kitchen table eating her sparse breakfast, sipping tea, while on a napkin she doodled the names of possible suspects for the murderer of Jed. Keith was at the top of the list followed by Shirlee, Javier the gardener, Mystery Man at Froggy's and followed by a question mark, Scott. Reconsidering, she crossed off Scott's name. She then circled Keith's name and dropped the pen.

She finished her toast, swallowed the last dribble of tea and put the mug, spoon and knife into the sink. When Tom was home they frequently had hearty breakfasts on weekends, blueberry pancakes or omelets filled with chopped ham and onions, oozing cheese. But those days were in the past, and this was her new life.

Davina took the interstate and then exited on North University where *Queen Anne's Lace* stood in a mini-mall wedged between a bakery and a florist shop. Only the locals knew the gift shop once housed a tobacco store. She parked in back and came through the rear door.

Leaning over a newspaper on the counter near the cash register, her gift shop co-partner, Meg looked up and smiled.

"Good morning, Vina." Meg was in her usually cheery mood. Broad shouldered, blond, and forty-five, she was reluctant to give up the page boy hair do that had originated from her years at Western Illinois University. "Jed's funeral was very well done," Meg said. "I've never seen so many flower arrangements at a funeral service. How are you feeling today?"

"Better," Davina said. "It will take time to get used to the idea that he's gone."

"I know." Meg turned the page of the newspaper and read for a few moments then looked up at Davina who still stood there as if she hadn't decided if she would stay, or go back out the door. "Listen to this-- my horoscope for today says: *Pluto has left your fifth house and Uranus is entering your eighth, so you are entering a prosperous period. Today should be a fruitful day.* It's a sign. Isn't it exciting, Vina? I think today we're going to actually make a profit."

"It's about time, now isn't it?" Davina stepped

behind the counter and set her bag on a lower shelf. Meg's buoyant outlook on life was one reason she had wanted Meg to be her business partner. She rarely complained about anything.

At first Meg wasn't sure if she was wanted in, but Davina finally convinced her that opening a gift shop was a worthy idea. Partially because her mother's name was Anne, Meg agreed they would name the shop *Queen Anne's Lace* as Davina had suggested. Although Davina's husband, Tom was skeptical of the idea of opening a shop that in his opinion, merely sold *doodads* and *thingamajigs,* Davina wouldn't be talked out of the plan. She and Meg took a road trip to Appalachia where they purchased unique handicrafts made by the local crafters to sell in the shop. Davina spent time researching on the internet and found a supplier in Arizona. And so in March she and Meg opened the shop.

In the beginning there was the usual surge of interest with a new store opening. A stream of customers came into the shop and the cash register rang up numerous sales. The two women felt giddy with their apparent success. Encouraged, they quickly expanded their selection of merchandise, including handmade pottery made by a retired doctor in Pekin. But abruptly there came a drop in sales. They would sit for hours playing Solitaire on the laptop computer, or wander around dusting and rearranging the merchandise, all the while anxiously awaiting the jingle of the front door bell that rarely came.

The slump in traffic through the door of *Queen Anne's Lace,* in addition to Tom's departure from their home caused Davina to join Meg in having doubts about the future of their new store. It saddened Davina that the new business never really took off.

"Things will get better," Meg said, repeatedly. "The holiday season is coming up. We can have another open house. We'll serve my little meat balls on toothpicks in sweet and sour sauce and you can make your pimento cheese spread."

That is one of our problems, Davina thought. Meg liked to spend money. She wanted to buy more advertising than Davina thought would be wise, but she didn't press the issue for Jed's murder was still heavy on her mind, more so than the troubles of the gift shop.

By two o'clock there had been two customers and neither had bought anything. Davina went into the back office where a lingering scent of tobacco from the former tenant remained. While eating a carton of strawberry yogurt from the mini refrigerator they kept there, she examined the debits and credits in the ledger on the computer. Fifteen minutes later Meg popped into the office with an anxious look upon her usually placid face.

"The mail just came- here's a bill from a supplier in Cleveland and they want payment *immediately*. Now when I mail them the check, we may be a little short this month."

"Again? Meg, you're depressing me."

"It's just a little cash flow problem," Meg said. "Now think about us having another open house. I'll put a sign announcing it in the window. And don't you bother about making the pimento cheese spread, although it's awfully good. I can take care of the food. Just be here."

Davina put in three hours and left when Josie, the part time clerk came in. They should not have hired any part time help, she thought. They couldn't afford it and with so few customers they didn't need an extra employee.

When Davina got back home she walked down the hall to the master bedroom where she saw the red light blinking on the answering machine. There were two hang-ups, a message from Police Officer Patricia Hansen to come pick up Jed's key, and a message from Maurice Wingate, the African-American vice president from BioChem where Jed had been employed.

"Ms. Reed, please call me, it's very important." Then he gave his home phone number twice. She tapped in his number but he didn't answer so she left a message.

Davina sat on the edge of the bed thinking that there was something she had been supposed to do, but she had forgotten what. A spider crawling across the wall got her attention and she smashed it with a shoe then wiped away the mess with a piece of tissue and flushed it down the toilet in the adjoining bathroom. She walked down the hallway and to the kitchen wondering what to fix to eat and then the doorbell rang.

Davina walked to the front door and opened it to find an unwanted visitor, the portly shaped Police Chief Leo Donovan, out of uniform, smiling broadly, a bouquet of roses and baby's breath sleeved in cellophane in his hands that he held out to Davina. "These are for you," he said. "You didn't forget our dinner date, now did you? I know I'm early but I was afraid you'd forget and go ahead and eat and then you wouldn't want to go out to dinner."

"Thanks," she said and took the flowers. She hoped none of the neighbors saw the uninvited man on her front porch. His stood there awkwardly with beads of sweat dotting his forehead.

"I did forget, but I'm sorry but I can't go out with you. I was going to call you-"

"Don't give me that, Ms. Reed. You were hoping I wouldn't show up now weren't you? Don't worry; this is a no strings attached dinner invitation. You'll want to come with me because I want to bring you up to date on the investigation of your brother's unfortunate death."

"Come inside. Can't you just tell me now? I'm not hungry. We can skip the dinner."

"I don't think so. We had a dinner date. Don't be rude." He stepped inside and after Davina shut the door he held out a key. "Here's your spare key to your brother's house," he said. "It turned out we didn't need it after all because Lieutenant Caldwell found Jed's key behind a sugar canister on his kitchen counter."

"Officer Hansen left a phone message for me to pick it up."

"Now you don't have to," he said and pressed the key into her hand. She took the key and invited him into the kitchen where he sat on a stool and watched as she pulled a vase from beneath the sink, filled it with water and plunged in the roses and baby's breath. She set the bouquet on the kitchen table.

"I don't think it's a good idea to go out to eat with you."

"I think it's an excellent idea." He patted a bulge beneath his sport coat. 'I'm armed but not dangerous, except to someone who dares to mess with you." He winked at her.

"You're asking me to go with you to a restaurant and you're carrying a gun?"

"It's perfectly legal. Beneath this coat is a holstered Smith and Wesson .357 Magnum," he said proudly. "With me by your side, you're safe. I'll protect you."

But who will protect me from *you?* Davina thought, but she said, "Alright, let me get my purse, but I'm warning you, I'm a vegetarian. I haven't eaten meat in over twenty years."

"Is that so? At times I'm a vegetarian, too," he said. "We'll get along just fine." He then proceeded to drive them to downtown Peoria and Michael's Steakhouse.

A hostess ushered Chief Donovan and Davina past the baby grand piano where a woman wearing rhinestone rimmed eyeglasses smiled a greeting as she played *Moon River*. They entered the dining room down two steps where all the tables had green cloths adorned with carnations in bud vases and thick candles in glass globes. They were seated at a table for four and a busboy hastily removed the extra place settings. Next a waitress handed them jumbo sized menus then proceeded to pluck from the tumbler in front of Davina the napkin, which she snapped open with a flourish and spread across Davina's lap. She repeated the napkin spreading movement for the chief. "May I get you something to drink from the bar," she asked.

"Would you like a daiquiri, or maybe a Tom Collins? Helen always ordered Tom Collins," Chief Donovan said. "Helen was my late wife," he added.

"I'll have tonic water with a twist of lemon," she told the waitress. Davina removed her bag from beneath the napkin in her lap and placed it on the empty chair seat next to her. "You must miss your wife very much."

The restaurant began to fill with mostly middle-aged couples. "I'm not always a vegetarian," Chief Donovan said. "Occasionally I cheat, how about you, Ms. Reed?" He winked at her and smiled. "Just kidding."

"No, I don't cheat, that would be my husband-*estranged* husband. But seriously, I've been known to devour a quarter pounder hamburger topped with bacon on rare occasions."

"There's nothing wrong with that!"

"I usually regret it. Now remember tonight we are going Dutch treat."

"If you insist, but it's not necessary. Don't get any ideas I'm putting the make on you, but you are one fine looking woman, Ms. Reed. Now is it okay if I call you Davina?"

"Yes, of course you can."

"I'd like us to enjoy our meal before I get to specifics concerning your brother, Jed's uh, murder."

"But I thought you felt it might have been a suicide."

"Not anymore,"

"Why's that?"

"I'll explain later. Now tell me about yourself. What do you like to do in your spare time? What type of books do you read and so forth?"

"I hate talking about myself. Current events and ordinary conversational topics are more interesting. What do you think of talk radio?"

"I only listen to country music on the radio," Donovan said.

"Okay then- how do you feel about combat duty for women in the military?"

"Let them fight hand to hand, them feminists," he said. "I don't like the way this conversation is going, Davina."

The waitress took their orders with Davina ordering a Caesar salad and vegetarian lasagna (Donovan wrinkled his nose in mock disapproval) and Donovan ordering salad with blue cheese dressing, a 16 ounce sirloin, medium with a baked potato topped with sour cream *and* butter. Although the chief was overweight, he definitely wasn't concerned with healthy eating, Davina thought, and she guessed his cholesterol level probably was dangerously elevated, too. As they finished their entrees Donovan turned serious.

"Don't be troubled by my question, but have you ever been fingerprinted?"

"Why do you ask?" She took a sip of water.

"I'd like you to answer my question please." She wished she were home in bed and reading a book awaiting the nothingness of sleep.

"It was a long time ago."

"So what was the reason? Did you have your prints taken when you applied for a government job? "

"No. I was in Chicago during the democratic convention in '68. I got arrested with some other protestors and we were all fingerprinted. My dad hired an attorney and I believe my prints were removed from my record."

"Your papa looked out for you," he said. "That's nice but somehow, I didn't figure you for a former hippie protestor."

"Lincoln Park was a long time ago," Davina said. " We were idealistic kids taken in by the rhetoric of the Chicago 7. It's in the past and I don't like to talk about it anymore."

The waitress approached their table and they stopped talking. They watched as she cleared the table then quickly returned with a tray filled with assorted desserts. She described each dessert enthusiastically as if all were not to be missed gourmet delights. Davina politely declined, while Donovan pointed to a large slice of cherry topped cheese cake.

"I take that one," he said, "and bring two forks just in case she changes her mind."

"I won't," Davina said, "but thanks."

"Well then, give the little lady some more tea, or would you like one of those latte things?"

"Tea will be fine." The waitress left the cheese cake for Donovan, and a busboy came with two mugs he set before them on the table. He returned to pour tea, and then coffee.

"Tell me what you promised," Davina said.

"What?" Into his cavernous mouth Leo Donovan shoveled a spoonful of cheese cake bearing deep red cherries. Davina twisted the napkin in her lap.

"What were you going to tell me about Jed's murder?"

"The pathologist's preliminary report points to homicide, so you'll be happy to hear that I've eliminated suicide as cause of death."

"I *knew* it wasn't suicide." Donovan explained that the angle of the arrow as it entered Jed's chest, and the depth of penetration suggested he was shot from about 30 feet away and likely through the screenless and open window by someone who had climbed up a nearby tree. With interest, Donovan listened as Davina then told the chief about returning to Jed's house and speaking to Alvin, the kid with the pet pot bellied pig. "Alvin lives in the green house near Jed's place. He was overprotected by his mom he said, so he likes to sneak out at night and roam the streets just to prove he can. That night when Jed was killed, Alvin said he heard animal sounds, sounds similar to a cow mooing but he didn't see anybody for Alvin claims to be blind, but I don't believe it. Maybe he has very limited vision."

"I'll send a detective to look up this Alvin kid and question him." He licked away a bit of cheese cake from his lips. "And what do you think? Do you have any thoughts about who may have killed Jed?"

"I don't want to accuse anyone, but I'm suspicious of Javier, the gardener who works for Jed's wife, Shirlee, and also there's Keith Thorne."

"Javier has an alibi," Donovan said. "Shirlee claims they were together all night- some grieving widow, right? I can't figure why would a smart man like your brother hang around with Thorne? He was just a drunk."

"The truth is they shared an addiction to booze. They were both going to AA meetings and both were off the wagon it seemed to me. Jed had it under control for a while but then his marriage problems caused him to start drinking again, and with that came depression. I think I should tell you I waited in my car after I left Paxtonia police department and when Keith came out I followed him to Grandma's Koffee Kup."

"I already know that. One of my officers saw you two together and came to my office and told me."

"Oh, I didn't know that. Anyway, I think Keith may be involved in some way in my brother's death." She related to Chief Donovan the details of the conversation she had with Keith at the café.

"Would you two like more coffee, tea, or an after dinner drink?" the waitress asked. "They make a great Grasshopper here."

"No thanks," Davina said. "It's tempting, but I'm finished-whenever you're ready, Mr. Donovan."

"Alright." He asked for the bill. "Forget about this Mr. or Chief Donavan business. You can call me Leo."

He looked at her anxiously. "Was everything okay? Did you like your meal?"

She assured him the dinner had been delicious. He seemed a decent man, still mourning his deceased wife, and lonely. The waitress placed the bill on a tray in front of Donovan. Davina quickly picked it up and insisted on paying half of the cost. His face crumpled in disappointment as she searched in her bag-futilely it turned out.

"Where is my billfold? This is so embarrassing."

"That's okay," Donavan said, happily.

He took out his well worn wallet, pulled out some bills. and laid them on the tray.

Before leaving the restaurant Davina went to the ladies' room located off the lobby. Besides being irritated for leaving her billfold at home, she felt perturbed that the chief hadn't really told her much, except that Jed's death was murder and she already knew that. She missed Tom and should have been more receptive to another man's attention, but clearly the portly police chief was not her type.

She returned to the lobby and was surprised to see Donovan reemerge from the dining room, an odd look on his face.

"I forgot my glasses," he said.

But she remembered that before she went to the powder room, he was wearing them. They stepped outside the restaurant and into the chill of November and walked to the parking deck.

"What do you know about Arkansas?" He asked. Davina felt the cold air against her face and wondered what he was getting at with his question. She took a deep breath and delivered her answer in a flippant tone.

"President Clinton is from Arkansas, a southern state located between Missouri and Louisiana. It's bordered by-oh yes, Oklahoma, Texas and Tennessee. People down there call handguns, pistols and some of them talk with a drawl. Am I right?"

"You forgot about Mississippi, and that Arkansas has beautiful lakes. It's always been my dream to retire in Arkansas."

"I sort of equate retirement with death," Davina said. Donovan unlocked the car door and swung it open for Davina. He slid the latch to open the remaining doors, shut the door and hurried to the other side.

"I don't plan to retire completely, just slow down and live at my own pace," he continued. He got in, started the ignition and leaned to push a cassette tape into a slot on the dashboard.

Frank Sinatra began singing, *Come Fly With Me.*

Fifteen minutes later Donovan pulled into Davina's driveway and shut off the engine. His large hands clutched the wheel as if he were still steering the car down I74.

"When I move to Arkansas I plan to open a small, private detective agency."

"You're going to be a private eye?"

"Yeah, this is bold of me to ask, but Ms. Reed-Davina could I interest you in a job, I mean when your divorce is final? I'll need a partner. You'd have to relocate, of course, but I think you'd love Arkansas; it's so beautiful."

His words shocked her. "The idea is ridiculous. I have no experience in detective work and I hardly know you," she said.

"This will be simple, not Sam Spade stuff. I'll supply security guards for businesses. I may do surveillances and try to get cheaters, both in divorce cases and workmen compensation. You have an inquisitive mind and a directness I admire, both qualities helpful to a detective."

"You mean I'm nosy?"

"Of course not."

"Thanks for the offer, but I'll have to say no."

"Why? I'm not difficult to get along with."

"My life is here in Central Illinois. I'm the co-owner of a gift shop that I am determined to make successful. My daughter lives nearby and some day I'm hoping for grandchildren for me to spoil."

"Don't reject my offer right away. Think about it, *please*. I might even consider opening my agency in central Illinois."

"Chief Donovan-Leo, I assure you no matter how much I think about it I will never, ever accept your job offer. I don't want to be a detective in Arkansas or Illinois!"

The corners of his mouth tightened. "As I said, think about it. Now let me walk you to your door." He was out of the car before Davina could say it wasn't necessary. The air smelled of wood smoke from a neighbor's fireplace and the amber glow of the porch light diffused into the night as they climbed the two steps to the porch. Flanking the front door, two pots held the frost killed remains of geraniums and salvia. She stuck the key in the door lock. A part of Davina wanted to offer to go inside and find her billfold and pay her part of the dinner check, but she knew it would offend the police chief.

"Thanks for the delicious dinner," she said. She expected to dodge a wet kiss, and with the porch light on, neighbors might see, but Donovan only grasped her hand and gently squeezed.

"Thank you," he said. But then his face turned serious. "Remember the glass of water I gave you back at the station when you gave your statement?"

"Yes."

"I lifted your prints from the glass and I got two matches, a print on the bathroom door, which was expected, but there was a fingerprint of yours on the murder weapon, on the shaft of the arrow pulled from your brother's chest."

"That's impossible. I'm sure I didn't touch the arrow."

"Maybe it slipped your mind because of memory loss from the bump on your head, or maybe you shot your brother and left a print."

"You're not serious. It has to be a mistake. If I shot him with an arrow, where's the bow?"

"Did you hide it in your car truck? We didn't search it. Maybe you put it there and came back inside and when you heard police sirens you hit your head with some object, pretended to be unconscious and then made up the story of someone attacking you. Those whirls and arches don't lie," he said. "It was your fingerprint."

"This is so stupid. I'll take a lie detector test to prove it."

"Relax Davina. I really had you going there, didn't I? I don't think you had anything to do with Jed's death. I don't know why but I think you made up that story about the attack. I think you came out of the bathroom and fainted and your head hit that metal cannon on the floor with such force you got a mild concussion. Play things my way and no one will ever know your fingerprint is on the murder weapon. I'm the police chief and I have access to all crime evidence. I can make it disappear. I can protect you. Now think about my offer. If you really don't want to move south, we can work out a plan to suit both of us."

He turned his bulky body and went down the steps and Davina went inside and shut the door and thought about what he had said.

CHAPTER 11

"No!" Davina shouted, and sat up. Her hands searched the bed beside her. Then she realized that she was alone, awakened abruptly from a dreadful dream.

She was not handcuffed to Chief Donovan and he was not next to her sleeping and snoring in her bed. The digital clock on the bedside table displayed the time as 6:09 AM. Heaving a sigh, she collapsed back onto the bed. She felt the back of her night gown damp against the sheet as she lay there and thought about the previous night and tried to figure out how her fingerprint could have gotten on the arrow that killed Jed. Maybe Donovan was correct when he said the trauma of hitting her head had caused Davina to lose the memory of her touching the arrow. She felt concern over the potential power he held over her. And now the chief had the arrow hidden some place with a threat of future disclosure if she didn't promise to seriously consider moving to Arkansas to work with him after her divorce from Tom. As far as Davina was concerned the police chief lived in a fantasyland.

After a hot shower she dressed, walked toward the

kitchen and caught her reflection in the mirror above the table at the end of the hall. She stopped and stared at her image and wondered why Donovan was so obsessed with her that he would compromise his job as Paxtonia police chief. She supposed she must remind him of Helen, his deceased wife.

In the kitchen she toasted a bagel and made herbal tea. The telephone rang and it was Rhonda, from the mini-maid service.

"Oh, I forgot to tell you," Rhonda said, "but since the house you want me to clean is located beyond our usual service area, I'll have to charge you an extra ten dollars."

With the thought of the blood stains on the bathroom floor that she had neglected to mention, Davina agreed. She felt certain that once Rhonda drove all the way to Jeb's place in Paxtonia, she might complain about the blood, but would complete the job.

"I'll meet you at the house. I'm leaving in five minutes" she said, and hung up the receiver. The extra fee didn't bother Davina, for her sister-in-law, Shirlee had promised to pay for the house cleaning. Quickly, she finished her bagel and tea and got ready to leave.

As Davina backed from the driveway and onto the street, she saw Margie, her neighbor from across the street, holding the newspaper she had just picked up. Simultaneously, they waved to each other.

Davina reached Jed's house before the arrival of the cleaning service worker. While she waited for Rhonda, she sat on the front steps of the porch and watched the squirrels playing in the yard. Her breath made white puffs in the chilly air.

Soon she saw a van approaching. The side panel of the van referred to its purpose- *Heartland Mini-Maids,* The cartoon figure of a grinning maid held a mop. The woman behind the steering wheel stopped the van and jumped out.

"Hi, I'm Rhonda and you must be Davina," she said, and they shook hands. Dressed in a sweat suit with *Heartland Mini-Maids* imprinted across her chest, Rhonda looked to be in her early forties. Her long blond hair was braided into a ponytail and the end fastened with a green rubber band that looked suspiciously like one that previously was used to hold a rolled up, home delivered newspaper. Davina caught the scent of the cinnamon gum Rhonda's mouth vigorously chewed.

"May I give you a hand with your equipment?"

"Sure, if you want to, I won't complain." Rhonda handed the vacuum cleaner to Davina, and then reached back into the van for a caddy filled with cleaning supplies. Lugging a mop and bucket and the caddy, she followed Davina up the porch steps. Davina set down the vacuum cleaner and unlocked the door and they went inside.

To access the job at hand, Rhonda looked around, and then she let out an earsplitting sneeze that almost blew the wad of chewing gum from her mouth.

"Bless you," Davina said politely.

"Thanks, this place must be full of dust and I'm allergic to dust. My mom keeps telling me to find some other way to make a living."

Davina suggested Rhonda start by cleaning the downstairs and begin with the kitchen.

"I'll stay out of your way. Call me when you're ready to clean upstairs and I'll tell you what I want done. It'll be quite a job up there."

"Oh, okay," Rhonda said and muffled another sneeze. Then she proceeded to put on a paper mask, and a headset attached to a portable cassette player she had stashed in her apron pocket. Adjusting the sound level occupied her attention briefly. Then they walked to the kitchen and Rhonda got to work filling the mop bucket with pine scented cleaner, and water from the faucet above the sink.

As she mopped the floor the pine scent infused the air and masked the scent of blood and death that only Davina seemed to be aware of. Davina walked into the hall and called Meg at *Queen Anne's Lace* on her cell phone. As she chatted with Meg, Rhonda busied herself swaying, mopping, and behind the paper mask, humming around the wad of gum to a tune only the cleaning woman could hear. Davina finished her conversation with Meg and flipped the cell phone shut. Preoccupied, she began tidying up the living room, and then stopped herself. She plopped down on the sofa and browsed through a Time magazine, then tossed it down and went outside to a beautiful, but windy day where the leaves danced across the yard like drunken ballerinas.

Davina breathed in the fresh air and walked around to the rear of the house. Beneath an oak tree she stood and looked up at Jed's bathroom window. As expected the window remained without a screen, and was now shut. Her eyes measured the distance from the window to the tree where many leaves still clung to the branches and could provide cover for anyone up there with a bow and arrow.

As Davina stepped away from the oak tree, the toe of her shoe bumped something hidden beneath the leaves. She squatted down and carefully lifted the leaves. On the ground lay a tubular, brown item about six inches long that she recognized as a deer bleat caller, commonly carried by deer hunters during rut season. Davina remembered Tom owned a similar deer caller. After inserting it into one's mouth and blowing, it made the sound of a bleating doe that aroused the bucks.

She examined the deer caller but recognizing potential crime scene evidence, she didn't touch it. Possibly it still held fingerprints. Then she looked at the tree trunk and saw scratches on the bark. She noticed the scratches were on both sides of the trunk and going upward. She guessed the marks were made by foot spikes of someone who had climbed the tree that crucial night. She looked up and noticed the tree with long and thick branches rose taller than the roof line of Jed's old, rented house.

As she imagined what could have happened the night he was killed, she felt sick. Up in the tree the assassin got his bow and arrow ready and waited. When the killer saw Jed enter the bathroom, a blow on the deer caller drew Jed to the window to investigate the noise. She realized that while Jed stood there, visible by moonlight, the person in the tree had a clear shot at him. As the scenario played in her head, Davina shivered. Now she knew how Jed probably was killed. But who was it?

Davina hurried back to the house to find a paper bag and paper towels. She needed to safely pick up the deer caller without disturbing any possible prints or dried saliva that might be still there and could identify the killer. She had watched enough crime shows on television to know the importance of protecting crime scene evidence.

As Davina came into the house and headed to the kitchen, she heard the whirring sound of the vacuum cleaner coming from midway up the staircase. Rhonda's back was to Davina so she was unaware of her presence. Davina knew she should have already told Rhonda about the blood in the bathroom. But her mind was on collecting what might be valuable evidence in solving Jed's murder.

If she hurried she would have time to collect the evidence and then tell the mini-maid about the presence of blood in the bathroom so she wouldn't be startled. Carefully, and walking on tiptoes so as to not leave footprints she walked across the freshly mopped kitchen floor.

Quickly, she looked inside the cupboards for a paper bag. Finally, beneath the sink she found a paper lunch bag. Then she tore a long sheet from the roll of paper towels on the counter.

Rhonda was no longer on the stairs, so Davina assumed she was cleaning the bedroom. Hurrying back outside, Davina decided to also preserve the evidence as she had found it with snapshots.

From her car trunk she got the Polaroid camera and proceeded to snap several views of the deer bleat caller, including close-ups of some of the scrapings on the tree bark. Then carefully, touching only the edge with a paper towel, she picked up the deer caller and laid it inside the paper bag. Davina then carried the paper bag to her car and put it on the front seat.

That was when she heard Rhonda's scream.

Shortly the front door banged open and Rhonda rushed out and ran down the steps.

"You didn't tell me there'd be blood to clean up! What happened up there?"

"I'm sorry. I was going to tell you before you started cleaning the bathroom. But then something important came up that I had to do right away and I couldn't stop and tell you before you saw the blood. But don't worry I'll give you some extra money to make up for it, if you'll just finish the job."

Rhonda pulled down her paper mask. "But was there an accident? Was someone murdered? I never read newspapers or listen to the news."

"There's an investigation going on. My brother died under mysterious circumstances and that's why there's blood in the bathroom. His wife begged me to get the house cleaned up before the out of state landlord found out about it and before any gossip about the bathroom condition got out. She's afraid of bad publicity. She was too upset to take care of the cleaning herself. I'm upset too, but I agreed to do it, mainly for my brother. I shouldn't say any more about it while the investigation is still going on."

"Rhonda folded her arms across her chest and stuck out her chin. "That's awful and I'm sorry, but why didn't you warn me? This place gives me the creeps. I don't want to go back up there. And I was almost finished. I just had the bathroom left to clean before I could pack up and leave and I opened the door and-"

"Please go back upstairs and finish cleaning the bathroom. I'll make it worth your while. Pretend the stains are spaghetti sauce and not my brother's blood," she pleaded.

"But-"

"Aren't you a professional cleaner?"

Davina successfully renegotiated the fee for the cleaning job and Rhonda said she would return to work.

"But I'll need more bleach," Rhonda said.

Davina searched the cupboards and closet and found a half full bottle of bleach.

By noon Rhonda had finished cleaning the house.

"I'm very pleased. You did a thorough job," Davina said. "Thanks so much. I know this has been a very unusual job for you." She wrote out a check and impulsively added a generous tip, and handed it to the mini-maid. "My brother's widow and I want you to keep details of the house cleaning private. You do understand, don't you?"

"Sure." Rhonda looked at the check and her eyes widened. "Wow, thanks."

She stashed her supplies in the van and got behind the wheel. She rolled down the window halfway.

"I would greatly appreciate it if you'd recommend my services to your friends that need a house cleaned," she said, and started the ignition, "especially houses that have stubborn stains. No disrespect to your brother meant."

Davina watched Rhonda drive off in the van. Then she locked the front door and headed down the steps and to her car with the intention of giving the deer caller and the Polaroid photos to Police Chief Leo Donovan. She drove to the Paxtonia Police Department.

At the information desk Davina spoke through the opening of the Plexiglas barrier to Nadine who had been a witness when Davina had signed her statement. Davina asked if she could meet with Police Chief

Donovan, but was told he had gone out for lunch.

"Maybe I can help you," Nadine offered. Davina felt perturbed and hesitated. She didn't know who she could trust with the evidence she had collected. Her roomy shoulder bag now held the paper bag with the deer caller inside. Perhaps she should turn it over to an attorney instead of the police. She spotted Lieutenant Jerry Caldwell emerging from a doorway but quickly decided to leave and turned away.

"Thanks, but I'll come back later," Davina said, and headed toward the exit. A lawyer was the person to trust, and not this small, and possible inept police department.

"Davina Reed," Caldwell called out, "Wait up. I need to talk to you. We can use my office down the hall."

• • •

Lieutenant Caldwell pulled a chair up in front of his desk.

"Have a seat, Ms. Reed. I've wanted to talk to you."

Davina raised her eye brows.

"Why?" The leather seated chair was worn, but comfortable. In her lap she clutched her shoulder bag containing the evidence she had now decided not to share with the Paxtonia Police Department.

Caldwell walked to the rear of his desk, pulled out a chair and plopped down, the force of his body causing the chair to give a loud squeak. Displayed on the wall behind him, framed certificates earned by Lieutenant Caldwell at various police seminars, attested to the seriousness of his ambition.

"How was your dinner at Michael's Steakhouse last night?"

"I didn't see you- were you there, too?"

"No, but this morning I got a call from an old

friend of mine who works at Michael's. She lets me know when the chief comes in as he frequently does. She tells me who he's dining with. It's his favorite restaurant. Her description of a middle-aged woman with red hair sitting at a table with Chief Leo Donovan made me think it was you. What were you doing there? Have you and the chief got a little romance going on?"

"Yeah, we're getting married next week! Come on- it was business. The chief and I were discussing my brother's death."

Caldwell rolled his chair closer to the desk and played with a *Bic* pen. "Ms. Reed, I'm not accusing you of anything, but why didn't you meet with Chief Donovan here at the police department?"

"Why don't you ask Chief Donovan yourself?"

Caldwell swiped a thumb across his nostrils, and blinked, a mannerism Davina noticed when he did it for the third time in her presence.

"The Chief doesn't know that I know he was at Michael's with you. Right now I'd like to keep it that way."

"It's certainly not a secret." Because she wanted to protect the love-struck police chief, she told a little white lie: "We met at a restaurant in Peoria, because he thought it was more convenient for me and he had personal business in the city earlier in the day anyway."

Her explanation was getting too detailed with false information, Davina thought. She hoped Caldwell's reporting friend hadn't seen them leave together in the chief's auto.

"Oh," he said, and considered her response. Davina shifted in the chair, feeling wary of the police officer. She wondered if Caldwell had noticed Chief Donovan's excessive interest in her.

"If you'd like to know, the police chief did not use any public funds for our dinners. We each paid half the bill." She thought why complicate her explanation by the truth about her misplaced billfold?

"It was an unpleasant dinner conversation, but we were discussing my brother's murder."

Caldwell dropped the pen. "So the chief told you the investigation is indicating your brother's death was a homicide, and not a suicide?"

"Our conversation was private and between Chief Donovan and me."

"By the way, did Donovan tell you that two years ago his wife died in a car-train accident?"

"He did mention she had died, but he didn't say a train was involved. That's really sad; it must have been an awful shock for him." A surge of sympathy began to modify Davina's opinion of the police chief.

"So you talked of things other than your brother's death, huh?"

"What are you getting at with these questions, Officer?"

"Oh, nothing," he said, his eyes on her spotted owl wristwatch. "That's an unusual watch," he said. "May I see?"

Davina extended her wrist. "It's a relic from the '60's," she said. Back then she had bought the watch because part of the cost went to a fund for the protection of endangered species.

"Hmm, no numbers, now what time would a quarter to that owl's feather be?" Caldwell asked.

Irritated and eager to leave, Davina stood up. 'I've got to go; I've got some things I need to do."

The smile on Lieutenant Caldwell's face faded.

"Hold on, Ms. Reed. One last question-do you ever do any bow and arrow hunting, or target practice?"

"No. I think hunting and shooting defenseless animals is disgusting."

"You must be one of those nutty animal rights people."

"I've got to go."

"Don't get huffy, I'm just kidding around. Did you know that some evidence concerning your brother's homicide is missing from the police department evidence lockers?"

"No, how would I know that? What kind of police department is this anyway, that evidence isn't protected?"

"I wanted to do fingerprint tests on the arrow the pathologist removed from your brother's body. I planned to do some fuming with Super Glue on the shaft, but now the arrow has disappeared."

So it *was* true, Davina thought, Leo Donovan was protecting her. And she wondered just how her finger print got on the arrow. "I guess we'll have to have an internal investigation," Caldwell said. He looked at the shoulder bag in her lap that she clutched protectively with both hands. "What's in your Brink-sized bag? You got something in there you want to show me?"

Not knowing what to do, Davina hesitated. Could she trust the deer bleat caller she had found beneath the oak in Jed's yard to a police department where evidence vanished? She felt sure the deer caller in her bag could be important in identifying Jed's killer. "Nothing, just the stuff a woman usually carries around in her purse," she said.

A suspicious Caldwell came around the desk and reached for the shoulder bag in Davina's lap. There was a brief tugging between them before Davina let go of the bag. "Please be careful," she said. "I found it beneath some leaves under an oak tree in Jed's back yard. I think it may have something to do with my brother's killer."

He zipped open the bag and took out the paper sack. Carefully he unfolded, and opened the top and looked inside. "What is it?"

"It's a deer bleat caller or grunt. It's a trick hunters use to fool deer. It imitates the sound of a doe during rutting, or mating season. Sometimes deer hunters rattle an old pair of deer antlers and sometimes they blow a deer caller like this one. There may still be dried saliva on it that may belong to the one who shot an arrow into my brother's chest. I was very careful when I picked it up because there may still be fingerprints or dried saliva on it. In his hurry to get away, the killer dropped it and then I found it today."

"Where do you buy something like this?"

"It's commonly found at sporting goods stores, and even at Wal-Mart."

"Ms. Reed, how do you know so much about deer hunting?"

"I come from a family of hunters. My dad, Jed and his wife all hunted deer with bow and arrows, even my husband who I'm now separated from. Will you send the deer caller to a lab for analysis? I won't leave until I'm certain it won't be lost, or misplaced."

As Caldwell wrote down her comments in a notebook, Davina explained exactly where and how she found the deer caller. He peered at the deer caller.

" How do I know where this piece of so called evidence came from and what does it have to do with Jed Davidson's death?"

She said she thought the killer was up in a tree and had seen Jed in the bathroom.

"He used the deer caller to draw Jed to the window where he could get a clear shot at him." She pulled the Polaroid snapshots from her bag. "I took these before I picked up the deer caller. And look at this photo of scrapings on the tree trunk. I think the marks were made by metal cleats on the killer's boots when he climbed the tree."

A curious Caldwell studied the photos and then looked at Davina. "You'd make a pretty sharp detective," he said. "Will you trust me with the deer caller and these snapshots? I'll personally drive over and deliver them to the state crime lab in Midville."

"I can drop them off. I think you know that I live in Midville. After I leave here I'm heading there."

"That would be highly irregular and I don't think they would even accept it from you. No, it has to come from our police department. There are procedures we have to follow with evidence to protect the chain of custody. I should put it in a larger evidence bag, seal it up and properly label it."

Davina realized he was right. "Okay, but I'd like to watch as you package and seal up the deer caller, okay?"

"You don't trust me at all, do you? Look at all my certificates on the wall. Can't you see how seriously I take my job? I follow the rules. Someday it will pay off for me."

"It's reassuring to me that you won't do the testing yourself." She thought better of adding, "A--hole."

"If it was a simple dusting of prints, I'd do it, but in this case considering it was found outside and beneath a layer of leaves, I'll leave the testing to the state crime lab people. And we're not equipped to do DNA testing in our lab here. In my opinion, I think it's highly unlikely they'll find anything. But you just never know."

"Is it okay if I check back with you to see what the crime lab finds?"

"No, we can't give out any information concerning an investigation. But I want to thank you for bringing this here, even though I had to wrestle it away from you."

"It's too bad the deer caller wasn't found earlier."

He ignored her comment with its hint of implied incompetence. "Back to the missing evidence in your brother's case—something odd is going on around here. I intend to find out what happened to the arrow the pathologist gave to me. I put it in the evidence locker. Someone took it out."

"I hope you find it," Davina said. "Lieutenant Caldwell, I have a question, I'm wondering if it is possible to lift fingerprints from say a drinking glass and transfer them to another object?"

"Sure, but that would be tampering with evidence." He stared at her intently. "Why did you ask me that?"

While Davina was at the police station talking to

Lieutenant Caldwell, Grandma's Koffee Kup bustled with noonday activity. A toddler threw a tantrum by the gumball machine.

"I want a gumball, gimme a quarter!" His mother slapped his behind and yanked him away from the globe of brightly colored balls. Laughter and chatter rose above the clinks of forks against china plates and a man in coveralls came to the machine.

"Hold on, little feller." Under the critical eyes of the mom he stuck a coin in the machine and turned the lever.

A thrilled little boy watched his chubby hands fill with gumballs. *"Tank you, tank you,"* he said.

Seated on a stool at the counter of the café, Police Chief Leo Donovan ate his lunch: a chili dog, french fries, a side of coleslaw and iced tea. As she refilled his glass, he kidded with the buxom June, but his mind was on Davina Reed. There was something about her that stirred up feelings like those he once held for Helen, his beloved, deceased wife. He knew it was inappropriate for him as police chief to be instigating a romantic relationship with Ms. Reed, the sister of a murder victim his department was investigating. He didn't care.

Last night on her doorstep he had told Davina stunning news: A fingerprint of hers was found on the shaft of the arrow that had killed her brother in his upstairs bathroom. Her prints were found on the bathroom doorknob and that was expected, but not her print midway on the shaft of the arrow. The prints matched those she had left on the glass from which she drank water at the police station, a glass that Donovan had preserved and tested himself, not sharing that information with anyone in the department. It could be incriminating evidence, but could she have stabbed Jed with the arrow, perhaps while he was asleep? Her body looked athletic and fit with strong arms so she could have done it, but even though Jed was drunk and passed out, there would have been a struggle. And if she had shot him with an arrow, as Davina had asked him, where was the bow?

The scenario he had recited to her sounded farfetched, he admitted to himself. No one would be reading Davina Reed the Miranda Rights anytime soon. In his heart he knew the idea she killed her brother was improbable and he shouldn't have removed the arrow from the evidence locker, but he would do almost anything to have a relationship with that woman, who seemed to have put a spell on him. June stopped and placed the bill on the table.

"June, are you trying to get rid of me?" He got pleasure in kidding around with the owner/waitress with the silvery eyelids and she responded in kind.

"No sweetheart, I forgot to ask, do you want dessert, maybe a piece of lemon meringue pie? Just yesterday, I made some fresh pies, strawberry, lemon meringue, and apple."

Chief Donovan patted his Santa Claus sized stomach. "You're tempting me, but I reckon not. I've been thinking maybe I should lose a few pounds."

He paid the bill with cash and placed a generous tip on the counter. Then he stepped outside the café. Overhead a flock of birds in the sky headed south for the winter. Someday I may join the migration south too, he thought, but if I do, it'll be one way. I won't come back. Then as he walked to his squad car in the crisp air, he mulled over his conversation the previous night with Davina Reed.

He had always prided himself on his integrity. Maybe he shouldn't have messed with the evidence. One thing was sure; when he discovered it missing, Lieutenant Caldwell wouldn't give up until he found out where the arrow was. Chief Donovan could plant the idea that the hotheaded police officer, Ron Hedges who had left the Paxtonia police force and moved away, had out of spite, taken the arrow. Of course, Hedges would deny taking the arrow, but with Hedges' vengeful, and contrary reputation, some in the department would believe he had indeed purposely taken evidence. Yes, Donovan thought, that scenario might work. Then as soon as he cleared up the case and the real killer of Davidson was found, Donovan could tidy things up by returning the arrow to some other place within the building. It wasn't unheard for evidence to get misplaced and then later be found in an unexpected place. By that time, no one would care that it had been temporarily missing. Yes, that's how this could turn out, Donovan thought. Then again, it might be better to wipe the shaft clean right now, and return the arrow to the evidence locker before anyone found it was missing.

However, for now the arrow would remain hidden under a blanket inside the trunk of Donovan's squad car.

CHAPTER 12

On Tuesday the temperature was a bone chilling 34 degrees. At the BioChem parking lot Davina pulled her Ford Escort into a visitor parking spot, got out and clicked the automatic lock on the remote. The sky was grey that November day with brown and yellow leaves windblown around the vehicles in the asphalt lot. Shivering, Davina hurried to the entrance where it took both of her hands to pull open the heavy door, whereupon a buzzer loudly announced her arrival. Behind the chest-high counter, an angular faced woman hunched over a computer keyboard, looked up and peered through lavender tinted lenses.

"May I help you?"

"Mr. Maurice Wingate is expecting me." The mustard color of the walls in the small and efficiently arranged lobby contrasted sharply with two blue chairs and an oversized fern that had outgrown its terra cotta pot.

"And you're-"

"Davina Reed. I phoned yesterday and talked to Mr. Wingate. We have an appointment." The clerk made a phone call and moments later Maurice Wingate opened a door and stepped into the lobby.

"Ms. Reed, it's a pleasure to see you again." He extended his hand to Davina. "Thanks for returning my call." Wingate's smile was engaging and friendly, the evenly aligned teeth, a highlight to his ebony skin. They shook hands and exchanged comments about the chilly November weather. The clerk in the lavender tinted lenses placed a visitor badge, sign in sheet and pen on the counter.

"Clip on this lovely badge and sign in," she said in a cheerful voice. Davina signed her name, unzipped her jacket and clipped the badge to the pocket of her tailored white blouse that she wore hanging over her black slacks. Then she followed Wingate back through the door he had entered.

"My office is upstairs and to the right. Follow me, please." Then they proceeded down a long hallway with many unexpected juts and turns. Wingate told Davina the building dated from the 1950's with many additions since that time as BioChem grew and expanded. He stopped before a door that bore his nameplate. "Welcome to my office," he said and opened the door.

On Wingate's desk next to a computer, keyboard and monitor, his paperwork mounded into a messy landfill. He removed a stack of books and papers from a leather armchair and invited Davina to sit down. "Please excuse the mess," he said. He went behind his desk and eased his long and slim frame into his chair.

"I'm not a picky housekeeper but I know where everything is-I think."

Framed photos decorated the wall above Wingate's head: Martin Luther King leading a civil rights march, Colin Powell, in his general's uniform laden with stripes and medals, and Michael Jordan slam dunking a basketball.

"Mr. Wingate, what was so urgent that you wanted to talk to me about? Has it something to do with my brother, Jed?"

"Please call me Maurice; I don't like this Mr. formality. And may I call you, Davina?"

"Sure. Please do."

His expression turned sympathetic. "I want to again offer you my condolences on the loss of your brother, Jed. He was a fine scientist."

From his desk he picked up a paperweight with a grasshopper encased inside.

He gazed at it briefly and then set it down.

She wished Wingate would get to the reason for his urgent summons to his office. She began to swing her crossed leg slightly, a mannerism of her impatience.

"I suppose you know that Jed helped develop Pro310, a birth control serum to help control the deer population?"

Davina nodded and stopped swinging her leg. She unzipped the opening of the shoulder bag in her lap and reached inside. Her hand shoveled through the contents and came up with a photocopy of the newspaper article Tom had given to her that day in his cabin in Spring Bay.

"Have you seen this article about Jed and Pro310," she asked as she handed him the photocopy.

Wingate glanced at the article. "Yes, I have. It was well written and informative, but caused some trouble for us here at BioChem." He returned the photocopy to Davina.

"After this article was in the newspaper, BioChem became the target of a letter campaign and crank calls. It was like someone posted a message over the internet to all the deer hunting kooks in the country. We got flooded with letters, and e-mails to our website, even nasty and harassing phone calls, all protesting Jed and the other scientists and their work with the deer serum."

Davina listened intently.

"Pro310 was proving successful in curbing the deer population on a small level but extremists in hunting clubs, survivalists' groups and nuts on the fringes of society protested, all because we wanted to curtail the deer overpopulation. They didn't seem to care about all the accidents and deaths they cause, including the damage too many deer do to corn crops, and soybean fields. For a time we even had pickets walking back and forth and carrying signs here in front of BioChem. Our employees were harassed when they arrived for work. It was so disruptive the management caved in and decided they didn't want any further research done in that field."

"What upsets me personally is how the local papers and the TV media tarnished Jed's name by suggesting he had committed suicide. I know he was murdered and it was probably because of his scientific work on deer population control. It may be someone who sent a letter to BioChem. May I have the letters to give to the police to examine?"

"I'm sorry, but they got thrown out and all the e-mails were deleted. It would be an impossible task to read through all those hundreds of e-mails and find a clue to a possible killer, even if a computer expert retrieved them from the hard drives in all our computers."

"Oh," Davina muttered, obviously disappointed. "I'm so mad and upset, I'd like to hunt down the person who killed Jed and even though I've never been a violent person- shoot an arrow through his evil heart!" She wiped away the tears filling her eyelids.

"I'm sorry to get emotional."

"I understand-well I can imagine how you feel."

"I don't have much confidence in that small town police department," Davina said. Then she told him about finding the deer caller beneath the tree. "It will be tested by the state crime lab."

"It's fortunate you found the deer caller, isn't it? Let's hope it was a rare oversight of the Paxtonia police."

"I wish I could do more to find Jed's killer."

"Usually Jed kept quiet about his personal problems, but sometimes he got moody-"

A loud knock on the door interrupted Wingate. The door swung open and a large framed woman with thick ankles came in. She wore a navy blazer over her broad shoulders that reminded Davina of a football player, and an orange wool skirt bulged by wide hips.

"Winny, you're wanted down the hall in Jim's office. He wants to show you the results of the electrophoresis tests. Whoops-sorry, I didn't know you had company."

When the hefty woman called him, Winny, Wingate frowned. "Ms. Reed, this is my secretary, Hyacinth Brock, who likes to barge into my office uninvited on a regular basis. She's the one who threw out all those protests letters and urged everyone to cleanse their computers of the e-mails from the kooks. I thought for our security the letters and e-mails should have been kept just in case we needed them."

"No telling tales out of school to strangers," she quipped.

"Hi, I'm Davina Reed," Davina said, "It's nice to meet you." But it wasn't, she admitted to herself.

Hyacinth's eyes honed onto Davina. "I have to explain my floral name," she said. "When she was procreating my mother was obsessed with flowers. I have a sister who's stuck with the name, Tulip. I used to want to change my name to Heidi, but with this body, I can't get away with it. Dainty, I ain't."

"Davina is Jed Davidson's sister," Wingate said.

"I'm so sorry about your brother," Hyacinth said. "He was a gifted scientist." Before Davina could respond Hyacinth tapped Wingate on the shoulder. "Did you ask her about the missing documents?"

Davina thought of the manila envelope back at her home containing the papers and floppy disk sent to her by Jed and now taped inside on a wall of the fireplace. Wingate took his secretary's elbow and steered her to the still opened door. Davina noticed the bulky ankles disappearing down into black oxfords like those she had seen on the feet of some nuns. Hyacinth was a woman with whom Davina wouldn't want to get angry.

"Did you finish typing up the letter to Stellar

136

Corporation?" Wingate asked.

"I'll get to it right away."

"Yes, you will, and tell Jim I'll be down in the lab in twenty minutes, and don't ever call me Winny again."

"Yes sir!" She saluted and clicked her heels together like an obedient soldier.

After she left his office, Wingate shut the door. "She's pretty obnoxious, but she can type 65 words a minute."

"That wouldn't be enough for me to keep her."

Wingate smiled but his face turned serious. "Davina, I'll get right to the reason I wanted to speak to you."

"I've been waiting. That's why I came."

"Jed was working on a new and improved animal birth control serum for deer that he called X267. Deer hunters would definitely not like X267. The old serum Pro310 could never have been utilized on a wide scale as each doe had to be shot with a birth control dart. Mainly, it was used to control the deer population in wildlife refuge parks located near residential areas. It was impractical to use broadly. Beside there aren't enough sharp shooters available to inoculate enough does to drop the deer birth rate significantly."

Vice President Wingate picked up the grasshopper paperweight from his desk. "But with the new serum Jed was working on-that was a different story."

"How is it different from the first formula?"

"I'm not exactly sure. But he was experimenting with a deer birth control immune vaccine and hoped to perfect it so that it could be sprayed on acorns, which deer love to eat, and dropped into areas populated by deer." He stared at the paperweight in his hand and Davina unexpectedly noticed something unusual about the grasshopper: It had three legs.

"Jed was secretive about the new formula. I'm sure he was already having it tested by someone with a crop duster."

"Isn't the spraying of strong chemicals dangerous to the environment? What about the birds and butterflies? Won't they get sick or die if they came in contact with it? And please tell me-why does that grasshopper have three legs?"

"Jed gave this paperweight to me after another project on insect control produced grasshoppers with three legs. I keep it on my desk as a reminder that things can go wrong if we're not careful."

He put down the paperweight. "I call him *Quasimodo*. Isn't that ridiculous, me naming a freak grasshopper encased in plastic, *Quasimodo*?"

"Yes. That grasshopper doesn't have a hump, or hunch on its back," Davina said, and smiled.

"I couldn't think of anything better than the character from Victor Hugo's novel," he said. He set down the paperweight. "X267 as far as I know, is perfectly safe. Jed told me it does only what it's supposed to do-make does infertile."

"So there's no danger of producing three legged deer?"

"That's funny," Wingate said, "but no, there will not be any three legged deer running, or hopping around because of X267 used on their feed. More likely the use of the formula would be a first step to possibly lead to the elimination of the sport of deer hunting."

"Deer are beautiful. It's something about the eyes, both innocent and wise."

"There's just too many of them."

"Although my husband hunted deer, and my brother and his wife did too, and also my dad, I could never understand how hunting is considered a sport. Deer can't shoot rifles or bows and arrows. They can't defend themselves. I've come to believe hunting is murder-*animal* murder."

"You surely put it strongly, but I'm inclined to agree these days now that I don't have to supplement my groceries by hunting for game. Now when I was a boy growing up in Kentucky I hunted not deer, but squirrels and possums to round out my family's diet of poke salad and grits. But now I buy my meat at the supermarket."

"I'm not familiar with poke salad, but I love that Southern specialty, grits, with lots of butter. By the way, I'm a vegetarian, for twenty years now."

Wingate leaned back in his chair and chuckled. "I know you're a vegetarian. Jed told me. Now can you help me out? I've searched Jed's work computer files, his desk and file cabinet and I can't find anything concerning X267."

However charming, accommodating and sincere Maurice Wingate seemed to be, Davina wasn't ready to turn over to him anything concerning Jed, just yet. Until she decided what to do with it, she wasn't going to tell anyone that taped inside the wall of her fireplace was Jed's X267 data.

"I don't know anything about Jed's formula," she fibbed. "But after Jed's murder, I phoned Andy Foley and Benton Cooper, the other two scientists mentioned in the newspaper article with Jed. I wanted to warn them to be careful, and that their lives might be in danger. Maybe you already know that Foley was killed in a suspicious bow and arrow hunting incident while mowing grass in his yard. Allegedly, it was an accident. Foley's property was located next to farm land where no hunting signs were posted, but hunters sometimes did anyway. Huntsville police still haven't caught the shooter. I don't think it was an accident. I believe it was deliberate."

"I heard about Foley's death, and I *did* think it could have a connection to Jed's death."

"Two out of three scientists who worked on a controversial doe birth control serum end up dead a week apart-it may have been a deliberate conspiracy to kill all three of them and send a message to the scientific community to not mess with deer hunting," Davina said.

"What about the other scientist, Benton Cooper? What does he think? You said you talked to him by phone."

"I couldn't convince Mr. Cooper over the telephone of any connection between the two deaths and their work on the deer birth control serum. He said it was most likely a coincidence. He said he was sorry and said how much he admired Jed and his work. Then he invited me to visit him in Tucson anytime. I may take him up on his invitation soon because I've got to find out who killed Jed. Maybe I can get information from Mr. Cooper that will help me."

Wingate tapped a pen against his desk top, thinking. "I guess you know that as Jed's employer, BioChem is entitled to rights to any research work he did here. There was some discussion about turning over everything to Jed to use as he saw fit because the rest of management decided they didn't want the controversy of being connected to deer control serum. They had a verbal agreement and were ready to sign the papers making it officially Jed's formula. Then some of them were reconsidering. Do you know anything about the whereabouts of the research on X267?"

"Weren't you listening? I told you I don't know anything about his work."

He looked at her intently. "Okay, I believe you. In fact, I've just got an idea. Why don't you fly out to Tucson?"

"Me, fly to Tucson?"

"Why not? You might find information from Mr. Cooper that will help solve Jed's murder. I only ask that you find out if Cooper will give you any data Jed may have shared with him that relates to the new formula X267."

"Suppose Benton Cooper doesn't have any X267 data? Suppose he does, but won't give it up?"

"I'll take the chance. Don't worry."

"I'm not interested in a reward. I only want to get

the evil person who killed my brother."

"Your mouth is saying you don't think so, but your eyes are saying you do want to go to Tucson. When can you leave? I'll call our travel agent and make arrangements for a round trip ticket. The company will pay for it, no obligation to you at all. Just promise me that you'll find out if Jed shared any info on X267 with Benton Cooper and if he did, get it and return it to me. If you don't find out anything, you will have had a nice trip anyway."

If Davina accepted the free ticket, it would be under false pretentions, she thought, for she already knew where the data was-inside her fireplace. However, she did not know for *certain* the manila envelope held the information Wingate wanted. She had barely looked at the contents and she didn't see anything that said X267. But suddenly a trip to Tucson away from the November chill appealed to her. Besides, hadn't Cooper invited her?

"Okay, if you arrange it, I can leave as soon as tomorrow," Davina said. "I'll call Benton Cooper to make sure he'll see me. But remember I'm making no promises. You may get zero information from this trip."

"Good, let's get everything coordinated as quickly as we can. You call Cooper and let him know you're flying out and want to meet with him."

"He may think it strange for me to fly out to Tucson so quickly after his phone invitation. But I could say it's a business trip for my gift shop."

"Oh, yes. Jed gave me one of your gift shop business cards. I have it on my Rolodex. He gave out your cards to almost everybody employed here. It's Queen something-"

"*Queen Anne's Lace.* I own it with a friend and business partner, Meg Hale. I'll feel better if we consider the paid airplane ticket a loan. After I return I'll reimburse your company for the plane ticket."

"That's not necessary," he said.

"I want to repay the ticket price. I'll make it a business trip for the gift shop. We need to stock up on some unique turquoise jewelry for the coming Christmas season. And while I'm there I'll try to convince Mr. Cooper that he should be careful because the person who killed Jed and the one who killed Foley may try to kill him too. I'll phone Mr. Cooper right now to verify he's going to be there and isn't on a business trip or vacation." She pulled her address book from her bag and found Cooper's phone number.

While Wingate fussed with some papers on his desk, Davina walked to a corner of the room and made a cell phone call to Benton Cooper who seemed surprised, but pleased to hear from her. In their brief conversation Cooper invited her to contact him when she arrived in Tucson.

"All set," Davina said. She stashed the cell phone in her bag.

Wingate then telephoned the travel agent and reserved an early morning flight to O'Hare with a connecting flight to Tucson. It's all arranged," Wingate said. "You can pick up your ticket at the travel agency. Here's the address." Wingate thanked her for coming to see him. "Have a good trip and find out all you can."

Then she opened the door and bumped into Hyacinth standing just outside. Davina realized she must have been listening through the door to their conversation. The Styrofoam cup of coffee in Hyacinth's hand sloshed over and to the floor and both women stooped down. With tissues Davina took from her shoulder bag they dabbed up the coffee. Davina wondered how long the husky woman with the thick ankles had been listening at the door.

"I'm almost done with the Stellar Corporation letter," Hyacinth said to Wingate. "I only need to spell check it and print out a copy."

"I should have had it on my desk by now. Goodbye, Ms. Reed." Wingate shut the door.

"I want you to know that I liked Jed a lot," Hyacinth said. "For a while, Jed was very kind to me. I'm gonna miss him."

"I miss him too," Davina said. The two women stood simultaneously.

"I can't believe I won't see Jed again," Hyacinth said.

Surprisingly to Davina, Hyacinth looked truly sad and teary eyed. It was a sight that caused Davina to reconsider her disappointing first impression of Wingate's secretary. She was stunned at the softness beneath Hyacinth's hard exterior.

Then unexpectedly, Hyacinth gripped Davina's forearm. Like the flame of a candle blown out, the softness disappeared and the tender look in her eyes was replaced by a cold and steely stare. "You wouldn't happen to know if Jed took some BioChem documents and a floppy disk home with him, would you?"

No, and take your hand off my arm!" Davina twisted out of Hyacinth's grip.

"There were rumors Jed was going to be fired."

"I don't believe you," Davina said and walked off. She felt anxious, but hopeful for a rewarding meeting in Tucson with Benton Cooper, the last remaining scientist to work on the doe birth control serum.

CHAPTER 13

Two rows ahead a baby began to cry as United Flight 248 descended through a sky fluffed by cumulus clouds. Davina felt her body tense up. Gazing out the window and past the stranger seated next to her, she whispered her mantra: *Still water, still water* and in her mind she became a figure in a Monet painting; reclined in a rowboat her hand trailed through water as her companion, (bearing a striking resemblance to Tom, her estranged husband) maneuvered the oars. As the 737 airliner bumped to a landing, she exhaled and mumbled, "Okay."

"Excuse me," said the middle-aged man seated in the adjacent window seat. "Did you say something?" The airliner rolled on, the speed slowing.

Davina felt embarrassed. "No, I was meditating-saying my mantra. I know it's silly, but takes offs and landings always scare me."

"Next time you fly, try a couple of gin and tonics," he said. "It always works for me."

"Thanks for the tip." Davina wondered if she would ever shake that fear, or the anxiety of being without Tom, and alone. And now she had the added burden to deal with, the loss of her brother, Jed.

In the terminal at an auto rental counter Davina

signed the contract for a Taurus automobile. Sunglasses shielded her eyes from the dazzle of the desert sun as Davina drove from the airport. She checked into the Hacienda Motel, a pink stucco building located on Speedway Boulevard near the University of Arizona. Outside room 302 Davina inserted the key card the desk clerk had given her into the slot. When the green light blinked, she quickly turned the handle and pushed open the door to a clean and inviting room with white stucco walls hung with paintings of blooming cacti. She unloaded her overnight case and shoulder bag on a cabinet where a printed note card by the ice bucket stated: *WELCOME! During your stay let me know if I can be of any service.* The card was hand signed in ballpoint pen, *Mariana.*

Davina looked around the spotless room and checked the bathroom where the first sheet of toilet paper on the roll was folded into a V, and bottles of lotion, shampoo and conditioner were lined up like toy soldiers on a tray by the sink. Mariana had done a professional job. With the remote Davina turned on the television set, found the weather channel and pushed the mute button. Davina walked over and peered out the window where below, the swimming pool looked inviting and empty. Except for a man sweeping a broom around patio chairs, the pool area was vacant. She removed her shoes and stretched out on the queen-sized bed covered with a spread of pink and sage swirls that matched the pattern on the curtains. The mattress was firm. That night when Davina went to bed, she thought she might actually sleep.

She sat up and eyed the telephone, remembering her daughter had asked Davina to phone when she had reached Tucson and got checked in. As the years had passed and Sunshine became an adult, Davina noticed their mother-daughter roles had shifted, ever so slightly. Now her daughter fretted over Davina as if she needed guidance and protection, like an overly concerned mom giving her unasked for advice, which Davina responded to by saying, "Thanks for your concern," then at once ignored. In their phone conversation the previous night, Sunshine had tried to talk Davina into cancelling the Tucson trip.

Now Davina tapped in Sunshine's phone number but got the answering machine. "Hi," she said pausing, "the snow bird has landed. I'm nesting in room 302 at the Hacienda Hotel and the temperature is-"she glanced at the TV, "102 degrees. Don't be jealous, bye, bye."

Then Davina made another phone call to Benton Cooper at his office. She sought any tidbit of information that would steer her in a direction leading to Jed's killer. She accepted Cooper's offer of lunch.

'I'll pick you up in front of the hotel entrance in 15 minutes," he said.

"What kind of car should I look for?" She thought of him as the sports car type.

"I'll be driving my Porsche, old yeller." Or did he say gold yellow? Did he really have a Porsche?

"I'll be out in front of the hotel entrance and I'll be wearing"-she looked at the clothes spread out on the bed-"a yellow outfit, so I'll match your Porsche." Over the phone line she heard a chuckle.

"See you very soon, Davina."

Davina shed her traveling clothes and stepped into the bathroom. At the sink she splashed water on her face, dried off with a hand towel, then refreshed her lipstick and flicked a comb through the red hair that she was getting used to; it seemed to have developed golden highlights. She put on the skirt and matching top and on her feet, espadrilles. Into her earlobes she attached silver hoops then scrutinized her mirrored imaged. Not too shabby, she decided, for a menopausal flower child. Entering the elevator, she felt as if she were going on a date.

She knew little about Benton Cooper but his voice

over the phone was filled with attributes that she prized-confidence and humor. It could be that he was married but like to flirt. This is business, she reminded herself. This is for Jed. Possibly Benton Cooper could give her new information. Near a saguaro cactus outside the motel entrance, Davina stood watching the traffic. Then she saw a yellow vehicle approaching, but it wasn't a Porsche. It looked like a Vega and as it came closer then rattled to a stop, she saw it *was* a Vega, possibly a '79 model. The man inside tooted the horn. She approached and peered into the window on the passenger side where she saw a husky man with a salt and pepper beard and corresponding hair, although receding, who could have once been a football player. He smiled broadly. He reached over and unlatched the door.

"Hi, Davina?" His eyes held a rash aspect that hinted excitement, or danger. She opened the door.

"Yes, and you must be Benton Cooper."

"Yep, hop in," he said. He appeared to be on the early side of fifty, but could have been younger. His casual dress yielded to the desert heat, no tie, short sleeved shirt, slacks and bare feet imbedded in moccasins.

She slid in and shut the door. "Hi, it's nice to meet you."

"Likewise." His quick handshake was firm and dry. "I can see the resemblance to Jed."

She fastened the safety belt and the Vega lurched noisily forward and soon into the traffic flow. "I'm sorry about deceiving you about my car. She may not be a Porsche- I've always wanted one- but old yeller is very reliable and has reached classic status. Is this your first visit to Arizona?"

"No," Davina said. "One summer in the '60s I tutored some kids on a Navaho Indian reservation near the Grand Canyon."

"Ah, youth! How well I remember those pot filled, I want to change the world days."

The suntanned fingers clutching the steering wheel were ringless, but that was never a guarantee a person without a ring on the fourth finger of the left hand wasn't married. And why did his marital state matter? She was here for Jed. And she was still married. "Uh, don't you have air conditioning?"

"Nah, the compressor went out a month ago. I should get that fixed. Roll down your window."

And let more of the heat inside? She'd try it anyway. The handle didn't turn easily but finally the window scraped its way down.

"Please call me Ben," he said. They drove past a bank where the digital letters on an electronic sign registered the temperature at 103. And inside the auto was proving to be a furnace. Davina's rented Taurus had air conditioning. She realized she should have suggested they switch cars back at the hotel. After passing through a 3-way intersection, Cooper parked the Vega on University Street.

"Leave the window open. It's okay," Benton Cooper said, and they walked toward a cluster of umbrella topped food carts.

"*Pedro's* has the best tacos in Tucson," Cooper said. "Or maybe you'd like a burrito instead. Just watch out that you don't drip anything on that pretty blouse."

At *Pedro's* food cart they ordered from the chalk board menu. Then they walked to a bench that was on the sidewalk facing University Street and shaded by a small tree. They set their lemonades in between them on the bench. Davina tucked a napkin into her neckline and very carefully ate the taco.

"Um, this is delicious," she said.

"I'm glad you like it. Sorry about the heat. I should have taken you to an air-conditioned restaurant."

Yes, maybe you should have, she thought. But she found the taco yummy and liked sitting on this bench next to this man in Tucson, even though it was 103 degrees. She steered the conversation to Jed.

"The roses you had delivered for Jed's visitation and funeral were lovely, thanks so much." The sun blazed down. Two University of Arizona students in shorts and flip flops strolled by.

"Sending flowers was the least I could do. I'm sorry I couldn't get away from Tucson and be there for Jed's visitation or the funeral."

"That's alright." She took a sip of mango flavored lemonade. "Now if you don't mind, I'd like to talk about the deaths of Andy Foley and Jed and my suspicions that their deaths are related."

"Okay." He was a fast eater and the last bite of his second taco disappeared into his mouth.

"Two out of three scientists who developed Pro310 end up shot by arrows under suspicious circumstances. As the third scientist, you may be the next target. I wouldn't take it lightly. I think you should be careful."

"It could be a coincidence."

"No, Jed was targeted. He was inside his house near an open window with no screen covering it. I think someone outside and up in a tree shot him with a bow and arrow. I found his body and someone attacked me." She told him what happened and he expressed his shock and sympathized with Davina for what she had been through.

"I won't let kooks on the fringe of society scare me. Some of them were picketing in front of the company where I work. But that didn't last long. I believe they couldn't bear walking all day in the desert heat."

"So I understand the Pro310 birth control was effective and reduced the deer population in areas where it was tested."

"That's right. We've even used the serum on wild boars in the desert. But deer are the pests we targeted for birth control. The deer are multiplying so fast they've become a real nuisance. During rut season the deer get frisky and run across highways, frequently colliding with cars."

"Yes, I know several people back in Illinois who

have hit deer. It usually totals their vehicle." Some pigeons swooped down on the sidewalk at their feet and Davina kicked a leg out in their direction.

"Shoo pigeons," she said, and as if they held squatter's rights the pigeons dispersed to a mere yard away.

"Yeah," Cooper said, "the deer wander into back yards in the suburbs and some homeowners will even start feeding them and treating them like pets. They'll give the deer names like they would give to cats or dogs. It must be the soulful eyes of the deer."

He lifted a paper towel toward Davina's lips. "You've got some taco sauce on your lip. May I?"

"Uh huh." Cooper dabbed the napkin to her upper lip and continued the discussion. "You can neuter the family cat or dog but with deer it's more complicated. And the serum is expensive, 80 bucks a shot. It's not feasible to send sharpshooters into every area where too many deer congregate, to shoot serum darts into every doe."

He crumbled up the wax paper from the tacos and stuffed it into the paper bag and continued.

"And then there was an incident with the serum used on the deer population in an area in the Sierrita Mountains. Personally, I don't think anything was wrong with the serum. But last spring a man from Tucson by the name of Joe Carter shot a deer in the Sierrita Mountains and later he fed some of it to his friends at a cookout in his backyard. His wife, Dawn who was pregnant, ate some of it and so did all the others at the gathering. First, his wife got sick, and later so did almost all the others at the cookout. Then Carter's wife had a miscarriage which they blamed on deer tainted with Pro310. Heck, it could have been the potato salad or something else they served. There was a write up in the *Arizona Daily Star* about the charges Joe Carter made." Davina made a mental note of the name, Joe Carter.

"So then what happened?"

"The Carters were talking about a lawsuit, but they couldn't prove anything connecting the serum to Dawn Carter's miscarriage. Then on the internet in chat rooms radical members of survivalists groups and hunters groups led by a man who called himself - let see, something like wolverine, or weevil, some animal-sorry I can't remember the name he went by- spread the rumor that the deer birth control serum was dangerous and that it had caused Mrs. Carter's miscarriage. For a while I got hate mail and prank phone calls at CSS Institute, but those crazies don't scare me."

"Do you think it's possible the serum *could* have caused Mrs. Carter's miscarriage? How can you be certain it didn't?"

Cooper studied a pigeon approaching them on the sidewalk. "It's perfectly safe and is registered with the Environmental Protection Agency and the Food and Drug Administration."

"What exactly does this serum do?"

"It simply causes the doe to create antibodies so pregnancy during rut season is prevented for up to four years. Anyway, it doesn't matter. Because of all the negative publicity and the expense of each serum dart the use of Pro310 is being phased out. Your brother was developing a new improved oral doe birth control method."

"X267," Davina said. "Did you happen to do research with Jed on the new formula? The management at BioChem wants all the data on X267."

"No, I didn't. We became friendly competitors. I've got my own experiments going and soon, if I'm lucky, I may come up with essentially the same birth control formula as Jed's X267. How about you, Davina? Did he share any of his data with you? By the way, you look like a beautiful sunflower in that outfit."

"Jed was working on X267. That's all I know." She found herself sucking in her stomach. Why did he think she looked like a sunflower and not a rose? Did the yellow make her look fat?

"You should never play poker," he said.

"Do you think I'm lying about something?"

"I'm not sure, but your cheeks did flame ever so prettily when you said that's all I know."

"I know nothing about Jed's work." Nor, she thought, what he wanted done with his papers now hidden inside her fireplace chimney.

Cooper patted her hand. "Your brother Jed, Andy and I shared our research data in a government funded project with the aim of controlling the deer population and came up with Pro310. The idea was to develop an effective, inexpensive birth control method to control deer in wild life refuges, or in wooded areas near subdivisions. Deer were multiplying so fast they caused problems not only in suburban yards, but did damage to farm crops. Deer are cute until they invade home gardens. Animal rights people loved Pro310 and the deer hunters hated it. Then the Tucson incident happened and the image of Pro310 was damaged. It didn't help that it wasn't cost effective. Lately, I couldn't reach Jed at his office at BioChem and he never answered messages I left on his voice mail, or the e-mails I sent to him."

"Jed was distracted by personal problems these past few months," Davina said. "He and his wife split up and he began to drink too much."

Cooper glanced at Davina. "The last time we spoke by phone in August, Jed was slurring his words and sounded high. I kidded him about seeing too much of Jack Daniels, or Mr. Bud, but he brushed me off. Then he complained about being unappreciated by the management at BioChem. He mentioned he needed money. But he turned down my offer of a loan. He said he soon would make a lot of money. He confided to me that because of all the controversy surrounding the first deer birth control serum, Pro310, the management wasn't interested in X267. They planned to return the rights to him on any further scientific work in the area of deer birth control, so he alone would hold the patent on his work. I don't know if they ever actually did put it in writing and make it official." Cooper sipped the last liquid from his paper cup and began chomping the crushed ice. "I always admired Jed and his superior intelligence."

"A BioChem secretary told me Jed was going to be fired, but I can't believe that," Davina said. "He was a genius, at least to me he was, and an asset to BioChem and they ought to have overlooked his eccentricities."

"Even geniuses are expendable, if the use of alcohol interferes with—I'm sorry I really don't want to criticize Jed. With X267, I believe he was on to something important, a new and improved method of deer population control. He was ahead of me in his research in that area."

"In laymen's terms can you explain how his formula might work?"

"I don't know for sure, but I'm guessing he was working on a gene engineered vaccine designed to stimulate mucosal infertility inside the deer's gut and setting off a mucosal infertility reaction."

"Sure, okay. That's as clear as cement to me."

"Jed hinted it would be more effective than Pro310 and he would prove its safety conclusively. Humans could eat the deer meat of a vaccinated doe and not be sickened or harmed in any way."

Across the street a black sedan with tinted windows pulled to the curb. The door swung open. A figure in black, wearing a baseball cap and sunglasses jumped out and aimed a bow and arrow in their direction.

The action was so quick, that Davina could only yell, "Look out!"

The car door of the black sedan with the tinted windows slammed shut behind the person in black and sped off into the sunlight. Davina couldn't read the license plate that was smeared with mud.

Benton Cooper stood slowly, a puzzled look on his

face which suddenly contorted to pain.

"You're hit!"

"Keys, in pocket, drive me, hospital now." Cooper teetered toward the Vega and Davina walked alongside. She took hold of his arm but he pulled away.

"Get the door," he gasped.

She hurried and yanked the door open on the passenger side. She pushed the seat forward as far as possible. She opened the rear door and called for help from a woman in cutoff jeans. The two women eased Cooper with the protruding arrow into the back seat. Cooper's face was ashen and he was sweating. Davina jumped behind the wheel and fumbled with the key. The motor started then sputtered and stopped. She knew she must remain calm.

"Hurry," Cooper said his voice barely a whisper. "I don't want to die."

"Hold on," she said. Davina turned the key once more and the engine caught. She took off from the curb like a jack rabbit chased by a coyote.

Cooper directed her as she drove, to "Go ten blocks. Turn left at the Shell station." Then he passed out. As soon as they arrived at the hospital emergency room entrance a woman came out with a wheel chair.

"We need a gurney," Davina said. "Hurry!" Davina saw Cooper's skin tone turn bluish.

An aid uttered something into a handset radio, and then he turned to Davina. "How did this happen?"

"We were sitting on a bench on a sidewalk and someone jumped out of a car and shot Mr. Cooper with a bow and arrow. Do something!"

Davina watched the emergency room personnel swarm over Benton Cooper, and then gingerly lift him onto a gurney. No, she didn't know if he was allergic to any medications. She watched them running with the gurney down the hallway of the hospital. She could feel her heart pounding and she told herself to breathe, just breathe. Calmly, she hurried outside and got back into the Vega, shifted the gear and drove past the emergency entrance and into the nearby parking lot where she parked. She rolled up the window they had left open and locked all the doors. Then she hurried back to the emergency entrance.

Inside at the end of a very long corridor she came to double doors with a sign that stated, *Do Not Enter*. A nurse stopped Davina. "You can't go into the operating room. Are you a relative?"

"No, I'm a friend." Silently, she prayed that Benton Cooper would survive. From her shoulder bag she pulled out her small address book and told the nurse the phone number of CSS Institute. "Someone there must know who to notify," she said.

"Sit in the waiting room and don't leave," the nurse said. "The Tucson police will want to talk to you."

Davina flipped through an Arizona Highways magazine as Benton Cooper embarked on his unpredictable medical journey. Sitting there in the waiting room she was reminded of the time as a child when she waited with her mother in a similar room while her maternal grandmother underwent gall bladder surgery. To pass the time and to get their minds off what was going on in the operating room, she and her mom had worked on a jigsaw puzzle. She could see the puzzle now, a half finished scene of a mountain with pines and a waterfall. Right now she decided to leave before a policeman came and detained her. After all, she reasoned she had already given all the information about the attack on Cooper to the hospital attendant.

Davina got up and went to the admittance counter and laid down Cooper's car keys. His name and address were on a CSS Institute Tag attached to the key chain. The woman behind the counter engrossed in typing keys on a computer keyboard looked up.

"These car keys belong to Benton Cooper who's in surgery."

"And who are you?"

"Just a friend."

"Why don't you keep the keys for him?"

"I'm not family and you'll have to excuse me. I really have to use the rest room. Where's the ladies room?"

"It's down that hallway and to the left," she motioned.

"Thanks."

The woman took the keys and put them in a drawer behind the counter and Davina walked in the direction the woman had pointed. The woman went back to her typing on the keyboard of her computer. Davina didn't go to the ladies room. Instead she headed to the exit. Outside the local TV news crew was on the scene already reporting the strange attack on Benton Cooper. A shaggy haired blond in a red suit stuck a microphone beneath Davina's nose.

"Do you know the victim? Could you tell us about the attack? Were you with Mr. Cooper when he was shot with the bow and arrow?"

Davina saw the camera and the red light and knew she was being recorded. "I'm sorry I really can't talk right now."

She began walking away and she could hear the TV reporter speaking into a microphone and saying, "I can't be certain but I think that lady I just spoke to was the woman who was with Mr. Benton Cooper when he was shot by someone with a bow and arrow."

Davina got into one of the waiting taxis and told the driver to take her to Hacienda Motel. When she arrived at the motel she telephoned CSS Institute and told a woman in the personnel department that Benton Cooper was undergoing surgery at the hospital and that his car was in the parking lot and the keys were left at the admitting desk.

Full of nervous energy Davina went into the gift shop. She had decided to work off her anxiety by going for a swim. Rapidly she looked through the rack of swimsuits and chose a one piece suit and paid for it at the cash register. She asked the clerk to remove the tags.

"Have a refreshing swim," the sales clerk said as she handed her the bag.

Later Davina got into the pool and started doing the side stroke. Alone in the pool she glided through the water doing laps and felt the tension leave her body. For a while in the water she was in a timeless state, her mind free of any worry.

After her swim she dried off and wrapped the oversized towel around her swimsuit and returned to her room and the reality of what had happened that day. She phoned the hospital and asked about Benton Cooper's condition. She was afraid of the answer. Davina waited for a moment and then the hospital clerk came back on the line.

"Mr. Cooper is still in surgery," she said.

Later she watched the local news and Benton Cooper's face popped up on the screen. The photo was a younger Cooper, with a totally brown, not grey flecked beard, his youthful, wrinkleless face flashing a boyish and mischievous grin. Then Davina saw herself in a brief video with the woman with the microphone and she almost spilled her cola and wondered if it would be on national television. Heaven forbid. She listened closely to the broadcast, relieved that she was nameless, referred to only as Cooper's unidentified companion at the time he was shot. The reporter with the shaggy blond hair said that after surgery Cooper was in stable condition with around the clock police guard.

The next morning she telephoned the hospital for an update of Cooper's condition. Stable was the only information the nurse on duty would divulge over the phone. Davina was scheduled to fly back home that evening. She felt that nothing worth much had been accomplished. She had learned from Cooper about the Joe Carter incident, and about the chat rooms on the internet where a person with the name or handle of wolverine, weevil or something similar was a ringleader urging protests against the scientists who had developed Pro310 and the companies where they were employed.

Davina showered and dressed in a white T-shirt and black jeans. After she put on some dangle earrings, fussed with her hair and applied a minimum of makeup, she left her room and went downstairs. She stepped outside into the dry desert air where the sunshine seemed to blanch color from everything and fed coins into a newspaper machine. After removing the newspaper she returned inside and to the area set aside for the complimentary breakfasts. Seated alone at a table by the window she ate cereal from a paper bowl, drank black coffee and read the newspaper.

"Where are you from?" The voice came from a man at a nearby table wearing Bermuda shorts and a shirt with a design that looked to Davina like puke: brown, grey and orange spatters and swirls. A camera hung from a strap around the man's neck.

"Illinois," she said, not making eye contact, or smiling.

"We're from Des Moines, Sally and me. We're thinking about moving to *Areezona* next year when I retire."

Sally, seated across from him looked glum. She licked grape jelly from her lips. "I don't care where you move to, George. I'm not leaving my grandkids." George ignored his wife's comment.

'Wasn't that a terrible thing that happened yesterday to that fellow, him gettin' shot in broad daylight by a bow and arrow?" Davina nodded and took another spoonful of raisin bran. "This morning they showed on TV an unidentified woman who was with him when he got shot. She had red hair. Say, she looked exactly like you."

The chair made a noisy scraping sound as Davina backed from the table. "No, it wasn't me. I just got into Tucson late last night."

"It coulda been your twin."

She carried her disposable dish filled with the half eaten cereal to the garbage container and shoved it inside. Feeling as if the eyes of the man followed her every move, she refilled her coffee cup and left the room.

CHAPTER 14

Thursday morning, Paxtonia, Illinois.

In his office Police Chief Leo Donovan sat at his desk sneezing, wiping his nose with a tissue, and brooding over the message relayed to him by Nadine, as he had entered the Paxtonia police department. He had arrived at his office later than usual because he felt lousy and had overslept. Mindful of Caldwell's tendency to meddle when the chief was absent, he decided to go to work and so he had missed the phone call from Davina Reed's daughter, Sunny. While Davina was in Tucson, Arizona, this morning someone had left an anonymous and threatening message on Davina's home answering machine. The message so frightened her daughter, who had stopped in to feed Davina's tropical fish, that she reported the phone call to the Paxtonia police department.

That redhead is going haywire, the chief thought. Was she out in Tucson on some reckless hunt and interfering with his investigation? Donovan had to think about this situation. He sipped his coffee and swallowed two aspirin tablets. Then he picked up the phone receiver and tapped in the number where Davina could be reached that Sunny had left with the clerk.

"Yes, we have a Davina Reed registered in Room 201," the desk clerk at the Hacienda Motel said to Police Chief Donovan. "Would you like me to transfer you to her room?"

"Yes, please."

"Hold on a minute."

While Donovan waited the woman's voice was replaced by the recorded sounds of a strumming guitar, punctuated with a blare of trumpets that caused Donovan to cringe. If Davina would give him a chance, they could be so happy. What a great team the two of them could make, in Arkansas! He drummed his fingers to the Hispanic music and thought of Davina dressed as a senorita, twirling around in a flaring skirt, her heels clicking on a wooden floor. Abruptly, the music stopped, replaced by silence, a click, and then the dial tone. Disconnected.

He swiveled around in his chair and looked out the window to a grey and blustery day that looked as if snow was on its way. Was Davina a modern day witch casting a spell over him? All he could think about was Davina, and all Davina could think about was her dead brother and finding his killer.

There were no identifiable prints on the scene except for Davina's prints on the bathroom doorknob and a partial print of hers Donovan had found on the upper part of the shaft of the arrow a few inches below the fletching of feathers. He had found no other fingerprints or anything else on the shaft of the arrow, except for some dried blood. He wondered, if someone planned to shoot an arrow at a person, wouldn't he, or she wipe the shaft clean and then wear gloves?

In his mind he tried to justify why Davina's print was found on the shaft. It was probably because of the trauma of finding her brother dead, when she rushed in she had instantly touched it. Afterwards, she had forgotten. Or, she had come in contact with the murder weapon in some other way that could be explained when the killer was identified.

Now there were other matters to deal with. His muddled thoughts and the phone call to Tucson had delayed him from immediately opening the package on his desk that he had been eyeing since he had sat down. It was from the Illinois State Crime Laboratory in Midville.

He remembered Lieutenant Jerry Caldwell had said Davina Reed had found a plastic deer caller beneath a tree under leaves in Jed's yard and had brought it to the police department. Caldwell personally took it to the state lab for further testing for latent prints, or dried saliva and Donovan admired the speed with which the testing had been completed.

From a box in a cabinet Donovan pulled out a pair of latex gloves and put them on. He examined the deer caller. It was brown and palm-sized. He read the report enclosed with the evidence. There were no prints found but there was saliva residue present and DNA tests determined the sample to be that of a non-secretor. He stripped off the gloves and tossed them into the waste basket.

He mulled over the details of the mysterious death he was determined to solve: Jed Davidson, found on his upstairs bathroom floor with an arrow stuck in his chest, his older sister on his bedroom floor coming back to consciousness with a nasty bump on her head and telling a fantastic story about being chloroformed by someone in camouflaged clothing, Donovan finding a match from the partial fingerprint on the arrow shaft to the fingerprint on the tumbler from which Davina had sipped water at her police interrogation.

At first Donovan had been shocked to find that Davina had touched the shaft. Then he realized there was an innocent explanation. In her traumatized state of mind, wanting to remove the arrow as if she could save him, she had touched it leaving her fingerprint.

"Knock-knock," Pat Hansen said as she entered Donovan's office. "Good morning, Chief."

"Not for me. I feel lousy, and even with this cold

I've got, I can tell the coffee is way too strong."

"Sorry about that, Chief. I can never remember how many scoops to use. Maybe Caldwell should make the coffee. And if you don't water that fern, it's going to die." She walked to the file cabinet and stuck a finger into the soil in the pot. "Dry as Death Valley."

Donovan saw Helen's gift fading away, along with his memory of her, while a woman with red hair and a spunky demeanor increasingly occupied his thoughts.

"Did you hear that about an hour ago some workers on a barge near Pekin came upon a body floating in the Illinois River?"

"No, who was it?"

"An unidentified male, about 35 years of age."

CHAPTER 15

From the shelf beneath the bedside drawer Davina lifted the hefty Tucson phone book and opened it. She flipped pages to the names beginning with C. Then she ran a finger down a column of Carters. There were two Joseph Carters listed with different middle initials. Maybe they were father and son. Davina tapped in the first number for Joseph A. After five rings, a man answered.

"Yeah, whadda yah want?"

"Good morning," Davina said cheerily.

"Am I speaking to Joseph Carter?"

"Uh huh."

"Would that be senior or junior?"

"Which one do you want?"

"I'm Cindy Miller and I'm in charge of our high school reunion and I'm contacting lost classmates." Davina looked at the address listed under the other Carter, a Joseph M. "Does he still live on Skylark?"

"Yes, but I don't get it. My son went to a military school, all males."

'Yes, I know. I'm calling for my husband. Thanks, Mr. Carter." Quickly, Davina hung up and then punched the number of Joseph M. Carter.

"Hello, Carter residence." It was a high pitched

voice that sounded like a little girl's.

"Hi, may I speak to your mom or dad?"

"Why?"

"It's something I need to talk to them about. When should I call back?"

"I dunno. You're a stranger. I'm not supposed to talk to strangers."

Davina felt ready to hang up but a woman's voice cut in on the line.

"Hello, who's this?"

"Hi, Mrs. Carter, I'm conducting a telephone survey for a major supermarket chain. Could you answer a few questions concerning your grocery shopping habits?"

Click.

Davina hung up the receiver and immediately the phone rang.

It was Sunny.

"Mom, this morning you got a phone call from some weirdo. I had stopped in your house to feed your fish like you asked me to do whenever you go out of town. I had just dropped a food disk into the tank and was so interested in watching the fish feed that I let the machine get the call. Later, I went in your bedroom and played your messages. in case any were important that I should tell you about. The last one was a threatening message. I couldn't tell if it was a man or woman. He or she said you'd better stop investigating Jed's death or you'd be very sorry."

"And you couldn't tell if it was a man or a woman?"

"No. The voice was muffled."

Davina clutched the receiver tighter. "Don't worry, Sun, You didn't erase the message did you?"

"No."

"I'm glad you didn't. When I get back home I'll listen to the tape and see if I can recognize the voice."

"I called Police Chief Donovan, Sunny said. He hadn't yet arrived for work, so I left a message for him

165

about the phone call with the clerk on duty. I think her name was Nadine."

"You didn't tell her I was in Tucson or give her the name of the motel I'm staying in, did you?"

"Of course, I did. She asked for a phone number where Chief Donovan could reach you. He should be phoning you."

"I've got to go, Honey. Don't worry I'll be fine. I'll be home tonight."

"Mom!"

Davina hung up.

She left a tip for the housekeeper on the pillow, gathered up her luggage and went downstairs to the checkout counter. After getting her receipt she tucked it into her bag and headed for the motel exit. She passed the man named George who at breakfast had recognized her from the TV newscast.

"Checking out already?" George called out. "I know that was you who I seen on TV."

Davina ignored him and kept walking. Outside she put on her sunglasses and walked to the Taurus, and put her luggage on the back seat. She got in the auto and drove until the motel was out of view. Then she turned down a side street, pulled to the curb and stopped. Before she left Arizona and returned to Illinois, a visit to the Joe M. Carter residence was next on her to do list.

She opened the Tucson street map she had picked up from the rack of publications in the motel lobby.

Where exactly was Skylark Drive? Unable to find the street on the abbreviated map, Davina drove to the nearest service station. Inside and behind the cash register, a Hispanic teenaged clerk chewed on a toothpick. Displayed above the stack of cigarette cartons was a faded map of the city of Tucson.

"Can you show me Skylark Drive on that map?"

He scrutinized the map and shook his head.

"It may be in a new subdivision." He motioned to a rack of magazines and maps.

"Look over there. You need a new map."

Davina bought an updated map of Tucson and asked where the nearest shopping mall was located.

"Turn right and go two blocks," he said.

She thanked him and headed out the door. Like George back at the motel, there was a possibility Mrs. Carter had seen the television news footage. It might be smart to buy some items to alter her appearance. In a drug store in the mall she selected a pair of black rimmed reading glasses. Then she searched through a display of scarves and hats, selecting a turban to cover her hair. At the checkout counter the clerk smiled sympathetically.

"My aunt has cancer and she wears one exactly like this," she said.

"I'm healthy. It's for my bad hair days." She handed over her credit card and the clerk rang up the sale and as Davina instructed, cut off all the tags.

"Every day is a bad hair day for Aunt Jane," the clerk said sadly. "After the chemotherapy, her head was as bald as the back of a spoon." The clerk stuck the receipt inside the bag with Davina's purchases.

" Best of luck to you, Honey."

"Thanks, and I'm sorry about your aunt." Davina hurried out the door. So let the clerk think she had the big C.

Inside the car Davina put the turban on her head and stuffed all her red hair inside. She found Skylark on the map and started the ignition. As she drove toward the subdivision she mulled over how to deal with Dawn Carter. What would she say to this woman who believed the deer birth serum Jed had helped develop, had caused her miscarriage?

Upon entering El Castellos subdivision, she read the billboard advertisement of the amenities and options available: oversized lots, four housing designs, four bedrooms, a swimming pool and a club house.

In the middle of the maze of houses Davina found 803 Skylark Drive, a ranch with a pebble lawn accented by a five-foot tall saguaro. After she parked the car at the curb she walked up the sidewalk and sidestepped an overturned pink bicycle with training wheels. A standard black poodle ran up to the fence near the corner of the house, barked and wagged its tail.

"Good doggie," Davina said.

On the porch she stood before the door that was decorated with a swag of raffia tied chili peppers. She took a deep breath and pushed the doorbell button and silently rehearsed what she would say.

Shortly the door opened to reveal a petite brunette holding a tumbler with an iced drink. She wore shorts and a T-shirt that declared: *Yeah, Right!* She blinked at the bright sunlight and peered at Davina with a questioning look. Davina caught the scent of whisky on the woman's breath.

"What are you zelling? I don't want any magazines." The woman began to shut the door.

"No, wait, I'm not selling anything. I'm Davina Reed, and you must be Dawn. I'd like to talk to you about the deer your husband shot last spring in Sierrita Mountains, the deer that you said made you sick and caused you to miscarry." Davina felt safe in identifying herself, because on the brief TV news segment broadcast the previous night she hadn't been named, plus her attention getting red hair was hidden beneath the turban.

The woman almost dropped her drink. "Are you from the *Arizona Daily Star*?"

"No, I'm not from the newspaper. Writing freelance articles is what I do. I'm writing an article right now about the pros and cons of using birth control serum on deer and other wildlife. May I talk to you for a few minutes? It won't take much of your time."

The intoxicated woman wasn't convinced. "You got some identify-cation?"

Davina searched through her bag. "Oh, shoot, I can't find my billfold."

"Aw, forget it." She stepped back from the door and held up her glass. "Wanna a drink?"

"Just water, will be fine," Davina said. She closed the front door and followed a weaving Dawn.

They entered the great room where a little girl about five or six years old bounced up and down on a mini trampoline.

"Hi," she said, and jumped from the trampoline, almost hitting the nearby glass topped coffee table.

"Dawn turned toward the little girl. "Tiffany, timeout! Go stand in the corner!"

On a wide screen TV mounted above the fireplace, a soap opera, accented by music dispensed its drama. Davina glanced toward the kitchen area and noticed the sink filled with used dishes. She watched as Dawn Carter opened a cupboard door and pulled out a tumbler that matched the one she had been drinking from and set it down on the counter. After she slopped whisky on the counter, she swore as she topped off her drink and poured one for Davina.

Davina took paper toweling from the roll on the island counter and began to mop up the spill.

"Are you alright?"

"I'm a wee bit sloshed- drink up."

Tiffany leaned, nose first into a corner of the room, fake crying.

"Shut up!" Dawn said.

Although she detested the taste and only wanted water, Davina took a sip.

"I was goin' have another baa-by," Mrs. Carter said, 'but I ate the bad deer meat. Joe cooked somethin' he calls scrapple. I got sick and lost my baa-by." She disintegrated into tears.

"I'm so sorry. Would you like me to make some coffee for you?"

"Yes, you go right ahead."

"Yes, Lady, please make her coffee," Tiffany said. Unnoticed, she had quietly turned around and stepped away from the corner.

"Mommy, can I come out now?" Her face held a pleading, pitiful look. "Please."

"Okay, Tif, but no more jumping."

Davina found a filter and the canister of ground coffee and proceeded to prepare coffee. She poured tap water into the brewer and slid the switch on.

Tiffany came up to Dawn and hugged her. "Mommy you should go and see the doctor," she said. "Can I watch cartoons?"

"I'll find some cartoons for you," Davina said. "Is it okay, Dawn?"

"I don't care. I don't care about anything."

While Tiffany stretched out on the floor and watched cartoons, Davina questioned Dawn further. With Davina's urging, Dawn sipped coffee.

She related events concerning the suspect venison. Her story took a while to tell, but Davina wrote down all the details in a notebook she took from her bag.

When Dawn was treated at the hospital the doctors didn't think there was any connection to her having eaten the deer meat and her miscarriage. But when one of the guests at the Carter's cookout arrived at the same Tucson hospital complaining of being sick after eating meat from the same deer, followed by four others from the backyard party who had also eaten the deer scrapple, the doctors and all the staff took notice. Arrangements were made and samples of the leftover meat from the cookout were sent for testing to the Atlanta Centers for Disease Control.

In time all the sickened guests recovered with no lasting ill effects and the tests eventually came back from Atlanta as negative on the deer meat. The conclusion of the experts was that it must have been something else served at the cookout that sickened those at the gathering. And it may have been that Dawn's miscarriage occurred for reasons, other than bad food. But Dawn kept blaming the deer meat.

Dawn said her husband began to do research on the internet. In a chat session with deer hunters he traded talk with a deer hunter and former Vietnam veteran who had turned against the government. He went by the name, Weasel and he told Joe about three scientists who had developed a birth control serum called Pro310 that was being tested in various places on the deer population. Even though it was deemed safe by the EPA and FDA, Weasel said that was a terrible lie and Pro310 was poisoning people if they ate the meat from deer that had been inoculated with the serum. It was a conspiracy by the government, he claimed, to eliminate the sport of deer hunting. He named the three scientists. Weasel said a close relative worked with one of the scientists.

"Joe told Weasel he was sure because I had eaten meat from a deer he thought had gotten the deer serum, it had caused me to lose my baby. This person called Weasel told Joe if we wanted he would help us get rid of the scientists, for revenge, but Joe said, no, he didn't want to harm them. He wanted to sue them and make them pay."

Tiffany got up and quietly went outside.

"Do you remember the name of the chat room?"

No, she didn't. Outside the kitchen window Tiffany tossed a red rubber ball toward the poodle. The dog retrieved the ball and brought it to the child, who promptly threw it again.

"I know it's not any of my business, but why don't you stop drinking and try for another baby?"

"Not possible. Dr. Ramsey says I can't ever get pregnant again."

"I'm very sorry. Now about this person, Weasel-do you know in what state he lives? Did he ever tell your husband?"

"I forget. I think it was Iowa, or Illinois. Are you going to write about how the deer birth control caused me to lose my baby?"

"I'll think about that angle for my article. But it wasn't proved to be the cause of your miscarriage now, was it? Could it be that something else you and Joe served at the cookout that day with the deer scrapple caused everyone to get sick? Maybe a salad with mayonnaise that sat too long in the sun?"

A more clearheaded Dawn looked at Davina with distrust. "Who are you, *really*?"

Davina stood up and put away her notebook. "A freelance writer. Thanks so much, for talking to me. I'll investigate this further."

At this point, Dawn seized Davina bag, reached in and pulled out her billfold and flipped it opened.

"So you did bring it after all. And here it says on your driver's license you're from Illinois, not Arizona. Now I remember that one of those scientists was from Illinois. Was he related to you?"

Davina regained possession of her billfold and bag but in the tussle, Dawn lifted Davina's turban and exposed the rumpled hair.

"Hey, you've got red hair. At first I thought you were a cancer patient." Her eyes widened. "I've seen you before. Last night you were on the late news. Don't you want to finish your whiskey, Denise, or whatever you said your name was?"

"I'm sorry I lied to you. The truth is my brother was murdered. I came here to try to find out who killed him. He was one of the three scientists who developed Pro310. Two of the scientists, including my brother have been killed by bow and arrows. Yesterday, I was with Mr. Cooper, the remaining scientist when he was shot the same way. He's in ICU and I hope he survives."

"I'm glad your brother is dead," Dawn said. She pulled a steak knife from the rack of kitchen knives on the counter. She came toward Davina, who backed away.

"Stop Dawn, I'm leaving," Davina said. "You should get sober for Tiffany's sake!"

"And you should leave before you join your brother!"

Upon hearing the commotion, Tiffany came back inside.

"Mommy, no, please don't hurt the nice lady!"

Both women looked at Tiffany who stood just inside the back door, holding the rubber ball in her small hands, with a look of alarm on her face.

Dawn put the knife back in its rack. "Don't worry, Tif. We were playing a game. And now the lady is leaving, aren't you?"

"Sure, I'm gone."

"She wanted Dawn Carter to know her brother, Jed was a kind man who meant no harm and that there was no proof Pro310 had caused her miscarriage, or the sickness of those people who ate it at the Carter's cookout. But even if there was a possibility it had, that was no reason for the murder of the three men.

Davina hurried to her car. This was not the way she had wanted her meeting with Dawn to end. However, in her conversation with Mrs. Carter, she had gained new knowledge that might lead to Jed's killer-the name, Weasel.

CHAPTER 16

The previous day Davina had told the hospital emergency room staff everything that she had seen during the attack. Surely, all the details were passed on to the Tucson police. To reassure herself that he was okay and recovering, she now only wanted to see Benton Cooper, her new friend, wish him a speedy return to good health, and then catch her flight back to Illinois.

In the hospital parking lot Davina checked her appearance in the rearview mirror. If a newspaper, radio, or TV reporter, or a detective still hung around the hospital in hopes of getting more information from her as a star witness to the bow and arrow attack, Davina didn't want to be recognized and further questioned. She adjusted the turban. With the drugstore glasses framing her eyes, even Sunshine might not immediately recognize her. Once inside the hospital lobby she headed to the gift shop where she bought a chrysanthemum plant.

"Wasn't it awful about that man getting shot with

the bow and arrow yesterday? I wonder how he's doing," she said to the elderly woman tending the cash register.

"Mr. Cooper's out of intensive care, I know that. I've sent two flower arrangements up to his room on the 6th floor today."

"I'm glad to hear he's better."

Although there were no others in the shop, the clerk lowered her voice. "There's a police guard outside his room."

Davina paid for the flowers with cash and left the shop. She took the elevator to the 5th floor and got off the elevator and walked to the door leading to the stairs. On the 6th floor she opened the door, peeked down the hall and waited.

When the police officer stood up and walked down the hall toward the water faucet, she hurried down the hall and slipped into Benton Cooper's hospital room. Davina walked past an empty bed and saw Cooper in the adjoining bed who had recovered enough to be sitting up. He wore a blue-dotted hospital gown and with a spoon, picked halfheartedly at the lime gelatin shimmering in a plastic cup. At the sound of her footsteps he looked up.

"Shh-it's me, Davina. How are you feeling?"

Cooper dropped his spoon and smiled. "Not as strong as before I got shot, but much better since you're here. I wondered what happened to you. The arrow missed my heart by this much." He held up his thumb and forefinger almost touching. "The doctors say I'm very lucky."

"We should keep our voices low. I'm not supposed to be here. I saw the police guard outside your door. When he got up and walked down the hall I sneaked in." She lined up the chrysanthemum plant with the other floral arrangements on the window ledge.

"Thanks for getting me to the hospital in time and thanks for the flowers. I got your message about my car. You look funny."

"It's my disguise." She removed the drug store glasses and whisked off the turban. Using her fingers she fluffed up her hair.

"Much better," he said.

"My daughter called me this morning. She said a threatening phone call had been left on my answering machine. She discovered the message when she stopped over to feed my tropical fish. When she didn't reach me right away she called the Paxtonia police department and reported it."

"What kind of threat?"

"It was a warning for me to stop investigating my brother's death from someone altering their voice. It could have been the killer, or someone from the Paxtonia Police Department. Chief Leo Donovan is acting very strange towards me. First, he thinks I'm interfering with the investigation of Jed's death. Then he says my fingerprint is on the shaft of the arrow that was pulled from Jed's body. He seems obsessed with me. He told me he hid the arrow to protect me, so no one would know my fingerprint is on the weapon that killed Jed."

"You must have touched it when you found Jed."

"Could be, but with the bump on my head I've had some memory loss. Donovan said he's hiding the arrow to protect me. But he's using the hidden arrow as blackmail. He wants me to promise to go with him to Arkansas where he wants to go into semi-retirement, plus open a detective agency. He wants me to be his partner. I must remind the poor man of his dead wife."

"So you'll go under cover in your turban and help him track down thieves and killers in Arkansas?"

"More like straying spouses and creeps trying to get away with insurance and worker's compensation fraud. And just for me, Donovan said if I'd prefer not relocating, he will consider opening his office in Illinois."

"Looks like you have him totally under your spell.

So who do you think shot me?"

"I don't know." Davina glanced at the clock. "Before I leave I want to fill you in on what I've found out. I talked to Dawn Carter, who miscarried after eating deer meat that was later found to have the residue of the serum Pro310. Didn't you tell me the serum was safe?"

"Yes, and it is. But it doesn't matter now, because the serum won't be used anymore. It will be replaced by a new and improved deer birth control serum, possibly the one Jed developed if his research papers are found, or the formula I'm working on. It will be more humane to control the deer population scientifically, rather than by culling by bow and arrows and guns and bullets. Too many accidents happen every year and instead of shooting a deer, a hunter sometimes gets shot by another hunter. Or he goes out hunting alone and falls off his tree strand, or flips his all terrain vehicle. I once heard of a hunter who thought the arrow he'd shot into the deer had killed the deer. But when he got close and leaned down, the deer suddenly gave a final kick to the man. The kick was so forceful the man was killed. In time hunting deer may become obsolete. At least that's my opinion."

"There are many hunters who disagree, some violently."

"Clearly. One of them tried to kill me."

"From Dawn I learned the name of the leader of the online chat room, the name you couldn't remember. It's Weasel."

"That's it."

"Weasel is the alias of a person whom Dawn Carter said her husband regularly chatted with online. He's the instigator who started the protests against the use of Pro310. Weasel convinced Joe Carter and other avid hunters like him, to do the same. He influenced them to harass the companies who employed you, Foley and Jed because the three of you had developed the serum."

"So how long will you be in Tucson? When I get out of here, I owe you another lunch or dinner, but inside a pleasant, air conditioned restaurant."

"Sorry, I'm leaving on a flight tonight, if they let me on the plane. Just to cause trouble for me, Chief Donovan might have me detained."

"I think you're letting your imagination run overtime. Wouldn't he have to get a court order, or at the very least have a very good reason which in this case, is lacking? Whatever happens I'll be in your corner, Babe."

"I'm so happy you survived your attack, I was so worried. Jed wasn't as lucky. "

"I'm so very sorry about Jed getting killed."

"I know. You look tired. Is there anything else I can do for you before I leave? Should I push your table away, or refill your water glass?"

Cooper's eyes flashed mischievously. "If it's in your power, pretty lady, restore my health to where it was before we had lunch."

"Just rest up and follow the doctor's advice. I'm sure you'll be just fine."

"As an alternate plan, come here and give me a goodbye kiss," he said with a playful look on his face. Without hesitation she kissed his cheek.

"Not like my mom-here," he said, and he pointed to his lips.

And a rush of mixed up thoughts came into her head. But foremost in her mind was the guilt she felt. If she had not come to Tucson and met Benton Cooper for lunch, he would not have been attacked, at least not in her presence. And so they kissed.

For Davina, the kiss stirred mixed feelings. Other than Tom, the husband she was separated from, Benton Cooper was the first man she had kissed on the lips in 25 years.

"Now I really should go." Davina pulled on the turban and replaced the eyeglasses. "How do I get out of here past that cop sitting outside?"

"I'll take care of it." Benson Cooper pulled back the bed covers. He eased out of bed and slipped his feet into slippers. He grimaced.

"Are you sure you should be up so soon?"

"Maybe you're right." He sat down. "Go open the door."

"Okay."

He waited and then he called out, "Hey, Clifford!"

"Yeah, what's up? Should I get the nurse?"

The cop came into the room still holding the *Arizona Daily Star*. Surprise flashed across his face when he saw someone in the room standing next to the patient he was charged with guarding from harm.

"What are you-"

"It's okay. This is my sister, Joan. Don't hassle her. She didn't know she was supposed to check in with you. You must have stepped away from my door for a minute. She's leaving now."

"I thought I heard voices but figured it was the TV," Clifford said. His face flamed red with embarrassment. "Alright, I just went to get a drink of water. I couldn't have been gone over a minute."

"Don't worry, I won't tell anyone," Cooper said. Clifford looked at Davina with suspicion.

"Goodbye, dear brother," Davina said.

"Stay in touch, Sis."

Davina sensed Clifford still watching her, as she walked briskly down the hall toward the elevator.

• • •

In the remaining time before she left Tucson, Davina stopped in to see Lil, a vendor she had dealt with on the Internet and spoken to by phone. When they first stocked the shelves of *Queen Anne's Lace,* she and Meg had ordered an assortment of handmade turquoise jewelry from Lil, who operated a gift shop on Broadway Street. Into the shop Davina carried the bag she had previously folded and packed empty in her suitcase in anticipation for holding any items she bought from Lil. This trip would be a business expense income tax deduction for Davina and Meg. She was determined to repay Wingate for the cost of her round trip ticket to Tucson.

Inside the shop, Davina introduced herself to Lil and both agreed what a pleasure it was to finally meet. Lil presented some items for her inspection, and then invited Davina to look around the store for any merchandise that she found appealing.

Davina examined some unique, lightweight items including a rack of colorful and eye-catching, tie-dyed T-shirts imprinted with the whimsical figure of a man playing a flute. As Davina examined the T-shirts the shop owner and vendor came over.

"I can give you a good price on the T-shirts. They are washable in cold water and are not made in China. A woman and her two daughters from the Yaqui Reservation hand dyed these. I sell a lot to tourists and also to the University of Arizona students."

Lil said the ancient cave drawing depicted on the T-shirts was called Kokopelli, a legendary spirit and its image hanging in her shop on the T-shirts would bring good luck.

"I have some new ones in back that came in yesterday that I'd like to show you."

Davina liked them and bought two dozen in various sizes and promised to order more if they sold well. Lil helped Davina pack the T-shirts and the trinkets Davina had chosen into her suitcase.

Then Davina asked Lil if she could look up a number in her Tucson telephone book. Davina thumbed through the telephone book and found the phone number of Family Services. She jotted down the number, thanked Lil and left. Back inside her auto she made a call that had been troubling her since she had left the Carter home.

"I don't want to give you my name, but I want to

report a situation of possible child abuse. I'm very concerned about the welfare of a child named Tiffany Carter who is about six years old," she said to the woman from Family Services who answered her call.

Davina explained why she was troubled and gave details she had observed from her visit that day: the mother's intoxication and the little girl's absence from school. After Davina revealed the parents' names and the address she hung up the receiver with the hope the family would get help.

CHAPTER 17

Fortified with coffee and two glazed donuts, Lieutenant Jerry Caldwell pushed open the door to *Queen Anne's Gift Shop*, setting off a tinkle of bells. Wearing the uniform that gave him importance and authority, he carefully moved his massive, muscular body between shelves cluttered with figurines, bud vases and various knickknacks. In this typically feminine territory he knew if he wasn't careful, there would be a disaster.

The woman standing behind the counter near the cash register looked up and smiled. The perfection of her teeth would have impressed an orthodontist. "May I help you Officer?"

Caldwell flashed his identification. "I'm investigating the murder of Jed Davidson in Paxtonia. I'd like to talk to Davina Reed the owner of this establishment."

She glanced at the photo ID and then his Paxtonia police uniform. "I'm Meg Hale. Davina and I are co-owners of this shop." She handed him a business card accented in one corner with a tiny sketch of the wild flower that shared its name with the shop.

He took the card, gave a cursory look and put it in a pocket. "Do you know where your partner is, right now?"

"Tucson, Arizona and I don't know a thing about her brother's death. What I do know is that his death has devastated Vina."

"Vina?"

"That's Davina's nickname."

"When do you expect her back?"

"I'm not sure, tonight or tomorrow."

"How often does she come into the shop?"

"We did have a rotating schedule, but she hardly works since her brother died."

"If I were you, I'd be mad." He glanced around the shop. "How's business?"

"Slow as you can see today, but with Christmas coming soon, I'm sure traffic will pick up. May I help you pick out a gift for your girlfriend or wife? We have some lovely jewelry."

"I don't have a steady girlfriend, or a wife," he said.

"But you have a mother. We have quilted aprons, and our handsaw painted with barn scenes are popular sellers. We have something for all tastes and ages."

"Maybe some other time, when I'm off duty. Now did your partner ever discuss her brother with you?"

"Yes, for sure. We're friends. She was close to her brother and quite proud of him. He was a brilliant scientist and had several patents."

"Do you know if she was a beneficiary to his will? Do you think she could have had anything to do with his murder?"

"She won't even swat a fly if one gets inside this shop. She'll shoo it out the front door. And I think Jed's wife and son would be beneficiaries in his will. But how would I know? Why don't you ask Davina when she gets back?"

Meg grabbed a miniature broom garlanded with ribbon and dried roses, meant to decorate a front door and to Caldwell's surprise, swatted him on his shoulder. "Go on and get out of here," she said. "This isn't Paxtonia. You have no authority here."

His face turned red, yet he forced a smile. "I'm

going, but I could arrest you for assaulting a police officer."

"With this tiny broom?"

Caldwell shook his head in exasperation and headed for the front door. While passing the corridor of display shelves, his elbow brushed against a cloth doll with an embroidered smile attired in a gingham dress and it fell noiselessly to the floor. Quickly, he picked up the doll, and replaced it on the shelf. The tinkle of bells on the door confirmed his exit from the shop.

Possibly Meg Hale was right about the complete innocence of Davina Reed, Caldwell surmised as he got into his squad car and headed back to Paxtonia. But a thought nagged at him:

Chief Donovan was shielding Ms. Reed. Since the day Caldwell had joined the Paxtonia force whenever he stood next to Donovan's desk, the photograph of the face of Mrs. Donovan beamed up at him. But yesterday, Caldwell had noticed the chief had removed his dead wife's photo from the top of his cluttered desk.

It was obvious Donovan was infatuated with Davina Reed. Caldwell wondered if he was so taken with Ms. Reed that he would remove evidence that might involve her in Jed's death. Possibly. The laxity of rules and sloppy work habits had long plagued the police department. Except for a few employees, all had access to the evidence locker. Caldwell refused to believe the scenario suggested by Chief Donovan: Ron Hedges who quit the police force had moved back to Ohio taking along with him stolen evidence, including the arrow that had killed Davidson. To strengthen his insinuation, the chief had pointed out another missing item, a nickel bag of marijuana confiscated in August from a stolen car abandoned on a country blacktop in their jurisdiction. Lieutenant Caldwell vowed to himself that he would solve the mystery of the missing arrow. Furthermore, he would talk to a member of the

Paxtonia City Council and see if he could get Donovan fired from his job as police chief. Caldwell was friendly with one of the council members named Thane Greer. They frequently went target practicing together. He planned to inform Councilman Greer of his suspicions that Donovan was trying to protect Davina Reed by stealing from the evidence locker. Then in the daydream his mind concocted, he imagined the town council holding a closed door investigation. If things turned out in his favor Lieutenant Caldwell might soon become the next police chief of Paxtonia.

• • •

In the backyard of the house he had once shared with Davina, Tom Reed mowed through leaves still falling from the oak trees. The chore he had once disliked now brought him contentment, as he pushed the mower pulverizing the leaves, and planned how to get Davina back. The next time he saw his estranged wife he would try extra hard to work things out between them. Life without her was like wearing his loafers without his lucky coins, like breathing without enough air. Whatever problems they had, whatever had caused the severing of their bond, he wanted Davina back in his life.

Where was Davina, anyway? Tom had phoned Meg at *Queen Anne's Lace* and Meg would only say that Davina wasn't in the shop. He supposed he'd have to call their daughter, Sunny. He wasn't sure that Sunny would tell him. He was the scoundrel, not Davina.

Although Nicki denied the allegation, Tom suspected Nicki had been harassing Davina and had even tried to run her car off the road that day Davina drove to his cabin. No matter how much fun it had been, he was finished with flirting with his young female students. He wanted his Davina, with all her quirkiness to return to him.

Near the ravine where the tiger lilies once bloomed but were now shriveled to the ground beneath a layer of leaves, Tom reversed the mower. He bulldozed through the remaining leaves and headed back toward the house. The mower bag bulged and made the pushing difficult. Tom began panting with the effort.

A surprise visitor came around the corner of the house, Margie Jager the nosy, but friendly neighbor from across the street.

"Hi, Tom. Did you move back home?"

He shut off the motor. "Pardon, I didn't hear-"

"I said it looks like you and Davina are back together, seeing how you're doing the fall cleanup." Sunlight highlighted the braces on her middle-aged teeth.

"No, no, I'm just helping Davina out with the leaves. Do you know where she is?"

"She went on a trip."

"Oh, where to?"

"I don't know. I saw her leave with a suitcase in her car. I guess she just wanted to get away for awhile. She's been under a lot of stress with Jed's death and she always has to put up with you know who. She nodded toward the house next door."

"I'm hoping to talk to Davina as soon as possible. If you see her tell her to call mc, will you?"

"Sure. I guess you still have a house key, getting into the garage for the mower and all?"

"I'd better finish up with these leaves I've bagged up. Davina always liked for me to spread them around the bushes and on the flower beds as mulch." Sure he had a key and a garage door opener that still worked. Why did Margie want to know, and what business of hers was it anyway?

Margie waved good-bye and to his relief left. He spread the mulched leaves around the perennials and shrubs with the hope Davina would notice, be pleased and think better of him. Then he went inside and took a nostalgic stroll through the house.

In the master bedroom a bra left on the comforter reminded him of Davina's bounteous breasts. In the kitchen a faded apron on the hook by the refrigerator reminded him of her homemade pizza. In the family room he sat down in his favorite chair, a recliner and imagined Davina forgiving him.

At the window through the crack where the drapes refused to meet, sunlight came in and illuminated the water in the aquarium. Something from the miniature treasure chest sparkled so intensely that Tom got up, walked to the tank and peered down. Among the miniature jewels in the toy treasure chest, he saw the gold wedding ring he had given Davina so many years ago.

• • •

When Davina arrived home from Tucson that night she found a box of chocolates on the kitchen table. A sticky note attached to the cover held a familiar scrawl: *Davina, I still love you. I took care of the leaves for you. Call me, Tom*

His intrusion angered her. Why hadn't she changed the locks on the doors and reprogrammed the garage door opener? She crushed the note and tossed it into the waste basket beneath the kitchen sink. If the chocolates hadn't been her favorite brand she would have passed them on to Margie, her neighbor across the street, or Meg, her co-partner. Greedily and without guilt she tore off the cellophane and lifted the white and gold cover. She chose a globular mound and popped it into her mouth; it was a yummy coconut cream. She ate another chocolate and then another as if to prove she could eat the candy Tom had given her and not feel any love toward him.

In the bedroom she shed her clothes, noticed the answering machine with its red eye blinking and pushed the button. It was Tom's voice, humble, professing love, begging forgiveness, pleading to come back home.

"Thanks, but it's too late," she said aloud to the four walls.

Then another obviously altered voice came on with the message Sunshine had warned her of: *I'll kill you, like I did Jed. He deserved to die, messing with deer hunting. Back off investigating his death or you'll be next.*

Two hang ups followed, then a call by Meg asking, "Are you back home? If so, come to work tomorrow. I need some relief." The frustration was apparent in her voice.

The next recorded message was from Maurice Wingate: "Did you get back from your Tucson trip? Please give me a call." He was sure to be disappointed at the unsuccessful trip and also shocked at the attack on Benton Cooper.

Then she heard the voice of Benton Cooper: "Hi Babe, Ben here. I just wanna say I miss you already. Phone me sometime. Another day or two and I'll be going home. Adios, for now."

Davina pushed the button to save the messages. She then replayed the threatening call. She listened carefully. Who was the owner of the low pitched, throaty voice with its hated filled message?

• • •

"All the town council members are concerned about the loss of evidence in the Jed Davidson murder case," Thane Greer said over the telephone to Paxtonia Police Chief Leo Donovan. Greer, a grocery store manager and town council member told Donovan that he had recently talked to Lieutenant Jerry Caldwell concerning all the circumstances surrounding Davidson's death. Then at the Tuesday night meeting he shared Caldwell's concerns about the missing evidence with his fellow council members.

"Who says there's missing evidence? Has there ever been a complaint about my job performance in all the years I've been police chief?"

"Leo, some of us members feel that the last couple of years you've been coasting along in your job as police chief. We've sensed a lack of commitment and interest in your job. Now, I know your wife's death has hit you hard, but we expect you to do your job. We want you to come to a closed door session of a special town meeting next Tuesday at 8 PM after our regular meeting."

"Exactly what's the purpose of the meeting and is this Jerry Caldwell's idea? Don't you know that Jerry's after my job and will say anything negative about me?"

"We want to discuss with you missing evidence from the police evidence locker, specifically the arrow pulled from Davidson's chest by Appolini, the pathologist who did the autopsy. You'll be there?"

Sweat beads sprouted across Donovan's forehead. "Sure, I'll be there, but didn't Caldwell tell you that I figured Ron Hedges took the evidence from the locker just to spite the police department when he quit his job here? You may have heard about what a hothead Hedges is."

"Why don't you follow up on that idea? If it's true Hedges took evidence then he should be prosecuted. We'll be expecting you, next Tuesday 8 PM."

If it's true. The words echoed inside Donovan's head. Donovan hung up the receiver and rotated in his chair. Outside the window, the rain turned into sleet and on the street a boy pedaled his bicycle fast, his shoulders hunched against the icy pelts.

Deep inside Donovan's chest, tightness gathered as he recalled the evidence he had taken and hidden beneath a blanket in the trunk of his car. He'd better find a better hiding place. He began to feel guilt at what he had done. Always, he had been proud of his work and accomplishments. Only three years ago he had been named grand marshal of the parade celebrating the 26th annual Paxtonia Corn Festival. He and Helen had ridden in the parade in a convertible and people had clapped and cheered, some of them calling out *Hey Leo! Way to Go! Thanks, Chief!* Yes, he had done a worthy job for the citizens of Paxtonia and they appreciated him. *What an idiot he had been, messing with crime scene evidence!*

When no one was around to see his actions, Chief Donovan, who was overcome with remorse, put the arrow he had been driving around with in his car trunk, into an evidence locker that had been used before the latest remodeling to the building.

The arrow was now clean of any fingerprints or dusting powder. Since there were no security cameras monitoring the evidence room, no one could prove he had anything to do with the sabbatical of the arrow. It would remain an unsolved mystery. An absentminded Caldwell must have stored it in the wrong locker. Let Caldwell prove otherwise.

Davina, Davina, Davina...

CHAPTER 18

On Saturday morning Davina felt happy to be home and refreshed after a night of once again sleeping in her own bed. Outside, the rain fell relentlessly. She went into the living room and pushed back the coffee table and a chair to give more space for her Tai Chi exercise routine. Because of the wet weather she wasn't turning, bending and stretching outside on the deck or the pine-needled covered grass, but on soft carpet.

Moments later came an interruption with the sound of the door bell ringing. She went to the front door and saw through the gauzy curtain that covered the small window, Shirlee.

Jed's widow stood on the porch with her back angled against the November wind. Davina pulled open the door and a damp gust blew inside.

"I've got to talk to you. Is it okay if I come in for a few minutes?" In her black outfit of jeans, leather jacket and boots, she could have been the widow not an esteemed scientist, but of a biker. A worried look haunted her eyes.

Davina stepped back and invited her inside. "Can I get you something to drink, coffee, tea or soda?"

The scent of tobacco mingled with jasmine and peonies traveled inside with Shirlee. Davina followed her to the kitchen where Shirlee pulled a chair out from the table, sat down and unzipped her jacket. She looked tired.

"Coffee, please, if it's no bother."

"Where's your motorcycle?" Davina joked. She opened a canister and proceeded to prepare a carafe of coffee.

"I feel so guilty," she said, ignoring Davina's remark. "Jed might still be alive if I hadn't humiliated him by taking up with Javier."

"Speaking of Mr. Six Pack, where is he?"

"I don't know. That's all over." A weepy line of mascara marred Shirlee's otherwise perfectly made up face.

Davina watched as coffee filled the carafe.

"What happened?"

"After Jed's funeral, Javier made up excuses not to come around me anymore. Now that I'm a widow and available, he's lost interest."

Although she usually drank tea, Davina filled two mugs with coffee and brought them to the table. Then she pulled out a chair, the one Tom used to sit in, and sat down.

"What's on your mind?" She was finding it hard to be civil when what she really wanted to do was slap Shirlee in the face and kick her out of the house.

"The insurance company representative won't give me Jed's life insurance money. An investigator came to the house and when he saw the deer decoy in the back yard, he asked if I ever hunted real deer with a bow and arrow. I couldn't deny it. So now they insist I take a polygraph test. I had nothing to do with his death. I think Jed got drunk, sunk into one of his depressions and decided to end it all. I've never told you this before, Davina, but he once threatened suicide."

"That doesn't sound like *my* brother." Davina's

eyes narrowed and she asked herself, wasn't suicide a malady passed down in a family like a defective gene? There had never been a suicide on either side of her family.

"I knew you wouldn't believe me, but it's true. At the time he mentioned killing himself, I didn't believe he was serious, because he was drunk."

Shirlee gazed at the patterned wallpaper. " This is hard for me to say to you, but Jed wasn't perfect. I want to tell you my side of the story of our life together. He drank too much. He was moody. He neglected me. You know what too much booze does to the sex drive? That's why I turned to Javier. Now Jed's dead and I'm innocent of any connection to his death, but I have to take a lie detector test to prove it to the insurance company. It's embarrassing. What will people think when they hear about it? The inheritance and Jed's insurance, if I ever get it, won't last forever. I may have to get a job, and I've never worked, except for one summer when I was sixteen at a Dairy Queen."

"I'm sure you'll survive." Yes, Davina thought, one way or another someone like you will always survive.

"Do you hate me?"

"No, I don't, but you weren't exactly a loving wife. You may have driven him to the bottle."

Shirlee's face reddened. She zipped up her jacket. "I should go."

"No, I'm sorry," Davina said. "Please stay and try to help me figure things out."

Shirlee's voice went on tense and nervous. "Javier and I didn't have anything to do with Jed's death, if that's what you're thinking." Shirlee reached for a napkin from the holder on the table and dabbed her eyes. "We both have alibis the night he was killed. We were together, all night. The divorce was almost final. When Javier stayed over we always slept in the guest bedroom. And by the way, your brother was not perfect. He was the one who first broke our wedding vows. He was having an affair. It could have been with someone he met at a bar, or at BioChem."

Davina suppressed the urge to further chastise Shirlee. She pushed her chair back and stood. "What's happening with Scott? Did he move back home?"

Shirlee's shoulders sagged. "No, I think I've lost my kid."

"Did you know that Scott talked to his father the night Jed was killed?" Davina asked.

"No, he barely spoke to me at the funeral, or afterwards."

"It was at Froggy's bar on the outskirts of Paxtonia. The bartender there told me that Scott came in that night and borrowed money from Jed. But Scott never mentioned it to me when I spoke to him at his high school and told him of Jed's death," Davina said. "Maybe he was too upset and scared."

Shirlee took a sip of coffee. " You can't think he would kill his own father. If he wanted to hurt anybody, it would have been Javier. Scotty is not a violent person. For goodness sake, when he was a kid he wouldn't even step on a bug!"

"In the high school counselor's office Scott said that Javier could have killed Jed."

Shirlee's lower lip came out in a pout. "Did he accuse me too?"

Davina didn't answer.

"He did, didn't he? Well, he's wrong!" Maybe after Jed's murder was solved and if both Shirlee and Javier were proved innocent there could be reconciliation between mother and son. As least, Davina hoped so.

Suddenly the house seemed to come alive: the ice maker in the refrigerator freezer dumped ice cubes, the furnace blower blew noisily through kitchen floor vents and the house creaked loudly as if the walls would crack.

"Do you know a man named Keith Thorne who hung around with Jed? He met him at an AA meeting," Davina said.

"Yes, Keith was some lowlife, a drunken

taxidermist in Paxtonia. They used to go fishing and drinking together. I didn't know they had renewed their odd friendship. Keith's a creep, but really Davina you don't want to hear this, but I think Jed *did* kill himself. He had strong arms and hands, and as gory as it is to imagine, in his state of mind, drunk and depressed I wouldn't put it past him. Jed complained to me that your father always expected too much from him. That's why he became a scientist-to please your dad. But Jed always wanted to follow his other dream. Maybe that's why he drank."

"What dream?" Jed had many talents and interests but I always thought science was tops.

"Music. Jed loved music and composed songs. I have a stack of music he had composed saved inside the piano bench."

"I thought tinkering songs on the piano was a hobby, not an obsession. Although Dad was hard on Jed, Jed was a grown man and could have done what he wanted."

"Money meant little to Jed. I got caught up in the good life his salary bought. You may not know this, but as a kid I was dirt poor. Coming from a wealthy, upper class family that had lost everything in the depression was a story I dreamed up with my mother and the only connection to Jackie O was what I read in magazines. I feel guilty and ashamed. I could have been a better wife." She pushed back from her face the disheveled ebony hair that seemed overdue for a shampooing.

"I think Jed's scientific work on birth control serums for deer caused his death," Davina said.

"He never discussed his work with me."

As Shirlee went on wallowing in her new found guilt and shame, another thought came to Davina.

"Be back in a minute." Davina went down the hall and into the bedroom and shut the door. Once again she listened to the mysterious and deep throated voice that threatened her on the answering machine. How could she have thought it might be Shirlee? Shirlee's voice was too soft. She returned to the kitchen where she found Shirlee still at the table, holding a compact mirror open and dabbing coverup beneath her eyes.

Davina asked Shirlee to go to the bedroom and listen to the threatening message on the machine. "See if you recognize the voice," she said.

In the bedroom Davina fast forwarded the tape to the message and they listened. "Do you know who this is?"

"I'm sorry. I've never heard that voice."

Davina glanced at the bedside digital clock. "I've got to go to *Queen Anne's Lace*. Meg must be getting irritated with me for not putting in my share of hours at the shop."

"And I've got to make arrangements to take a polygraph test and clear my name. I need the insurance money, or like your neighbor next door, I may have to stick a for sale sign in my yard."

"Which house are you talking about?"

"The house on the left with the godawful pea green shutters."

Davina felt elated. Cosmos Harris had put his house up for sale. "The man living there is weird. He used to around walk naked in his back yard until I got a petition going around the neighborhood that ended up putting a stop to it."

Shirlee's eyes widened and she laughed. If he walked around naked outside today, his wienie might turn to ice and fall off."

Davina followed Shirlee outside to the porch. They professed no ill feelings toward each other and hugged.

The rain had stopped but the chill remained. Davina walked with Shirlee to her car. While there, she looked over at the plywood sign in Cosmos Harris's yard with its crudely painted letters: *For Sale by Owner*. Beneath was a phone number. Davina hoped his house would sell quickly and she would never see him again.

As Shirlee backed her car from Davina's driveway, a sport vehicle passed by and pulled into Cosmos's driveway. A large woman in a rabbit fur trimmed parka got out. She wore oversized designer sunglasses that covered half of her face and a scarf wound high around her neck. She hurried to Cosmos's front door and without ringing the doorbell, went inside. She must have had a key, or the door was left open for her to enter. Something about the woman nibbled at Davina's memory. In some way, she seemed familiar.

Davina went back inside. Never the type to spy on her neighbors, she now regretted there were no windows on the side of her house that bordered Cosmos' house. The length of the woman's visit could be determined only if Davina kept vigil through the kitchen window that faced the street and she could see her vehicle past by as she left. What would that prove anyway, and why did Davina care? She smiled at the thought that skinny Cosmos and the woman might be lovers. But Cosmos was antisocial and didn't love anyone, she thought. And besides, he was moving out of his house, and that was very welcome news for Davina and the neighborhood.

● ● ●

When Davina got to the shop she showed Meg her purchases from Tucson. Meg was not impressed with the T-shirts. "Who knows, *somebody* might like them, but I'd be surprised."

"What about all the Chinese stuff you insisted on buying? It's been sitting on the shelves collecting dust since we opened!"

They had their first argument as business partners and as a result, closed the shop an hour early, making halfhearted apologies in the parking lot before driving off in opposite directions.

Back at home Davina picked up the mail from the

mailbox by the street. It had happened again. The post office delivery woman had carelessly put mail meant for Cosmos Harris in with Davina's mail into her mailbox. This time it was a catalogue of weaponry for self-protection and hunting. Among the offerings on the cover was a special for a wicked looking knife with a long serrated blade. Davina walked over to her neighbor's mailbox, pulled the lid down and propelled the catalogue inside.

CHAPTER 19

Sunshine had phoned Davina earlier and said she would stop in for a short visit after church. Now the scent of cinnamon filled Davina's kitchen. The coffee cake baking inside the oven was from a mix but jazzed up with added vanilla flavoring and chopped pecans.

The doorbell rang and Sunshine came inside, shed her coat and from a plastic bag pulled out a small gift wrapped box. She handed the package to Davina insisting she open it right away. Inside Davina found what appeared to be a sheet of paper rolled up like a scroll, and tied with pink and blue ribbons. She removed the ribbons and unrolled the paper and discovered a joyful surprise. It was a sonogram.

"I couldn't wait any longer to tell you."

Davina was going to be a grandmother and she felt excitement, happiness and sadness all mixed together. "But Sun, I'm too young to be a grandma," she said, and hugged her daughter.

"Oh, no, you're not! Gary had to go out of town on business, or he would have been here, too." She stepped back and rubbed her stomach. "I can't wait for the next sonogram when we can find out if it's a boy or girl."

The oven buzzer sounded and Davina took out the coffee cake. "But that's like finding out what's inside a gift before you open the package."

"How else will I know whether to paint the walls pink or blue?"

"What's wrong with mint green or yellow?"

"Is that what they did in the olden days?" Mischievous Sunny implied she would do exactly as she pleased. Back when she was twelve years old, Sunny announced that she wanted to be called by her middle name, Marie. "I'm tired of being teased. Why did you give me such a stupid name?" But the years passed and now Sunshine was proud of her full and legal name, with the nickname Sunny.

"Mom, let's eat in the family room. Go turn the thermostat off and I'll start a fire in the fireplace. I'll get some firewood from the garage." She headed toward the door that led from the family room to the attached garage.

"No! I don't want a fire!"

The forceful outburst from Davina stopped Sunshine as if she had run into a wall. "Have it your way, *Mother*. It was only a suggestion. We can eat at the kitchen table."

"I didn't mean to scream at you, but building a fire in that fireplace is too dangerous. Sometimes I hear the sound of chirping birds coming down the chimney. There might be a nest up there. There could be a chimney fire." And she thought: *I'd better find another hiding place for Jed's papers.*

The oven timer buzzed and their attention turned from the fireplace to the sweet smelling coffee cake. Davina removed the pan from the oven and cut for them generous slices. Davina fixed a cup of tea for herself, and because she thought pregnancy meant a caffeine free drink was called for, she poured Sunny a glass of milk.

"Do you know what would make me happier than I am now?" Sunny asked.

"No. What?"

"I want you and Dad to get back together. W h e n

this little baby pops out, then he or she will have two sets of grandparents who are still together."

"Let's don't go there," Davina said. She took a big bite of coffee cake.

"Then tell me about your Tucson trip. Did you find some nifty merchandise for *Queen Anne's Lace*?"

"Yes, let me show you. I saved a T-shirt for you." She would not upset her pregnant daughter by telling her about the bow and arrow attack on Benton Cooper as Davina sat next to him. And so from the bedroom, she brought back to the kitchen a T-shirt with the figure of the flute playing, dancing Kokopelli and handed it to Sunny who thanked her and said it was the coolest T-shirt she had ever seen.

Later, Sunny left wearing her new T-shirt, and Davina turned her thoughts back to finding Jed's killer. She decided to not wait any longer before sharing what had happened in Tucson with the police chief.

She phoned the Paxtonia Police Department and asked to speak to Chief Donovan. She was told he didn't work on Sunday. Davina thanked the clerk and hung up. Then she searched inside her shoulder bag and found the scrap of paper with his home phone number Donovan had insisted she have the night they had gone for dinner. She tapped in his number and after three rings he picked up.

"Davina it's so good to hear from you," he said.

Before he could imagine the call was anything other than something concerning her brother's murder, Davina plunged ahead. She told Donovan about the bow and arrow attack on Benton Cooper in Tucson who, luckily, survived and was recuperating. Then she mentioned the person called Weasel, who had prowled online chat rooms spewing hateful rants against environmentalists and in particular, the three scientists including Jed, who had developed Pro310 the birth control serum.

"You put yourself in a dangerous situation by

going to Tucson. When your daughter called the department and said someone had left a threatening phone call on your answering machine while you were gone, I was worried about you. You won't listen when I tell you to let-"

"I want to take a lie detector test," Davina said, "to clear up any suspicion you have about me."

"That's not necessary," Donovan said. "Forget what I said to you that upset you. The missing arrow has been found. It seems someone in the department, maybe Jerry Caldwell, had accidentally put it in a locker we used to store evidence in, before the recent remodeling."

"What about the partial fingerprint you said belonged to me that was found on the shaft?"

"Let's just say the rediscovered arrow has no prints, full, or partial on it."

"What about the fingerprint card?"

"It must have gotten lost."

"How did my print get on the arrow?"

"I think you got excited when you saw your brother's body and touched it. Then you ran back into the bedroom and fainted. When you fell you hit your head on the metal cannon that was on the floor. It was quite heavy, as I recall."

It greatly annoyed Davina that the police chief still dismissed her account of the camouflage clad intruder, but she said, "I got a concussion when my head hit the cannon, so that's probably why I can't remember."

"I didn't realize it was that serious. Are you okay now?"

"Sometimes I get a headache but when I do it's not as bad as before."

Chief Donovan thanked Davina for sharing the information about Weasel, and also for the details of the attack on Benton Cooper.

"I still think you would make a sharp detective–assistant partner, but I won't hold you to the job offer. I think too much of you to make you do anything you don't want to do." There was a melancholy tone to his voice.

For the first time she felt compassion toward the police chief. "I'm flattered by your attention, "she said, "but my life is too complicated and unsettled for any major changes." Surely he now understood.

For a moment he was silent then he cleared his throat.

"It's highly irregular, but I'd like to share some information with you as now I'm certain you are completely innocent of any involvement with Jed's death other than finding his body."

He then told her the tests had come back from the state lab and that the dried saliva residue left on the deer caller had been positively determined to be that of a secretor.

"That information would help in identifying Jed's killer. Twenty per cent of the population is classified as secretors. The remaining are non-secretors. We still don't have any solid suspects. Also Alvin, the kid with the pot bellied pig denied he had ever talked to you."

CHAPTER 20

Just before daybreak in the semidarkness on the frosty November morning, a deer hunter in camouflage clothing walked along the perimeter of a field and poured granules of doe scent on the ground. There was no human body odor to warn any possible bucks in the vicinity, for the hunter had showered at home using no scent body soap and shampoo.

The hunter looked around to make sure no one else was present, selected a sturdy tree and attached a climbing tree stand to the trunk. The camouflage clothing blended into the bark as the hunter went up the climbing tree stand to a height of 30 feet where there was a wide view of the spot where deer would likely approach.

The hunter reversed the seat, secured it, sat down and pulled up the rope that held the bow and quiver of arrows. Through binoculars the hunter scrutinized the surroundings and waited. The sky lightened. If the scentless soap happened to be ineffective, there was no wind to betray any human presence. The hunter rattled old deer horns together and blew the new deer caller that sounded out doe bleats. The deer caller replaced the one lost the night the hunter killed Jed Davidson. A dead leaf fluttered down to the ground, then another. The hunter watched as in the distance a buck, mouse brown in color with magnificent antlers approached, then stopped, immobile except for its twitching ears. The hunter remained still, felt the adrenalin surge and waited. The big eyed animal approached warily. Eight points on the antlers indicated a four-year-old buck. The hunter raised the bow, aimed, drew back the string and let go.

Twang! The arrow pierced below the shoulder of the buck that sprinted for the last time, then fell to the ground, mortally wounded. The hunter descended the tree, looking forward to the second best part of the deer kill, gutting the animal.

The hunter shivered in excitement, remembering the night in Paxtonia and the sight of the bare, strong torso bathed in dim light that met a similar fate. "I ought to kill the sister, too," the hunter mumbled, "that *bitch*-Davina Reed."

CHAPTER 21

As she did every night, Davina turned the wands, closing the mini blinds on the double window above the sink. Then she scrubbed the kitchen sink. Worn, scratched and no longer truly stainless, the scouring didn't much improve the shine. The volume on the TV in the adjoining family room was turned up and she could hear the news reporter say that because of prolonged rain the past month, the central Illinois corn harvest was later than usual. Now the farmers hurried to complete their harvest before the first snow arrived and blanketed the fields.

Soon it would be Thanksgiving Day. Usually family members gathered at Davina's and Tom's house for a traditional feast of turkey with all the trimmings b u t this year Davina had not made any plans. Too much sadness and anger because Jed's killer remained free with no rock solid leads to the murderer's identity occupied her thoughts.

The telephone ring interrupted Davina's unsettled state of mind. She answered the call, at once pleased to hear Ben Cooper's voice.

"Hiyah, Babe." His greeting lifted her spirits.

"How are you, Ben?" Life still held possibilities. She could even excuse Benton Cooper for calling her

Babe.

"I'm better, but mad as hell at the *shithead* that shot that damn arrow into me. I 've got a permanent ugly scar to remind me that someone tried to kill me."

"I wouldn't worry. Over time it will probably fade."

"I hope so."

"You could cover it with a tattoo."

"Nah, hey I've got some news. The Arizona state police did some investigating and found a witness who saw the car fleeing the scene when I was shot. A University of Arizona marketing student got the license number and wrote it down. It was traced to a rental car at Ace-Rent-A-Car near the airport."

"So they know the name of the person who rented the car?"

"No, it was a woman who used a false driver's license."

"I assumed it was a man."

"Beneath the ball cap, neck scarf and oversized sunglasses was a vicious gal bent on killing me and it might have been my ex-wife, Phyllis. Although Phyl wouldn't want to kill the golden goose who sends her maintenance payments the first of every month."

Davina had imagined he was a widower, for who would willingly leave such a fascinating and good hearted man? How little she knew about Ben! Was it only the lack of affection in her own life that made him so appealing to her?

"So, you're divorced."

"Isn't most of the adult population?"

"If they're not, then maybe they're thinking about it, like Tom and me."

"Tom's nuts to leave a woman like you."

His sincerely expressed words flattered her, but wasn't that his intention? Davina hadn't wanted to discuss with him her severed marriage but she said, "Tom wants to reconcile." There was a silence in the phone connection between Arizona and Illinois and she wondered who would speak first to fill the void.

"I was sitting here in my apartment looking out the window-don't laugh-when I had a vision of you," Ben said. "I looked up at the sky and it was filled with fluffy clouds and you came out of those clouds looking like an angel with red hair. Then I remembered how you saved my life by getting me to the hospital quickly before I turned my toes up permanently. What I'm trying to say, is I want to see you again, real soon, Davina. Another week or ten days and I'll be healed enough to fly out to see you, or you could fly here, or we could meet halfway, maybe in Tulsa, Oklahoma. Whaddaya think?"

"Have you been drinking?"

"Only pineapple juice."

"I don't think I'd be good company. I'm still very depressed over Jed's death. I'm frustrated that the Paxtonia police don't seem to be getting anywhere in the investigation."

"I'm wondering if the woman in the rental car who attacked me took a flight and followed you from Illinois to Tucson."

"I never thought- I don't know."

"You were sitting right next to me. You may have been the intended target."

Suddenly Davina blurted out an invitation without thinking: "Why don't you fly out here for Thanksgiving Day?"

"That might be a problem for you. I wouldn't want to intrude on your plans."

Davina thought of how unhappy she was. Ben Cooper was the person who could cheer her up. Besides she felt a connection to him through Jed.

"On Thanksgiving Day I'm roasting a turkey for dinner at my house. It may only be me, my daughter, Sunny and her husband, Gary. I'd love for you to join us if you're feeling up to it, but you'd have to stay in a motel instead of my guest room. Midville is a very conservative town. People would gossip."

"We can't have that. Are you sure you want me to

come there for Thanksgiving, Babe?"

"I am, or I wouldn't ask- that's if you've recovered enough."

"Count me in. I feel better already."

CHAPTER 22

Margie, the neighbor across the street who sought perfectly aligned teeth, phoned Davina. "Hi, guess what?"

"The orthodontist removed your braces?"

"Don't I wish," Margie said. "No, he told me that I have two more months to go with wearing the wires. Then I have to use a retainer at night for at least six months. Ed will love that! Did you notice the For Sale sign in Cosmos' front yard?"

"Yes and I couldn't believe it."

"I've got some more news about that oddball."

"What?"

"I know how you feel about hunting, that you think it's cruel, blah, blah, blah, but listen to this: Last weekend Ed went on a hunting trip near Lacon at a lodge called Wilwood, or Wildwood, something like that. Ed's not here or I'd ask him. Anyway, hunters will pay a premium to hunt in a controlled environment like that, where the odds are in their favor to bag a trophy deer. And do you know who Ed thought he saw there?"

"Not Cosmos!"

"Yes! Can you imagine him acting like he doesn't live right across the street from Ed? I suppose he thought since he shaved off his bushy beard, Ed wouldn't recognize him, but Ed did."

"But is he sure it was Cosmos? They say everyone has a twin somewhere in the world."

"He's positive. Ed thinks Cosmos may have been part of another group who had just finished their hunt, or that he was an employee at the lodge. Ed was walking by a storage building near the main building and almost bumped into Cosmos when he came out a door. He got a clear look at his face and said hello. But the guy didn't answer and kept walking like he was deaf. At first Ed thought he was mistaken, but when he got back to his room he decided the man actually was Cosmos, our nutty neighbor, looking different because he had shaved off his beard."

"Maybe he's trying to change his image."

"You're talking major renovation, *kiddo*. We just can't understand why he would act like he didn't know Ed. Was I thrilled to see that For Sale sign in his yard! He can't move fast enough for me."

"Me too, but sometimes I feel sorry for Cosmos."

"Why?"

"He was always peculiar, but he got worse after his wife died. Moira would have been mortified if she had seen the way he carried on, mowing his yard buck naked," Davina said.

"I think that he abused Moira. Remember me telling you how one night about 2 in the morning, she came over and pounded on our door and woke me up? You and Tom were on vacation and Ed was visiting his sick mom in Ohio, or I would have let her in. I still feel guilty that I didn't. Instead, I told Moira I'd call 911 and she said not to do that. I asked if Cosmos had been beating her and she said in that little mouse voice, no. I watched her go back across the street and hide in the shrubbery and then Cosmos was on their front porch calling her name. By the time the cops arrived she was back inside. Moira and Cosmos must have convinced the police that nothing was going on other than a little argument. They drove off without ever knocking on my door. Do you think Cosmos poisoned Moira?"

"No, Moira died of pneumonia. One time I drove her to a doctor's appointment and she was coughing and wheezing. The man's a nut case but I don't think he's crazy enough to have killed her."

"I can tell you one thing Ed's not *ever* going hunting again at that lodge. It was a rip-off. He never saw one deer. The man leading Ed's group said he couldn't figure it out because the previous day he had seen three trophy bucks."

"So hunting there wasn't like shooting ducks in a pond?"

"It was a bunch of BS."

CHAPTER 23

As Thanksgiving Day approached more often the Indian bells on the front door jingled at *Queen Anne's Lace* and the cash register keys clicked at a steady pace. Much to their delight the buying customers increased dramatically. Meg said the sudden upturn in business was simply due to the approaching Christmas season, plus the word of mouth about the unique merchandise in the shop.

But Davina was convinced *Queen Anne's Lace* was under a magical spell that flowed from the Kokopelli image of good luck on the T-shirts displayed in the window and hanging on a rack just inside the entrance.

Then, one night Davina almost fainted when she saw a commercial about *Queen Anne's Lace* on a local television channel prior to the 10 PM news. The exterior of the shop was televised, with close-ups of merchandise in the window.

The camera followed a customer into the store and scanned the aisles displaying the offerings of the shop. Josie smiled as she held up a T-shirt with the Kokopelli figure playing its flute. Davina phoned Meg, who phoned Josie, who then phoned Davina and relayed the sequence of events that resulted in the commercial: The TV crew had arrived when only Josie was tending the store. Tom had called ahead and plotted with Josie for the pricy surprise he planned. He promised Josie she could be in the commercial if she would not tell Meg or Davina in advance. Josie agreed and went out and bought new makeup for her TV debut.

It ran every night for a week, sometimes at the 5:30 PM news. The commercial must have cost Tom plenty, she reasoned, but he couldn't buy back her affection. Reluctant to credit the television spot entirely for the booming business, Davina still believed the shop to be under a magical spell that flowed from the Kokopelli images displayed on the T-shirts from Tucson.

On the eve of Thanksgiving Day Davina set the table in the dining room. She had extended an invitation to Shirlee and Scott and both had accepted. After Jed's murder Shirlee seemed a changed person. She was an inept cook but promised to bring two pumpkin pies for the feast. It didn't matter to Davina the pies would probably be store bought. Davina's parents didn't feel up to making their usual Thanksgiving Day visit so soon after the trip for Jed's funeral.

Gary and Sunny would come, but not Ben Cooper as she had expected. Two days ago a local florist had delivered a beautiful amaryllis plant. The note was obviously handwritten by the florist on a card decorated with the image of a turkey.

So sorry, something came up and I can't make it to Illinois after all. Ben.

She was disappointed. The last time they had spoken by phone Ben had said he would come, but he never followed up with a confirming call.

Davina told herself she really didn't care. Those who did sit at her table would get a delicious meal because cooking was one of her talents. After she received the plant from Ben, she phoned Tom as Sunny had begged her to do and invited him to come and join them, for Sunny's sake. He gladly accepted, but Davina felt glum.

She watched the commercial for the gift shop again and sat through the local news. Then she brushed her teeth and went to bed.

While hugging a pillow, she plummeted into a deep ravine of sleep where she became Alice in a strange wonderland where a midget in a puce top hat beckoned with his silver cane. When she tried to escape through a giant field of gladioli the petals unrolled and morphed into a tongue licking her face- She awoke, startled and wrinkled her nose.

Onion. Garlic. Tobacco. Someone with putrid breath was nearby. A gloved hand clamped her mouth and she tasted oily leather.

"Quiet." It was a man's voice in a rough and mean tone that chilled Davina with fear. Through a gap between the blinds and window frame street light eased inside. "If you do what I say, I won't hurt you." To make his point he pressed a knife blade against her neck, sharp and cold. "No fast moves. Get up and come with me."

She now recognized his voice. Cosmos Harris was in her bedroom. Frantic, she sat up. The light from a pen flashlight beamed into her eyes.

"Don't try anything funny. Get dressed and do it fast."

To Davina's racing mind an escape strategy proved elusive. Jarred awake from her sound sleep, she felt disoriented, confused. And she thought if only Tom were here this wouldn't be happening. "I'll put on my sweats," she said. "They're on the chair."

He threw the pants and top at her.

As she pulled the sweats over her pajamas then pulled on the top, he tugged at the telephone and sliced his knife through the wires. She slipped her feet into the Nikes and rose from the bed, balancing the unexpected sway. She always locked the doors, so how did he get inside?

Cosmos pushed Davina through the bedroom doorway and down the hall. "Do you need money? I have a hundred and fifty dollars in my billfold. Take it and I'll pretend this never happened, that it's just a dream."

"Shut up, we're going outside. Where's your jacket?"

"In the front hall closet."

In the shadowy light he pulled open the closet door and Davina reached in and pulled a jacket with a scarf entwined around the collar off a hanger. Cosmos contorted Davina's arms into the sleeves of the unlined jacket. Her winter jackets and coats were still in the basement hanging on a rack under plastic. He jostled her into the kitchen where the digital clock on the microwave glowed 3:05 AM.

"Why don't we put on some lights and talk things over? I know you've been upset with me and the neighbors. I can make some coffee and-"

"Shut your mouth." Although he was a thin framed man, he was strong and with his body he pinned her against the refrigerator, clamped the pen flashlight between his teeth and proceeded to wrap duct tape he had pulled from his pocket, around her wrists. Instinctively, Davina pushed her wrists against the tape. The effort was futile. His foul breath rushed like a bad omen into her nostrils and sickened her. If Cosmos planned to harm her immediately, he wouldn't have allowed Davina to get a jacket, she decided. But head to toe a fearful feeling engulfed Davina and she dreaded how the abduction might end.

"Cosmos don't do this. You'll be sor-"

"Move! Don't scream or I'll slit your throat." He pushed her out of the kitchen, and past the table set with the gold rimmed china. Then he unlatched and slid open the door and shoved her onto the deck.

The night air chilled Davina's feverish cheeks. She felt nauseated. It was important to remain calm. If she got sick and threw up, he would get angrier than he already was. In the moonlight, their bodies made shadows as they crossed the deck and went down the steps and onto the frosty grass.

He shoved her toward the tall hedge that separated their properties and forced her into his backyard. Growing more alarmed, she thought of Jack the Ripper, John Wayne Gacy, Ted Bundy.

Davina struggled to escape but Cosmos held on tightly. He pushed her around his house to the front and hurried her across the lawn and into his open garage where his truck was parked. She resisted getting into the truck but was no match for his strength. In an attempt to loosen the duct tape Davina continued to push her wrists against it but the sharp edged tape cut into her wrists. Her angry and nutty neighbor opened the truck door and forced her inside. No interior light came on. Cosmos yanked the safety belt across her arms and latched it.

Quickly, Cosmos went around the truck, got in and turned the ignition key. The motor caught and he backed the truck from the garage, braked and pushed a button on the remote. The garage door lowered as he reversed the truck. Across the street Margie Jager awakened by her husband's snoring, heard the rumble of the garage door and the sound of the truck motor. She pushed open the curtain, looked out and saw Cosmos's pickup backing from the driveway. As the truck turned into the street, beneath the street light, Margie's keen eyes read the large cursive lettering on the door panel, *Wildwood*, and through the front passenger window, she caught a glimpse of red hair. Davina! Riding off into the night with Cosmos.

She hurried back past Ed and to the front door where she stepped outside on the porch and saw the truck make a left turn onto the highway. Darting back inside she shoved her feet into her shoes and put a coat on over her nightgown. There was no time to wake up her snoring mate for if it must be Davina who she had seen. She must follow the truck and find out if Davina was being kidnapped. Margie lifted Ed's keys from the bowl on the kitchen table.

Inside the attached garage she quickly got into the Toyota, pushed the remote and when the door opened she backed the auto out, once more pushing the remote. She sped down to the corner and took a left turn and accelerated. Soon she saw tail lights of the truck ahead. She picked up her cell phone and pushed in Davina's speed dial number, just to make certain the person in the truck really was Davina.

"Pick up, pickup," she muttered, but there was no answer. She was certain it was Davina she had seen in Cosmos's truck. Margie had noticed Davina's bedroom light go off earlier around 11 PM when Margie had gone outside to retrieve the garbage can that Ed had forgotten to bring in.

She watched the truck go through the flashing yellow traffic signals ahead in front of the mini mall. Ten minutes later still lagging behind, she followed the truck, crossed Murray Baker Bridge, and took the first exit and headed north as the truck had done.

She switched to the parking lights and followed at a prudent distance. There was no way Davina would go willingly with that kook. The truck was getting too far ahead of her car, she noticed, as she saw the tail lights go around a curve in the road.

Then at a crossroads Margie found she had lost sight of the pickup. She wondered which way to turn, but suspected Cosmos was headed to the *Wildwood Hunting Lodge*. With the hope she guessed correctly, she made a left turn and pressed her foot down on the gas pedal.

Too late, she saw a piece of wood, a tree branch, or a two by four lying on the road and hit it full force. The car began vibrating. What a horrible time to get a flat tire, in the middle of a freezing night on a deserted country road with a crazy man abducting her friend! Margie pulled the auto to the shoulder of the road and reached for her cell phone.

• • •

He kept the knife on the seat between them. "Why don't we go back? Or drop me off somewhere and I'll forget this ever happened." If he released her, she would gladly risk hypothermia.

"No way in hell. Now shut up."

"Why pick on me?"

"Your mouth was the loudest one. You caused the most trouble for me."

"I wasn't the only one in our neighborhood complaining about your public nudity."

"You're one to talk. What was that you were always doing in your back yard, prancing around with the squirrels?"

"Tai Chi, it's a form of Chinese exercise. You might find it more beneficial than nude lawn mowing."

"You really looked dumb, ballet dancing outside. But I didn't complain to the cops that you were acting crazy, not even the time on your deck you played that oddball music on a cassette player loud enough to scare away crows."

"It's New Age music." If there had been a squad car on the highway Davina could have tried to draw attention by jamming her foot on the brake or slamming her body against the steering wheel but no vehicle lights pierced the darkness. Once she thought she saw dim lights reflected in the side mirror but when she looked again, they had disappeared. Cosmos began driving on back country roads.

"I bet you don't even know I've been inside your house before tonight." Cosmos laughed and slapped her knee. D a v i n a pulled away and leaned against the door. She hoped it would open and she could tumble out safely and run into a tall cornfield.

"I don't think so. I always lock my doors and windows."

"You should check the locks on your basement windows. I came through a basement window. It was a tight squeeze, but I got inside, twice. One time I ate an ice cream bar from your freezer. I've always liked redheads." He reached out and fluffed a curl of hair above her left ear. She twisted her head away from his touch.

"You weren't home when I came inside. I looked all over but I couldn't find what I was looking for. You've got some lacy underwear in your dresser drawer, now haven't you?" He lit a cigarette. "Mind if I smoke? I don't care if you do. This is my truck and it's a free country."

Through the windshield Davina saw the moon at intervals appear and disappear as he drove around the curvy road. She suspected they were near Paxtonia, or Lacon, for he had headed in that direction. Finally, he turned the truck onto a gravel road where a sign with an arrow stated: *Wildwood Hunt Club.*

"Jed Davidson was an enemy of all people who like to hunt deer," Cosmos said.

"You knew my brother?"

"Let's say I knew who he was, and what he did for a living. But I didn't know you were his sister until someone told me. Your bro wanted to stop deer hunting with that formula he and the other two geeks concocted." He stopped the truck in front of a padlocked gate posted with a sign: *No Trespassing-Guard Dog on Duty.* Cosmos took only a minute to unlock the gate, push it open and return to the truck cab.

The secluded area and the duct tape around Davina's wrists complicated any escape. If she ran, surely he would catch her. And her clothing was inadequate for the frigid Thanksgiving Eve night. If her hands were free, she could pull out the tiny pepper spray canister she always carried in her jacket pocket. She pressed her elbows to her sides and could feel the lumps- her car keys and the pepper spray- inside the pockets of her jacket.

Cosmos pulled the truck in front of a log lodge and turned off the ignition switch. The building could have been a cabin where Girl Scouts snuggled in sleeping bags or on cots, watched embers in a fireplace burn down to ashes and told ghost stories all night. But Cosmos was real. Davina was his captive and she didn't think he planned to make S'mores with her.

Cosmos exited the truck and came around to the passenger side and pulled open the door. "Get out," he ordered.

The sign had posted a lie; no guard dog was in sight.

"My wrists are numb. Could you take off this tape?"

"Good try, but shut up."

As they walked past the truck, she noted the license plate and silently repeated the number to memory. He unlocked the front door and shoved her inside.

He flipped a light switch that revealed a cozy and inviting living area. Under difference circumstances, she would have found it quite appealing: Overhead lights on a wagon wheel fixture illuminated the spacious room with burlap curtains hung over the windows. Above the fireplace a mounted deer head with sable colored eyes gazed out over chairs of Naugahyde. To the right of the fireplace a staircase led to a railed loft.

"Sit down." Cosmos shoved her onto a wooden chair. " You can yell all you like. No one can hear you, except maybe a wild turkey or a deer."

It was obvious that Cosmos enjoyed the control he had over her. He touched the point of his knife to her cheek. "Behave or you're going to get hurt."

Warily, she watched him move a chair alongside her chair. Cosmos pulled a roll of duct tape from his pocket and proceeded to cut off two long strips and placed them sticky side up on the chair seat. Suddenly Cosmos slapped Davina hard across her face and as she sat stunned he cut through the duct tape holding her wrists. He roughly ripped the tape off her wrists. Quickly, he secured one of her wrists and then the other with duct tape to the arms of the chair in which she sat.

But Davina felt a jagged nail head that protruded slightly from the left chair arm, something her captor had not noticed. Whenever he turned away, she rubbed the tape on her wrist against the nail. With a little luck and a lot of effort the nail head might be her ticket to escape.

"You offered to make coffee for me before, but now I'll make some for you. See what a good host I am." He headed over to the kitchen area and flipped a light switch.

"You've got something we want."

"I don't know what you're talking about. What?"

"You'll find out soon enough." While Cosmos prepared coffee, Davina studied every area of the cabin interior, all the time sawing away the duct tape on her left wrist against the jagged nail.

"Sis should be here soon."

"Who is sis?"

"My sister, Hyacinth."

"Does she work as a secretary at BioChem?" She tried to comprehend what was going on.

"You've met Hy, haven't you?"

"Yes, in Maurice Wingate's office there. She said that your mother named all her kids after flowers."

"Mom so loved flowers." He crossed himself and looked upward toward a heaven he imagined her spirit inhabited.

"Wingate is Hy's boss and a real peacock. She said he only wears custom made suits."

"Does he have anything to do with you kidnapping me?"

"Nah."

Cosmos carried back two Styrofoam cups filled with coffee. "I think you'll like my coffee. Have a sip," he said, and put one of the cups to her lips.

She had seen his hand pass over one of the cups in the kitchen and she wondered if he had spiked her coffee with some drug. She turned her head away from the cup and some of the hot liquid ran down her chin.

"Now see what you've done!"

"But Cosmos, it's too hot." She kept her voice calm, steady and pleasant. "It would be easier for me to drink if you cut off the tape from my right wrist. After I drink the coffee you can retape my wrist to the chair arm. I can't get away. I don't even know where I am."

"No way, *Jose*," Cosmos said. But he gazed at her as if he were considering her suggestion. Suddenly he set down the two coffees on a nearby table and approached with his knife. He slit the duct tape off on both sides of the right chair arm, leaving the tape stuck across her right wrist. He brought her one of the cups and put it in her freed hand.

She blew on the coffee and faked a sip.

"That's better."

"Did you and Hyacinth kill Jed?"

"Do I look like a killer?"

Yes, you do, she thought. "Jed was a good man. He only wanted to control the deer population, not end deer hunting."

Cosmos got up and paced the floor. "This government is getting power hungry and taxing us to death. They want to take away our guns. When I think about it, I get so all fired mad. And a man can't even exercise his right not to wear clothes in his own damn back yard in the summertime if he wants to."

"The neighbors didn't want their children-" She heard the sound of a car arriving. Moments later the door opened and a gust of wind blew in. A woman bundled in a fur trimmed parka wound with a scarf around the neck stepped inside, wiped her feet and unwound the scarf. Davina saw it was Hyacinth.

CHAPTER 24

On the night before Thanksgiving Day Lieutenant Jerry Caldwell was off duty and spending an evening with a singles group he'd recently been encouraged to join by Phoebe, his sister. Talking and laughing the group spilled out of a bar adjacent to the historic Madison Theatre. Some stopped to read the names of three prominent locals, including Sam Kinison, who had found fame nationally, their names now embedded on the sidewalk. In the adjoining bar, Caldwell had flirted with a blond nurse named Ashley, whose acceptance of the daiquiris he bought for her, gave him hope. But when the group dispersed in the parking lot, she left not with Caldwell, but with a twenty something guy with bleached hair, wearing Zirconium earrings. Upset, he went to a downtown strip club. Nursing a beer and his bruised ego, he stayed until almost closing time.

It had not been a lucky night for Caldwell, but as he drove from Peoria and toward Paxtonia in the early morning, his angry mood dissipated. Soon he'd be conked out in his bed between flannel sheets, sleeping late because he was off work for the holiday. Then he'd get up and drive to his folks' house for Turkey Day.

Yawning, he drove past a drying field of corn still not harvested. He supposed the farmers would be scrambling in early December to finish gathering the corn. The headlights of his auto caught the image of a car ahead at the side of the road. As he got closer he saw a woman behind the wheel. He stopped to investigate and rolled down his window. "Do you need some help?" he asked the woman who proceeded to roll down the window an inch. She held up a cell phone as if it were her protector.

"I'm calling my husband now," she said. He noticed she had braces on her teeth.

"It looks like you've got a left front flat tire. I can change it for you. Don't worry, I'm an off duty police officer." He didn't intend to make a pass at the woman who, despite braces on her teeth, looked old enough to be his mother.

The woman looked afraid, and rumpled as if she had just crawled out of bed. "You're a police officer- in what city?"

"Paxtonia," up ahead. If you turn left at the next intersection, and go about five miles, you can't miss it. If you're sure you don't need my help, I'll get going."

"Wait, I do need help. I've never changed a tire. I tried but I couldn't get 911 to answer."

"That's because we don't have 911."

She turned on her interior light. "May I see your identification?"

"Yes, if you'll let me see your driver license. After all, I am a police officer. I'm wondering what you're doing out here this time of night when you should be home in bed, or getting your turkey ready to roast."

He pulled ahead of her car, parked and came back, his photo ID and badge in his hand that he held up to her window and shined a pen light on.

She was satisfied, thanked him and held up her driver's license for him to read.

"Marjorie Jager- pleased to meet you. May I have the key to your trunk so I can get the car jack out and change your tire for you?"

"Yes officer." She rolled the window back up and got out and handed him the car keys. Then she followed him to the rear of the car and watched as he removed the jack and tire iron from the trunk.

"I'd like to explain to you what I'm doing out here on this country road wearing just a coat over my nightgown."

"Yes, I'd like to know what brings you out in what Frank Sinatra in a song called the wee, small hours of the morning."

As Lieutenant Caldwell jacked up the wheel and changed the tire, she told him her account of the reason she was there. She had witnessed what she believed to be the abduction of her neighbor who lived across the street from her in Midville, by another neighbor named Cosmos Harris who was weird and had been arrested in the past for public nudity.

"I think he was taking Davina to Wildwood Hunt Club because that was the name I saw on the door of the truck they were riding in. I followed them until I hit a board with a nail in it. I have a general idea of where the club is because my husband Ed was there recently and saw Cosmos. He didn't look familiar at first because he had shaved off his beard. If you don't do something to stop it, I think Davina may be killed just like her brother was."

Davina Reed-Her nosiness has finally gotten her into trouble, Caldwell thought. "I've met her at the Paxtonia police department. I think I know exactly where the hunt club is located," he said. "It's over on the old highway C."

Quickly, he finished with the tire and let the jack down. He put the jack, tire iron and the damaged tire in the trunk. Then he asked to use her phone.

His cell phone call woke up Chief Leo Donovan. Caldwell explained the situation and repeated the story Margie had told him.

"Yes, I believe her," he said to Donovan. "Yes, I

will."

"I'd better get back home before Ed wakes up and finds me missing. But I really want to know if Davina is alright. Please hurry out there and save her!"

"Listen, Margie, I want you to drive to the Paxtonia Police Department and make out a report. Just tell them at the station what you told me. I'll return your cell phone to you later either at the station or your home. You can phone your hubby from the police department. Now like I said, turn left at the next intersection and go five miles. You'll see the police department on the right side of the road. Now go!"

He watched the woman drive off toward Paxtonia and then he headed his car toward highway C and the *Wildwood Hunt Club* at a high rate of speed. Lieutenant Caldwell had long wanted to demonstrate to the citizens of Paxtonia that he could outdo Chief Donovan. This might be his chance to prove it.

CHAPTER 25

Davina scooted to one side of her chair and poured her coffee into a nearby scuttle filled with ashes. She let the cup slip to the floor and tried to push it beneath the chair with her foot. As the brother and sister conversed in whispers near the door, she strained to listen. She thought she heard Cosmos say, "When do I get her? You promised me"-followed by "Sh!" uttered by Hyacinth. Then Hyacinth walked over to Davina and noticed the empty cup on the floor.

"I see Cos has been taking care of you. Want some more coffee?"

"No, I'm trying to cut down on the caffeine."

From across the room, Cosmos chuckled and muttered something that sounded to Davina like *fat chance.* Now she was certain he had spiked the coffee. She pretended to doze as she tried to connect the puzzle pieces that had brought her to this terrifying night.

It had been a quick glance that day in Tucson, but Hyacinth was similar in height and body build to Ben Cooper's attacker. A sympathizer in Tucson could have supplied Hyacinth with the weapon that would have been difficult to get through airport security. Possibly the supplier of the bow and arrow she used was Joe Carter, the husband of Dawn who had suffered the miscarriage that they both blamed the scientists for, because of their creation and dispense of Pro310.

Davina opened her eyes. "You listened outside the door of Wingate's office while I was there and heard of my plans. You follow me to Tucson, didn't you?"

"Why would I follow you?"

"To kill Benton Cooper, the remaining scientist connected to Pro310."

"I can't say I've ever heard the name."

"He's one of the enemies, Sis."

Cosmos crept up and got in Davina's face. "Boo!" His breath fanned out to her face a rotten odor. "You and me are going have us some fun real soon."

Davina leaned her head back. "Don't you ever brush your teeth?"

"Shut up. "

"Cut it out, Cosmos. Go out and bring in some more logs for the fire. It's going out and the furnace isn't working. When all of this is over, we'll have to call a repairman. Take your time and bring in lots of logs," she added.

Cosmos opened the door and the wind rushed in and flapped pages of a calendar hanging on the logged wall. The picture for November was a hunter in an orange vest and camouflage clothing, smiling and kneeling by a dead buck.

"I wanted Cosmos to leave so we could talk without his interruptions. At times, Cos is hard to control but he'll usually do anything I tell him to do, like on the internet where I got him to use the name, Weasel and rev up the converts. He has recruited many followers for our cause, hunters and others who feel the same way we do. Some local people find Cosmos weird, and apparently you do too."

"If walking around in public dressed only in boots and a cowboy hat is weird then I'd say, yes. If spying on me and throwing things in my back yard is-" The fog lifted from her memory loss.

In full clarity Davina remembered *the arrow she*

saw Cosmos shoot into her yard. It was a week before Jed's death. She waited to retrieve the arrow because she was afraid he might actually shoot at her. She had planned to phone the Midville police, but she had hesitated, waiting to see if he would do it again so he could be caught in the act. She had her camera ready.

And then Jed was dead, and she had been hit on the head and lost part of her memory, including the part about touching the arrow. But now she remembered how, using only her thumb and index finger she had picked up the arrow, touching only the shaft mere inches below the plastic fetching and then she had pushed through the hedge that separated their back yards and threw back the offending arrow. The partial print on the arrow that killed Jed had been hers, now wiped off by Police Chief Donovan who had been obsessed with Davina and wanted to protect her.

"Are you deaf? I asked throwing what things into your yard?"

"Nothing important, some little rocks." Davina wondered if Cosmos had been trying to get her fingerprints placed on the shaft of the arrow that he was planning to shoot and kill Jed with, so she could be then be blamed as the killer. Or, was it merely his usual crazy harassment?

Hyacinth brought a kitchen chair and set it down backwards in front of Davina. Her sturdy legs straddled the chair seat and she sat down, and gazed coldly into Davina's eyes. "Now it's time for some girl talk. You can make this easy," she said. "Tell me where the papers Jed gave you are located."

"I don't know what you're talking about."

Hyacinth slapped Davina on the face hard. She cringed but resisted lifting her right hand that Hyacinth appeared not to notice had been freed. Maybe the duct tape still stuck across Davina's wrist fooled her eyes.

"Cosmos searched your house at night while you were in Tucson, but said it was hard to find anything in the dark with only a flashlight. He didn't dare turn on a light for he knew your nosy neighbor across the street might call the Midville police. So tell me, are the papers with the new deer birth control formula hidden at your house, or did you put them in a safe deposit box? Did you copy them to a computer disk?"

"Jed didn't give me *anything*."

Hyacinth said she didn't believe Davina. "When I met you that day in Maurice's office at BioChem, I knew Jed much better than I let on. When he started having trouble with his wife, I saw an opportunity. For a time, even I looked attractive to your brother. Imagine with this chunky body, my thick ankles, this face that no man, other than my ex, has ever looked at twice-we were lovers."

As if remembering the bliss of her sexual relationship with Jed, Hyacinth hugged herself and smiled. Then abruptly her face changed from happy to angry. "Unfortunately, Jed got bored with me. He was courteous, but I took being dumped, personally. I knew he was working at home on X267, a new and improved doe birth control serum, for he told me. Jed knew his job was at risk."

"Why was it at risk?"

"I know you think Jed was a genius, and maybe he was, but he was acting erratic Sometimes he only showed up at work three or four days a week, and always late. He got in a habit of leaving before anyone else did."

"Why didn't someone at the company try to help him?"

"I tried, and so did personnel. He'd be okay but only for a week or two. Then management got fed up. But I know Jed never stopped working on the new deer serum. He was obsessed with perfecting it. He wanted to test it on deer here at Wildwood, but I said no. I think he may have tested it here anyway without my knowledge. For a while he had the run of the property. And we don't seem to have as many fawns as before.

232

He almost had me convinced to turn Wildwood from a hunt club into a wildlife refuge park. I may work at BioChem but I come from a family of avid hunters and patriots. There are many like minded people across the country. Waco, Ruby Ridge, the bombing of the federal building in Oklahoma, we true patriots hate big government. I don't care about the reward money offered by BioChem. I want the research papers of the new formula. I want to destroy X267. Now, tell me- where did you hide them?"

"Maybe he gave them to Shirlee, his wife."

Davina realized they planned to kill her. "No, *you* have the papers, or know where they are stashed."

Whenever she wasn't observed by Hyacinth, Davina continued to work the duct tape against the nail. Soon she would have both hands free.

"What's the use? Another scientist will eventually develop a similar deer birth control serum." She was almost through the tape.

"*Wildwood Hunt Club* isn't much now, but some day it will be a huge success, most of the year a legitimate business, and occasionally a place for like minded patriots to gather and plan for the coming revolution."

Davina felt the tape release her wrist from the chair arm. Impatiently, she waited for a chance to make the move that she hoped would ultimately save her life. It would have to be quick, for Cosmos would soon come back with the logs. As if obliging Davina's wish, Hyacinth got up from the chair. "Damn, it's freezing in here. I need some coffee."

She headed to the kitchen area.

Davina eased her hand into her jacket pocket. Her fingers found the pepper spray canister and untwisted the lock. It was ready to use. With her back toward Davina, Hyacinth busied herself in the kitchen. Silently, Davina rose from the chair and tiptoed toward Hyacinth. She stepped around the kitchen counter and aimed the pepper spray straight toward Hyacinth.

The woman turned. Davina pressed the tab hard but the spray missed its target.

Hyacinth lunged at Davina. Davina dodged and re-aimed. The pepper spray blasted into Hyacinth's eyes. Hyacinth slammed shut her eyes.

"Ohhhh."

She stopped, pressed her fingers to her eyes, and then fell to the floor, moaning and rolling.

"You want more?" Davina couldn't resist giving another blast to the woman writhing on the floor. Then she scooped up Hyacinth's car keys from the counter, ran and opened the door, and escaped outside just as Cosmos approached from the dark and into the moonlight with his body hunched against the wind.

He peered over his load of wood. "Hell, how'd *you* get loose?" He charged forward on his long legs. There was no time to get to Hyacinth's car and flee She aimed the pepper spray at Cosmos's eyes and pushed down on the tab.

Empty. She threw the depleted canister at Cosmos where it hit his cheek bone and bounced off. When he came within her reach, Davina shelved his chin with her hand and pushed violently. Cosmos's lower body came forward. She kicked him in the crotch. He winced and fell to the ground.

The wind whipped her face as Davina raced to the car. Fumbling, she unlocked the door, slid behind the wheel, dropped the ignition key, but quickly picked it up. When she turned the key, the motor grumbled, then caught and hummed. Pushing her foot against the gas pedal, she turned on the headlights and headed toward the gate ahead.

A glance in the review mirror. Cosmos running, closing the distance. A pitch of his body onto the trunk with a *thump*. Davina pressed hard on the pedal, gunning the motor. Then the auto rammed through the gate. Splintered wood flew off, shot into the air and to the ground. Tires spinning, she twisted the steering wheel sharply and Cosmos flew off and to the ground. The car rolled along the shoulder. *She must not end up stuck in a ditch!*

• • •

With a popping sound, and the reeking smell of smoking motor oil, the auto suddenly slowed down. Engulfed by a sinking feeling, Davina pulled onto the shoulder of the country road, where the motor died. Frantically, she tried to restart the engine. Only minutes had passed since she had made her escape from the lodge, as she sped down the gravel road with a wonderful feeling of elation as she turned onto the highway, stepped on the gas pedal, and made several turns on side roads, just in case Cosmos and Hyacinth were in pursuit. Now she sat stalled in a useless sedan in a flimsy jacket, with no socks on her feet, lost in the dark. In frustration, she beat her fists against the steering wheel.

Then she heard a buzz that grew into a rumble. A single headlight appeared in the rearview mirror. She hoped rescue was near, and that some youth on his motorcycle was coming and would help her. She twisted her body and looked back. What she thought was a motorcycle, was in fact, a truck. Davina's joy crumpled into fear. She recognized the truck, with one of the headlights now burned out. Behind the wheel sat Cosmos Harris.

She opened the car door and jumped out just as an albino buck with a wide rack of antlers, bolted across the blacktop. Without any hesitation, Davina followed the ghostly deer into the cornfield. As she ran in the moonlight, plunging between rows of dried corn stalks, the wind chilled her bones. Her toes became like ice cubes. Once she dared to look back to the highway. She stopped, turned around, and jumped up. Over the dried corn stalks, with horror, she saw Cosmos with a bow and arrow in his hands, raised and aimed in her direction.

She zigzagged through the field with the hope he would give up and leave her alone. But an arrow whizzed past, barely missing her neck. To escape was her only intention as she ran on and on, the dried stalks stinging her face and hands. Pushing forward, she drank frigid air and her mouth grew dry. She thought she caught occasional glimpses of the albino buck still guiding her away from Cosmos and his bow and arrows.

Davina heard a swishing sound, followed by hoof beats and the rustle of corn stalks. The scene she came upon was unexpected and beautiful.

• • •

The fading moonlight shone on the flattened circle of corn stalks, an area deep inside the field where a group of does were bedded down. Like an image on a poster, or calendar, stood the albino buck several feet beyond the circle. Abruptly, the albino buck grunted, turned and galloped away. All the deer stood up and scattered into the field away from Davina. Left behind, a pregnant doe struggled to stand up. For a mystical moment, animal eyes and human eyes met in a universal connection. When the pregnant doe finally succeeded in standing, she turned and ran after the other deer into the cornfield.

Then Davina smelled smoke. She pivoted and saw smoke curling upward inscribing the sky with swirls that slowly dissipated.

Cosmos must have set the cornfield on fire. She tried to stay calm and think as she left the deer bedding area and walked the way the deer had gone. The deer had left a trail that she followed that eventually turned back in the direction of the highway but a safe distance from the flames.

She left the deer trail and soon, like a wary doe, parted the cornstalks and peeked from her hideout. When she reached the highway and began walking back along the edge of the field she recognized Jerry Caldwell, out of police uniform and in casual clothes. She watched as he walked to Hyacinth's disabled auto and looked inside. As fast as her numbed feet in her dirt caked Nikes would carry her, she got on the highway, ran toward him, and called out his name. Corn silk and bits of husk decorated her messy hair.

"Davina, is that you?"

"Yes, it's me. Cosmos Harris, my insane neighbor kidnapped me and brought me to *Wildwood Hunt Club* and his sister, Hyacinth-right now I can't think of her last name- was there and I escaped and he tried to kill me and he must have set the field on fire. Where did he go? I want him arrested."

"Get in my car over there and I'll bring you a blanket from the trunk and start the heater." Moments later he opened the car door and Davina sat down on the front passenger side. It was daybreak. Smoke from the dying fire still rose skyward and Davina knew she was safe.

"Thanks." Out of the cold, she felt better.

From his trunk Caldwell removed a blanket. It held a woody scent, was raw edged, and wrinkled, but clean. He wrapped the blanket around Davina and asked if she were comfortable. Then he slipped back behind the wheel, started the engine and turned the heater blower on high.

"Do you need to go to the hospital?"

"No, I'll be okay when I get warm." From her blanket cocoon, she studied the blackened cornfield through the windshield. The flames had died down as had the wind.

"Your neighbor, Margie Jager told me about your abduction. She followed you and Harris, but got a flat tire. It's just as well. I don't know what she could have done to help you, if she managed to get to the lodge.

After I fixed her flat, I directed her to the Paxtonia Police Department. She may still be there. I got all turned around trying to find *Wildwood Hunt Club* or I would have rescued you. That was my intention. I'm sorry. I thought I could find it. Margie lent me her cell phone and I called Chief Donovan and got directions to the club. He remembered Clyde Woolsey sold his farm two years ago, to someone who planned to turn it into a hunting lodge. I was headed there when I saw this cornfield burning."

"Cosmos set the fire. He shot some arrows at me, too. Did you see Cosmos in his one lighted truck?"

"I saw tail lights of a vehicle a ways up the road, but I stopped to investigate the situation with the abandoned car and the fire. I'm glad I did. It's lucky there aren't any nearby houses or barns."

"I saw some deer in the field back there."

The approaching squad cars didn't look like they were going to slow down. Forced to jump out of the way, he swore. Two squad cars whizzed past. Then the third squad car braked and stopped alongside Caldwell's auto. Davina rolled down the window and Caldwell, red-faced with anger and embarrassment, walked toward Donovan seated in his squad car. The chief rolled down the window. Concern mingled with happiness reflected his feelings and he ignored the fuming Caldwell.

"Are you alright Davina, Dear?" Donovan asked.

"Yes, don't let Cosmos get away. He's up ahead."

"I won't, now you just wait for me at the station. Lieutenant Caldwell will take care of you, won't you? When we finish this business if it's not too late, I'll treat you to breakfast."

"I think Davina's okay. Can't we follow you?"

"Definitely not. Check her out at the station and if necessary you drive her straight to the hospital emergency room."

Donovan sped off.

Davina appreciated the chief's concern for her

welfare, but was uncomfortable for being the cause of Caldwell's frustration.

• • •

With her feet in a pail of warm water, Davina sat near a heat register drinking black coffee, still wrapped in Caldwell's blanket and thankful he had come upon the scene, causing Cosmos to flee and probably saving her life.

"Thank you for helping me. I'm sorry my presence and the fire kept you from chasing Cosmos down, or going with the others to the hunt club."

"Me too," he said. "Don't get me wrong, my first priority was your safety. The Chief would make my life hell if you were harmed. Are you sure you don't want to get your feet checked at the hospital?"

"No, my feet are fine."

"I thought your neighbor, Margie would still be here, but Officer Cooper said she left without phoning her husband. She said she wanted to get back before her hubby woke up and missed her. He must be some sound sleeper. She'll have an interesting story to tell later on today around the Thanksgiving Day table."

Me, too, Davina thought, remembering the thawed turkey, its skin seasoned and oiled in her refrigerator waiting to be baked. Nothing was going to spoil her plans for the annual feast.

Davina asked for paper towels to dry her feet. Officer Hansen brought the towels, along with an extra pair of socks she said she always kept in her desk. Then Davina folded up the blanket, returned it to Caldwell, and asked to use a telephone so she could phone her daughter, Sunny.

"Mom, what do you want?"

"Sorry to wake you, but I have a favor to ask. I need you to get up and get over to my house ASAP and preheat the oven to 350 degrees and get the turkey baking. Can you do that?"

"Sure, but why aren't you home? Where are you?"

"It's a long story, but I'll tell you later. I have a list, stuck on the front of the refrigerator. Just read it and do what it says. The green bean bake and the dressing for the turkey are in the refrigerator. And don't forget to bring rolls and carrot sticks and dip. The table's all set. And peel ten potatoes and put them in a pot of water, but don't start cooking them until the time on my list. I'll call you back later, or I'll see you at home. Nothing's going to spoil our Thanksgiving dinner!"

She replaced the receiver. Caldwell was talking with Officer Patricia Hansen and Davina went over to thank him again.

"It's okay," he said. "I can't talk; I've got to get my dog Sherlock and get out to *Wildwood Hunt Club*. Donovan thinks that woman, Hyacinth Brock, is hiding somewhere on the property."

"Did you tell Davina about the body pulled from the Illinois River being identified as Keith Thorne?" Officer Hansen asked.

"No," Caldwell said, and hurried off leaving Davina, who was stunned by the news of Keith's death, to continue the conversation.

"We'd been trying to reach Keith and so had his parole officer. Keith had a huge bump and a deep gash on his head. His parole office identified the body. Of course an autopsy hasn't been done yet, but it looks like it wasn't an accident."

"It's a shame. What about Cosmos? I hope he gets caught."

'I'm sure he won't get far," Hansen said. "We've notified all state and local law enforcement in the area to look for a truck with *Wildwood Hunt Club* on the door panel, the license plate number, and a man behind the wheel. But now that it's daylight the one headlight won't be on. As soon as Caldwell gets over to the hunt club with Sherlock, Donovan said he'd come back to the station. The chief said he wanted you released to him personally. She winked at Davina. "He's got his eye on you.

• • •

Davina had been anxious to get home to help Sunshine prepare the Thanksgiving Day dinner, but Chief Leo Donovan insisted she needed breakfast after her ordeal, even if it was a *small* breakfast. Now she sat across from him in a booth at Grandma's Koffee Kup.

'I think you've met Davina Reed," Chief Donovan said to June, who handed menus to them.

"Oh, yes, I have," she said. Silver iridescent shadow covered her eyelids and somehow seemed appropriate for the friendly-faced proprietor. "I really didn't expect any breakfast customers so early this Thanksgiving morning but I'm happy to serve you. I always stay open on Thanksgiving Day because I don't want to disappoint the seniors who are alone. I usually get 12 to 15 for turkey and the trimmings and it's free for them. It's my way of paying back for all the blessings I've received in my life. There'll be plenty today. I have two 25 pounders baking right now."

Donovan sniffed the air.

" I can smell them. You're a kind person, June Bug."

"Thanks, more coffee, Chief?"

"Yes, but the lady likes tea, and do you have any of your pumpkin muffins? Davina's in a hurry and I've offered to drive her to Midville."

"Yes, I do," June said. "Do you want your usual breakfast?"

He looked down and patted his stomach. "I've decided take off a few pounds," he said, "and so I'll take just a muffin also."

"Chief, you are breaking my heart, but as you say."

She brought muffins for each, with foil wrapped

241

butter patties, refilled Donovan's cup and then retreated to her usual spot behind the counter, where she occasionally looked their way, studying the situation.

"Where are you having Thanksgiving dinner?" Davina asked.

"At home," he said, "maybe a turkey TV dinner." And then Davina surprised herself by asking Chief Donovan to have dinner at her place, and when he accepted, she was again surprised.

"You are driving me there. You may as well stay and join us. You can mash the potatoes and help my daughter in the kitchen, or watch TV. I may take a short nap before the others arrive."

A wide smile spread across Donovan's face. "Alright, if you insist, I'll stay. But you must be tired after being awake all night. I don't want to cause you any extra work."

"It's surprising, but I'm not tired at all. I think when I saw Hyacinth brought into the police station in handcuffs a little while ago, I got energized. Then as we were leaving we heard they'd caught Cosmos-you saw how happy that made me, didn't you?"

"Thanks to you, finding and bringing in the deer caller you found on the ground at Jed's, we may nail Cosmos, or Hyacinth with the DNA on the dried saliva. Now finish your muffin and we'll get going. June, may I have the bill?"

Davina excused herself and went to look at the pies offered for sale in a display cabinet. Donovan paid the bill and walked to the entry way to wait for Davina.

Suddenly a middle-aged man in a trench coat came through the front door. Excuse me," he said to Donovan. "You're the police chief, Leo Donovan, aren't you?"

"Yes, I am. How can I help you?"

"Officer Hansen said I'd find you here. I'm Jim Logan, Keith Thorne's parole officer. The two men shook hands. Logan nodded to acknowledge Davina who had joined them. "What can I do for you?"

"Here," he said. He handed the chief, a sealed business-sized envelope. Thorne's sister found this letter last night after she went to his apartment above the taxidermy shop where he worked. She thought it might be important and gave it to me this morning. I'm on my way to Milwaukee and will be out of town until Monday. I didn't have time to read it. I think it may speed up your investigation of Jed Davidson's death.

"Thanks," Donovan said.

He read the handwriting on the envelope: *If anything hapens to me give this to Paxtonia Police Cheif Donovan*

"Do you think you should read it now?"

"I think I should get you home, first. It's a holiday. It can wait."

Donovan drove, and Davina sat beside him and through the windshield watched the Midwestern landscape slipping by. Some people who considered themselves superior or cool called the Midwest *fly over country,* an insinuation that the Midwest wasn't as important a place to live as New York City, or Los Angeles, but she knew better.

Chief Donovan kept his eyes on the road, as Davina explained how her fingerprint had come to be on the shaft of the arrow. She was certain the arrow that killed Jed was the one Cosmos had shot or placed in her yard with the hope she would leave her print on it and toss it back into his yard, as she had done.

And then Donovan told her he had never really believed she had anything to do with her brother's death. But Davina didn't hear. As she watched the drying cornfields slip by, she had dosed off to the comforting drone of the motor and the wind humming past the vehicle.

• • •

Sunny and Gary had listened in astonishment as Chief Donovan and Davina related the exciting events of the past night, beginning with Davina's kidnapping and ending with her rescue and the capture of the apparent killers of Jed, Davina's neighbor, Cosmos and his sister, Hyacinth. Now Chief Leo Donovan watched football with Gary in the family room. Davina checked the progress of the turkey and the trimmings being prepared in the kitchen, as Sunny told Davina that Tom would be coming for the Thanksgiving Day dinner. Furthermore, a man named Benton Cooper had phoned and said for Sunny to tell Davina that he would be there for the Thanksgiving Day dinner after all.

Mr. Cooper asked if I thought it was still okay with you and I said, sure, for I didn't know what was going on. I gave him directions to your house from the Peoria airport. This seems crazy, Mom. You're like a middle-aged bell of the ball, with Dad, a police chief, and some guy you met on a quick trip to Tucson all coming to your house today for your Thanksgiving Day dinner." And Davina thought, maybe it is crazy, but *interesting*.

"After Thanksgiving I want you to stop in, *Queen Anne's Lace*, "she said to Sunny, "and pick out anything in the store. You've been such a great help getting this dinner ready. In some small way I want to pay you back."

Then Davina decided there was nothing more to do at the moment, so she told Sunny to wake her in an hour, and immediately went to bed.

• • •

When Davina awoke and came down the hall she met Police Chief Donovan who handed her the letter from Keith Thorne. "You may as well read this now before the turkey gets done, he said. It won't take long. I'll be in the kitchen mashing potatoes or in the family room with your other admirers."

Davina said hello to Benton Cooper, and nodded at Tom in the family room. Neither looked comfortable being in each other's presence.

She excused herself and went back to the privacy and quiet of her bedroom, shut the door, unfolded Keith Thorne's letter and began reading.

What hapened the night Jed was killed. Around 11 PM he picked me up and we went to Froggy's and ate burgers, and drank beer for hours, and shot pool. At the bar Jed started to talk about his new deer birth control formula he called X267. A man at the end of the bar heard and got mad and said Jed was un-American to mess with the deer population. They almost hit each other but Travis, the bartender calmed them down and the man left. Then Scott came in and asked his dad for some money. He left with a twenty dollar bill. Around 2 am I drove me and Jed in his Corvette to his home. Jed said I should sleep on the sofa. He said, after we take naps, let's go fishin because he needed a day off.

He said his life was a mess. Maybe I should kill myself and I said don't do that man. And he said, okay. I'm going to check my e-mail and he went upstairs and I fell asleep. I guess that's when he may have typed the suicide note.

Davina thought I typed it but I did not. When I woke up I saw he was not in his bed. I pounded on the bath room door but he wouldn't answer. I opened the door about an inch and saw he was on the floor with the arrow in his chest. I knew he was dead. I thought maybe he stabbed himself because he was deprest but then I got to thinkin someone might beleive I killed Jed. I have been in trouble and served prison time and we were together that night at Froggy's. I found his sis's number in his addres book on his table.

I jumped on his bike and rode up to the phone

245

booth on the corner of Third Street and called Davina. I told her she should come and bring a key and check on Jed. I pretended I didn't already know he was dead. I'm on parole and I don't need no trouble, especialy suspicions about murder.

But while she was on her way, I thought up this crazy plan to make police think there was an intruder. I know it was wrong and a bad thing for me to do. After I hung up, I rode the bike back and leaned it against the side of the garage and went inside and upstairs. I remembered Jed had chloroform in his closet and I thought to change my plan and put some chloroform on a cloth and knock her out. I put Jed's camouflage shirt over mine and the camo hat and scarf.

I hid behind all the clothes in the closet with a blanket over me. I waited for Davina to come and find his body. When she did I came up behind and put the cloth over her nose and mouth and she fought me and fell, and then I ran out. No one saw me when I got on Jed's bike and rode as fast as I could.

I took a short cut on a path through the woods and then I called the police from the phone booth on Third, and said there was a burglar breaking in the house. I knew they'd go and find her and she could explain things, not me. I rode on home and hid the bike under a tarp. I planned to get rid of it later.

Then I heard the sirens. I waited a few minutes and then drove back in my truck and acted like I had never met her, cause no one ever saw us two together that I can think of. I'm sorry if she hurt her head.

I've been getting phone calls asking me where Jed's new formula is, and that I'd better tell them or I'm going to get killed too. Sometimes the phone rings and nobody says a word but I can hear someone breathing. I'm scared. I think I may leave town.

Keith Thorne
PS Tell Davina I'm sorry

Davina refolded the letter and in the hallway returned it to Donovan. Sunny called out from the kitchen that all should immediately sit down at the dining table. "Gary and I will serve everyone," she said.

Tom took what used to be his usual chair at the head of the table, but Davina steered Shirlee to sit at Davina's customary spot opposite Tom at the other end of the table. Davina took a chair as far from Tom as possible, on the end and next to Scott and across from Donovan. Benton Cooper, from Tucson sat next to Donovan. Sunny said a brief grace then she and Gary served everyone and seated themselves opposite each other, close to Tom.

To be seated at a table with three men who had professed romantic interest in her made Davina giddy. It was only because of her presence that all three men gathered at the same table.

If she could forgive Tom, Davina could give Sunny what she (and he) wanted, unwavering grandparents to the baby when he was born, still together, carrying on.

With Benton Cooper, she could live in Tucson and pursue a new life with a man as capricious as she.

Or, as inconceivable as it seemed Davina could romantically, or in companionship only, begin a new adventure doing detective work with Leo Donovan, either in Illinois, or Arkansas, wherever she desired.

With laughter and friendly chatter, the dinner went much better than she expected, or maybe it was because of the effect of the champagne.

EPILOGUE

The following July:

"Are you sure you don't mind watching the baby?" Sunny asked Davina.

"Who wouldn't *love* to take care of Jeffrey Jed, the sweetest, most *beau-ti-ful* baby in the world, while his mom and dad go out for pizza and a movie?"

'You won't need to feed him for at least two hours. His bottle is in the refrigerator. It's better to heat the bottle in a pan of hot water until room temperature, because the microwave-"

"Come on Sunny, your mom's brimming with experience," Gary said. He pushed his wife toward the door.

Jeffrey Jed yawned and closed his eyes. Davina lifted the flannel wrapped bundle to her shoulder and patted his back. The talcum powder scent brought back faded memories of other babies, Sunny and Jed, when as a girl of ten, she helped take care of her infant brother.

Justice for Jed came swiftly. Cosmos, *AKA Weasel* Harris, was convicted of kidnapping Davina, murdering Jed, and Keith Thorne, and Hyacinth Brock was convicted of the attempted murder of Benton Cooper in Tucson. Both Cosmos and Hyacinth awaited sentencing in jail cells.

With considerable thought, and after consulting an attorney, Davina turned over the X267 data and floppy disk to Maurice Wingate at BioChem. The reward she received funded the annual Jed Davidson Scholarship to be given to an outstanding high school senior who planned to pursue a career in science.

She put the baby down on his back in the portable baby bed and carried it out to the deck. The air was fresh and pleasant. As baby Jeffrey slept, Davina went down the steps and out onto the grass. With the divorce settlement, the house was hers alone, but she hadn't decided if she would keep it. She felt free, powerful, wise but a bit sad.

With her feet carefully balanced, Davina raised an arm in slow motion and turned. Half the way through her Tai Chi routine she heard a familiar voice.

"I thought you'd be back here." Leo Donovan came walking from the side of the house toward Davina. Newly retired, somehow he had convinced Davina Reed she would make an excellent detective.

"Will you teach me that dance you're doing?" He had shed 20 pounds.

"Sure," Davina said. "Come on."

He followed her movements, although not quite as fluid of movement as Davina, but he was trying.

Then much to Davina's surprise, and to Donovan's dismay, Tom strode around the side of the house and into the back yard. He walked right up to Davina and tapped her lightly on the shoulder.

"May I have just one dance? There was in his eyes an expression of hope and affection. "You don't mind, do you?" he asked the former police chief.

Suddenly Jimmy, a little boy who had just moved with his family into what was once the Cosmos Harris house next door, squeezed through the hedge. They watched as he ran to pick up the ball rolling toward the ravine where tiger lilies grew in abundance.

"Look," he said. "There's a white deer down in the ravine. Wow, it's got antlers!"

ABOUT THE AUTHOR

Irene Sedeora is a James Jones Short Story Award winner in the seventh annual Illinois Emerging Writers Competition. A published writer of poetry and short stories, her work has appeared in various publications and anthologies including *The Aurorean*, *Dupage Valley Review*, *Downstate Story*, *Parting Gifts*, *The Writer*, and the anthologies, *Love Poems for the Media Age*, Ripple Effect Press and *Working Hard for the Money*, Bottom Dog Press.

ACKNOWLEDGMENTS
Thanks to family and friends for their continuing support in my writing endeavors.

"Fortune favors the brave."

Virgil

www.ingramcontent.com/pod-product-compliance
Lightning Source LLC
Chambersburg PA
CBHW051427170626
46809CB00006B/2356